Hot Gossip

'Anyone who falls asleep sucking on my breast has no right to call me a good girl!' said Suzy. 'And you, Squire, have been a very bad boy.'

In the mirror behind her, Clifton could see how high Suzy's skirt had risen up, displaying her translucent blue panties. He swallowed hard, all composure gone, raw anticipation in his eyes.

'What do you want from me?' he asked hoarsely.

'I want you to give one hundred per cent effort to get on your feet, or you won't get your reward.'

'Who the hell do you think you are?' His voice shook with anger and desire. His eyes were vivid with lust.

'You're hurting, aren't you, Clifton?' she said. 'Well, whilst you are pissed off you might as well use the energy to get back on your feet. Then you will be able to catch me and give me the punishment you think I deserve for tormenting you. That's what you really want, isn't it? To give your "maid" a spanking?'

Other books by the author:

Wolf at the Door
Stormy Haven
Driven by Desire

Hot Gossip
Savannah Smythe

BLACKLACE

Black Lace books contain sexual fantasies.
In real life, always practise safe sex.

First published in 2004 by
Black Lace
Thames Wharf Studios
Rainville Road
London W6 9HA

Typeset by SetSystems Ltd, Saffron Walden, Essex
Design by Smith & Gilmour, London
Printed and bound by Mackays of Chatham PLC

ISBN 0 352 33880 6

1

'So you've never had eighteen hands between your legs before?' Clifton McKenna said as he lay down in the warm hay. 'Tell me how it made you feel.'

Suzy sighed happily, watching the hay dust circle gently around in the single shaft of cold sunlight coming through the old barn's broken roof. It was warm in the hayloft, and redolent with the smell of cut grass and clover. Below them Clifton's black stallion, Sentinel, moved around in the dry straw and munched rhythmically at the carrots he had been given as a form of appeasement. He had to stay in the barn so that no one would see him from the path leading across the field in the distance.

Before that, Suzy had been running, her breath catching painfully in her throat as she hurtled across the frozen field, putting the hounds off the fox's scent. The trick was in not being seen, but the Master of the Hunt had already spotted her, and she had ducked into the woods to try and escape him. Her feet sounded fearfully noisy crunching through crisp mounds of fallen leaves, but not as loud as the baying hounds, and now she was the one being pursued, not the fox.

She tripped on a hidden oak root and went sprawling, landing hard enough to wind herself on the flinty ground. As she staggered to her feet Suzy realised the game was over. She was surrounded by curious, sniffing hounds and enraged men on horseback; puce with anger, some of them were, and it was all directed at her. Despite her dishevelled hair and her sweater falling off one shoulder, she stood tall and defiant.

'Oh no, got you outfoxed again?' Suzy's tone was mocking.

The Master looked formidable on his black stallion. His eyes were slitted with anger and frustration. Suzy could see the riding crop tremble in his hand, and read as clear as day the desire to use it on her.

'Go back. I'll deal with her,' he barked back to the others.

There was no dissent. They melted like shadows through the bare trees, taking the hounds with them. Within moments they were left alone. Suzy stepped forward, striking an alluring pose with one hand on her hip, the other pushing back her tangle of black curly hair.

'So how exactly are you planning to deal with me?'

Clifton McKenna, the Master of the Hunt, was a man of very few words. As he shifted in the saddle she heard the creak of his mahogany leather boots against the girth. He looked resplendent in full hunting regalia: tight cream breeches, cream silk shirt and red jacket, with a silk stock tied around his neck and a black velvet riding cap. The way he slowly released the stock from its knot and loosened the top two buttons of his shirt was enough to set her juices flowing. Then he leant forward and held out his hand.

'Get up here,' he said.

Of course, never having been on a horse in her life, she knew exactly what to do. She fair flew up on to the horse's back and landed snugly in Clifton's lap, without any ungainly scrabbling whatsoever. Then the horse lurched forwards and they were off across the field, their hair tangling together as she held on to the horse's mane. She was breathless, terrified, totally exhilarated. Riding into the unknown with a man she barely knew yet had lusted after for so long, she felt as if she were on the brink of a huge adventure there was no turning back from.

And now they were in the barn, and she was considering his question.

'It felt huge and very frightening,' she said, but her blue eyes flashed with mischief. 'I've never felt anything quite like that before.'

'Have you ever felt anything like this?' Clifton McKenna's slim, elegant hand feathered its way up her bare leg, under the flowing gypsy skirt, to stroke the soft skin on her inner thighs.

'No, Master, I haven't.' She let her legs drift apart slightly. She saw the flush on his high cheekbones as he registered her compliance. His hand slid higher and pressed gently between her legs, where a flood of moisture from her already aroused state had soaked her panties. Pressing against her hip, she could feel something very hard and hot. It had been there when she was up on the horse with him, pushing against her buttocks as they galloped away from Great Clutton.

Now he was taking her hand and placing it palm down on that hardness, and as her hand curved naturally around it and gave it a cheeky squeeze he uttered a strange, strangled moan.

'Have you ever felt anything like that?' she whispered boldly, knowing now that she had control.

'Horny little wench,' he rasped, cupping her head in his hand and drawing her down for a long, deep-throated kiss. The sunlight gleamed on his raven hair, flowing down to his shoulders. The shirt he was wearing was now unbuttoned to the chest. She undid the last two buttons and flipped his shirt open, exposing a sculpted, creamy-skinned torso, lightly dusted with silky black hair. His nipples were very dark, like tiny chocolate buttons, and when she ran her tongue over one it immediately hardened. She continued to lick each nipple, her hand still firmly squeezing his cock under the riding breeches.

'Suzy, Suzy,' he purred, slyly undoing the breeches and guiding her hand inside. He was smooth and silky, hot and heavy in her palm. She felt a twinge of apprehension, barely registered, then growing tremors of excitement. Her mouth watered, and her nostrils flared as she breathed in his musky fragrance. Her lips eased over his cock as if they had been lovers for ever, and as she took him all the way in his hips trembled. His jaw was clenched, forcing back the cries of joy her warm mouth muscles had wrought in him. As she knelt to her blissful task he flipped up her skirt and let his finger delve into her pulpy depths. His breath caught.

'You're unbroken,' he said huskily.

'Of course, Master. I was saving myself for you.'

His eyes glittered in the soft light. 'I fear I may hurt you very badly, my love.'

She laughed scornfully. 'If I thought you were afraid of anything at all I would not be here!'

'Then I shall treat you as the woman you believe you are.' He kissed her again. She felt his finger gently probing her, and thought of his cock, and the driving force behind it, soon to forge its path into that private place. She was so wet that the thought brought nothing but wanton anticipation. He pushed her back into the hay, his knee nudging against her. Then he was pushing into her, gently at first, but only because he wanted to savour the unique experience of plundering virgin flesh. Her breath caught as he drew back, knowing that the time was almost upon her. Her fingers dug into his back, her legs tightened around his. She bit her lip as –

* * *

4

Suzy's fantasy came crashing to a halt seconds before she did, rear-ending a huge Scania truck that hardly felt the impact.

'Shit!' She couldn't believe she had done it. Not when stuck in traffic on the M40, with amused and exasperated business people all around her. The traffic had only moved a few yards before stopping again with nowhere to go, but some drivers were still hooting at her.

'Give me a break, will you?' she muttered, climbing out to inspect the damage. There was none to the truck, although the driver insisted on running his hand thoughtfully along the bumper, looking for infinitesimal dents.

'Oh dear, I really saw that coming. In the land of the fairies, you were. I knew you weren't going to stop.'

Suzy bit back an impolite comment and concentrated on her poor little Golf GTI. Fortunately they were only going at five miles an hour, but she had still managed to pop the lights on one side and ding the grill. It wasn't worth getting her insurance company excited about. It was just annoying, and humiliating. She glanced up and saw the man in the Audi TT behind her, laughing his head off. She flipped him the bird and he climbed out.

'You OK?'

'Pride sorely bruised, otherwise A1,' she said ruefully.

'That was priceless, even by your standards. What were you thinking of?'

She could hardly tell him she was fantasising about being deflowered by his father. 'I was just thinking about this decision you've talked me into,' she said hurriedly as he checked the Golf to see if it was still roadworthy. It was. The truck driver climbed back into his cab, still shaking his head.

Jem grinned at Suzy's anxious face. 'Don't worry. We'll get it fixed by the end of the week.'

'It's not that. I'm not running away, am I?' She suddenly felt very apprehensive.

'Running towards,' Jem McKenna replied firmly. 'And we better get going now, we need to be home before dark.'

In the car Suzy was preoccupied, now with financial matters. Her bank balance didn't look too good, but that was the price she paid for choosing beauty therapy as a career instead of law. At least her savings were healthy. Her parents had sold everything they owned to buy an Airstream so they could spend their lives travelling around the United States. They had put some cash in an account for their pension, and the rest they had given to Suzy. That was her inheritance, her father had told her. Use it wisely. So far she had not touched it.

So she had some backup. She began to relax, thinking that maybe she had not been so rash after all. Or it could just have been the sun flooding the green fields surrounding the M40, and the promise of something unknown waiting amongst the bluebells of Great Clutton.

It was hard to believe that at lunchtime that day she had been staring at the hairy rear end of a commodities broker, applying wax to said backside, and wondering, although not literally, if there was light at the end of the tunnel. As his screams had been consigned to distant memory she went on to one of her favourite customers, an ageing rock star called Sammy, and the day had brightened somewhat. He was the frontman for a glam metal group called Meathead, and was incredibly sweet – coked to hell, but like a lamb under her touch. She had given him a pedicure and manicure, complete with black nail lacquer, massaged him all over and had finished with a facial, for which he was supremely grateful and showed it with a generous tip. Even so, he had been the only good thing that had come out of her year's employment at Grooming For The Discerning.

The clunky name should have warned her when she applied for the job. After a year she had seen more back-stabbing than a decade of soap operas, but she had stuck it out because she needed the money and it seemed prudent to stay in a job for more than six months, as her previous track record wasn't that great. She had been brought up to think that life was too short to be tied to a job you hated, but now she knew that life was too long to be broke all the time.

Her main problem was Sheena, her boss, and her perception of Suzy as a threat. She was popular with the punters, but instead of seeing that as an asset, Sheena had decided to get girly and jealous. Consequently, Suzy's cards had been marked for some time.

When Sammy and Suzy emerged from the cubicle the girls from the salon were clustered at the window, universally condemning a woman walking by in a short skirt and kitten-heeled boots because she was the wrong side of forty.

'I want to be put down when I'm twenty-nine,' the youngest member of staff proclaimed, unaware that a very wealthy forty- (and the rest) year-old customer was standing right behind her.

'I'll do it for you,' Suzy said sweetly.

'But you'll be long dead by then, won't you?' She smiled bitchily back, then saw Sammy the star scowling at her. He flipped out his platinum Amex and gave it to Suzy.

'Next time, come to the house. You can do the missus as well.'

They agreed on a date, he gave her a quick kiss on the cheek and left. She was still grinning as she checked the diary for her next client. It was a male name she did not recognise, in for a manicure. The others had gone back to tending their clients in their private cubicles. The resident age-fascist was sweeping the floor, as befitting her lowly seventeen-year-old status.

Suzy sat at the reception desk to wait for her client, and surreptitiously checked her reflection in the mirror. She didn't subscribe to the heavy lip liner that her contemporaries favoured. She was still a country girl at heart, with clear skin and naturally red lips, and an untameable riot of curly black hair, enhanced with wild blue highlights. Snow White with a scrotum, Jem called her. Her figure wasn't bad either. She had a few hang-ups at a certain time each month, but usually she was a convenient C cup, with hips to match. As she was a woman, it seemed pretty reasonable to her to look like one, rather than like a Marlboro Light. It was another point she argued with her colleagues on a regular basis. Actually, more and more she wondered exactly what she was doing at a Camden beauty salon when her heart had always been back in the country. After qualifying she had acquired the job and the flat as a matter of rote. She enjoyed the work; it was the environment that wasn't doing it for her. That and the terminally bitchy company she had to keep.

The door opened with a chime of bells. The man was dark haired and wore designer tortoiseshell glasses, reminding her strongly of one of her oldest friends, but it could not have been him because he was in Australia, bumming around on Bondi Beach.

But not any more, it seemed.

As she let out a disbelieving squeal, he picked her up and swung her around the tiny reception area, knocking over a display for St Tropez tanning products. She was aware that the others had rushed out to see what was happening.

'What the hell are you doing back here?' she asked breathlessly.

'I'll tell you while you're doing my manicure.'

Whilst she pushed back creeping cuticles and scraped and buffed, he talked wistfully of the food, the heat, the cool blue sea. He had been gone two long years, but there had to be a damned good reason for his return. As yet, he hadn't enlightened her.

She went out into the shop to fetch some more moisturising cream. Liz was there, fiddling with the St Tropez display, setting it out again on the glass shelf.

'Perhaps you should dust that first,' Suzy said, wiping a finger along the top and showing her the resulting fluff. Liz wasn't the brightest of bunnies, though no one else seemed to realise it yet. She huffed and started removing the bottles again, muttering 'perhaps you should fuck off' under her breath.

'Ungraciousness is *so* last year,' Suzy said, flinging Liz's own over-used phrase back in her face. Jem looked up as she came back through the curtain.

'First things first. How's your love life?'

'Don't ask.'

'OK, I won't.'

There was silence as she applied cuticle softener to one hand. 'He was screwing my best friend, OK? I found them in my bed one afternoon three months ago.'

'Ouch.'

'Something like that,' she said shortly, hoping he would change the subject. It wasn't the best way to start a reunion.

'So you're single then?'

She gave him a patient look. 'Yes, Jem, I'm single.

Could you just rub it in a little more? It does wonders for my pain threshold.'

'Sorry. Just checking.'

'What about you?'

'I'm too busy being twenty-six, rich and eligible to be pinned down,' he said lightly. He looked around the small cubicle. 'What the hell are you doing in this place? What happened to the girl who loved chasing butterflies and saving foxes from my father?'

'She's still here.' She tapped her heart. 'But this pays the rent.'

'Yeah, on a shithole on the wrong side of the canal. You belong in the countryside. It's bluebell time in Lickfold Wood. I bet you haven't seen them for years.'

'Stop it. You know I can't afford to live around there.'

'Well, excuse me but what's wrong with living in Oxford? It isn't going to be any more expensive than this rat-infested city. And it'll be healthier.'

'There's rats in Oxford too, you know.'

'You know what I'm getting at.'

This was an old argument, and every time they had it, she weakened a little more. Now he was moving in for the kill, because he had this irritating ability to walk into a totally new situation and correctly assess the atmosphere within thirty seconds.

'Come on, Suzy, you could do this job anywhere. There's enough rich, bored housewives in Great Clutton alone to keep you occupied for months.'

'I'm sure there are, but things change. I have friends up here. The vibe's good.' But she sounded unconvincing, even to herself. The vibe had been good at first, but now it all seemed a bit superficial.

'It's good in Oxford as well,' Jem argued.

'How do you know? You haven't been back five minutes!'

Jem didn't say anything. She had the distinct impression that he was holding something back.

'What is it?' she said, concentrating on his ragged cuticles. 'If you don't tell me I'll pull your fingernails out.'

'I've been back six months already,' he said finally. 'That's why the tan has faded.'

Until then, she hadn't noticed his tan, or lack of it. She stared at him. 'Six months? Why the hell didn't you tell me?'

Jem squirmed. 'There's . . . stuff going down. I've been at the stables, working my bollocks off. There never seemed to be a right time.'

The hurt must have shown on her face. Their relationship was based on friendship, not need and expectation, but to come back and set down roots again and not tell her seemed a bit much.

'So why is now the right time?' She tried not to sound sulky.

'Come back to Springfields with me. I'll explain everything.'

She laughed at him. 'Right now?'

'Right now.'

Suzy had to admit she was tempted. There wasn't much to keep her in London. She hated her job, her flat was a hole and her friends were getting obsessed with capturing a man to set them up for the future.

'Where am I going to live while I look for a job? And what am I going to do for cash until I do get one? I won't take any off you.'

'But you can live at Springfields until you find somewhere. There's plenty of room. You'll find work easy. Until then you can work for me, mucking out the stables.'

'Thanks a lot. And I think your mother might have something to say about it.'

'She's in Cannes. Won't be back for three weeks at

least. Look, you don't have to work at the stables. I'll be there twenty-four-seven but we'll have a good time. Come on Suzy, where's your sense of adventure?'

This was beginning to sound more and more like one of Jem's grand ideas. Because he never had to worry about money he assumed that no one else had to either. Maybe that was true of all his polo-playing friends, but not Suzy. Even so, the gentle jibe about her adventurous streak hurt. She took her time in easing back his stubborn cuticles. It would take a lot of work before his fingers rivalled those of a Wall Street banker.

'Are you game or not? Afraid of taking a risk?'

'No,' she said indignantly, 'it's just that . . .' What? She had nothing apart from a very high insurance premium on a very old Golf GTI and a lot of girly friends that she never talked to when she went out clubbing because the music was too loud. Besides, she hadn't made any rash decisions since ditching her degree, six years before. Her wardrobe was good, but she could take that with her. And she could make new friends because she was that kind of girl. Suddenly she realised that she had forgotten how to live. Even so . . .

'It's different for you. I need to work –'

'To live, not live to work. Come on, Suzy. In a couple of years you'll start panicking about a husband and babies. Now is the time to take a leap into the unknown, before it's too late.'

'It's never too late. Look at my parents.'

Jem threw his hands up, knocking the cuticle cutters out of her hands. 'All right! Do it for me instead. I'll pay you to do it.'

She laughed at him. 'Why?'

'Because I need you to save my sanity,' he said simply.

'Why?' She asked again.

And that was when he mentioned his father.

2

When Suzy first met Jem, she threw up on him, courtesy of an iffy hotdog at the village fête in 1990. Her mortified mother sent her round to Springfields the next day to apologise, and they had been friends ever since.

Clifton McKenna owned a prestigious racing and hunting stables, as well as sizeable tracts of land in Oxfordshire. He also nursed a passion for Jaguars and blood sports, and he tolerated Suzy's pointed remarks about murdering foxes with effortless grace.

'I would gladly demonstrate to you the realities of cold-blooded murder, if you so desire,' he had said once, after one of her barbed comments. She had been speechless, not with fear, but the with the way he had said 'desire', as if he had seen her thoughts and had read them out loud. After that she did her utmost to provoke any response she could from him but he never rose to it. He would doff his velvet riding hat and smile coldly, and she would retreat unsuccessfully back under her woolly student scarf and sensibilities to nurse her confused feelings for him.

He did at least acknowledge her presence though, however sarcastic she chose to be. Alice McKenna, Jem's eternally frosty mother, offered her no such courtesy. Suzy's name was Suzanne Eugenie (after her grandmother) Whitbread, but when Alice found out she wasn't the heiress to a brewing dynasty she immediately dismissed her as a waste of her precious son's time.

How such people had managed to produce such a

joyous free spirit as Jeremy was a mystery. He even looked different, with wide myopic brown eyes and a cute button nose, and floppy brown hair that always fell into his eyes. Men dismissed him as a dweeb, but girls loved him because he made them laugh. Thus he stealthily reaped the benefits, snatching stunning women from under their beefcake suitors' noses. Unlike his father, he was no academic. He had scraped through Oxford with a meagre third in English Literature and had crashed out of the accountancy training his mother had insisted on. Briefly he had entertained the notion of becoming a vet, but on seeing the amount of studying needed promptly dropped that idea and went for a building apprenticeship instead. Whilst Clifton was happy to humour his son, Alice was appalled and let him know about it every day. For three years he put up with it, grafting solidly and coming home every evening with calloused hands. People in the village were quietly amused by the whole thing. When he had learnt enough to get decent work anywhere, he booked an open ticket to Australia. Soon after he had written to Suzy saying he was never coming back.

So what had driven him back so soon? Infuriatingly, he still had not told her. He had known, damn him, that mentioning Clifton would be enough to pique her interest.

She had fallen in love, or rather, hormone-charged raging lust, with Clifton when she was thirteen. Until then anyone of the male species had been treated with the contempt they deserved. Everyone except Jem, of course. He was her friend who just so happened to have a penis.

She would always remember the day it happened with cringing embarrassment. They were in the kitchen one Sunday morning making popcorn when Clifton strode in. He never walked, his bearing was too imposing for anything as inferior as walking. He was dressed for the hunt – cream jodhpurs, white shirt, riding crop tucked under one arm. She could not stop staring. He looked lean and hungry, with slim hips and long legs encased in highly polished mahogany leather boots. His black hair stopped just beyond the razor sharp collar of his shirt, and when he turned around, the shirt was still undone, exposing a fine covering of silky black hair on his chest.

Don't look down, she distinctly remembered willing herself, but it was no good. Discreetly she let her gaze drop to his crotch. She had meant to look back up immediately, but the discipline to do so just wasn't there. The tight riding breeches revealed a discreet but notice-able bulge like that under the jacket of a bodyguard armed more than adequately to deal with any situation. She felt Jem kick her under the table and the spell was broken, but not before she saw what could have been a fleeting smile cross the great man's lips. Then he was gone, leaving her burning with shame.

She was blushing again as she and Jem walked along the banks of the tranquil River Cherwell. It was now Friday evening, a world away from London. A family of ducks paddled away from them, leaving a spreading vee of ripples to lap silently against the grassy bank. Even her minor accident seemed unreal, as if it had never happened.

'What are you thinking?' Jem asked.

Suzy tried to gather her thoughts. It wasn't just the thought of seeing Clifton again. For years she had chosen money and career instead of adventure and bluebells. Now she felt stronger, fuelled by the satisfaction at seeing the horror on Sheena's face as she dropped her white tunic on the floor at her feet with the words, 'I quit.'

'Money, career, bluebells. Adventure, bluebells, money,' she mused dreamily.

'Always work in alphabetical order. It makes life much simpler,' he said pragmatically.

She laughed freely. 'Same old Jem. So full of shit.'

'Make that horseshit.' Jem admired his newly buffed nails. 'Shame these won't last.'

They sat down on an old log and stared across the river. It was too hazy to see the spires of Oxford that evening.

'OK, so you've alluded to family trouble, but what's so awful that you've had to come from the other side of the world to sort it out?'

Jem sighed heavily. 'There was a meet last Boxing Day. They converged in the drive, as usual. The hunt began and at the furthest point, where they were spread out all over buggery, Dad takes a fence that was too high and came off. He broke five ribs, bruised his spinal cord so badly that his legs were paralysed, and dislocated his shoulder. The real blow for him has been the wheelchair. He hates it. You know what he's like. Always full-on, never resting for a minute. The doctors say he could walk again, but it's as if he doesn't want to try. I guess he's depressed.'

He looked down and shuffled an old cigarette butt around with his toe. 'We've had the house modified as much as we can, but he never goes out. Some of the owners aren't pleased. We've lost two already. Spring-fields is going to run into trouble soon if something isn't done. Meanwhile Dad locks himself away and listens to bloody opera all the time. I don't think he's seen daylight since he came out of hospital.'

'Shit, that's awful.' Suzy couldn't think of anything more profound to say. Only that it was a wicked waste of such a virile man to be rotting away in a wheelchair, especially if it needn't be. 'Funny question, but why isn't

Alice here? Surely she should be looking after him? And what about the stables? Who's looking after them?'

'Take a wild guess,' Jem replied wryly. 'Mother thinks I'm in my rightful place but it's my idea of hell, to be honest. As for Dad, she's really pissed off with him.'

'What, for falling off? How did it happen, anyway?' An experienced equestrian like Clifton McKenna didn't just fall off his horse for no reason.

Jem rolled a spliff. 'Well, there's the rub. We don't think he did fall off. He was rogering half the female population of Great Clutton, according to my mother. Any one of their husbands could have helped him off his horse. Mum has been a prize bitch ever since. Even worse than usual.'

'Can't say I blame her.' It wasn't in Suzy's nature to side with an enemy but she knew firsthand how it felt when someone she thought she could trust was screwing around behind her back.

Jem shrugged. 'They're as bad as each other. She and Dad have never been happy. They should have called it quits years ago, but it suits her to stay now and play the martyr, even though the atmosphere between them is bloody Arctic.'

'So why doesn't he divorce her?'

'I don't know. Anyway, that's why I'm here. I couldn't just . . . you know.' He trailed off, drawing fiercely on the joint. 'I feel like I'm in a bloody prison here. He doesn't want my company, but if I don't see him no one else will. He's been so bloody rude to everyone they've all given up on him.' He shot Suzy a quick glance, filled with guilt.

'So I'm here to save the day and wallow in horse manure.'

'Well . . . yes. Sorry.'

Suzy folded her arms tight across her body and huddled on the tree stump. They sat in silence, staring at the river. In the distance, the church clock informed them that it was six o'clock.

'Pub's open,' Jem said gloomily.

Suzy glanced at him. 'Oh lighten up, would you? Suzy the saviour of sanity isn't going away any time soon.'

Jem laughed then. 'Anyway, you owe me one.'

'How come?'

'Do you remember that day when you embarrassed yourself in front of Dad? Staring at his dick like a hungry lioness, remember?'

Suzy reddened. 'I have no idea what you're talking about.'

'Did you realise you actually licked your lips? It was the most blatant display of lust I've ever seen,' he continued mercilessly.

'And your point is?' Suzy's cheeks burned fiercely.

'I went upstairs a few minutes later and he was jacking off in his bathroom! It scarred me for life, it did. My inadequacy in the bedroom department has haunted me ever since.'

'You're having me on!' Suzy shoulder-shoved him off the log. He fell backwards, roaring with laughter. After a moment Suzy joined him. They lay together, their legs propped over the log, sharing the crumpled remains of the joint.

'You are having me on,' Suzy said again.

'Nope. My dad is the five-knuckle shuffle *meister*. He's gonna be delighted to see you again.'

'Are you sure about that?' Suzy was serious again.

'If he isn't, I'm on the next flight back to Sydney.'

The McKenna house had a respectable façade of Georgian splendour, with wisteria twisting up the wall on each side of the grand white oak doorway, and meeting in the middle to surround a square verdigris sundial. The driveway was long and straight, leading directly up to the house and encircling a round bed of white roses, just coming into bloom. The large Jaguar that always used to be parked in readiness by the front door had gone.

'I bet he misses driving.'

'Yeah. The XKR he ordered came two days after the accident. It's in the garage. Hasn't been touched. Mother keeps nagging at him to sell it.'

Inside, the furnishings reflected the age of the house and its strong equestrian connections. There were oil paintings on the walls, mostly hunting scenes, some the profiles of proud horses past. Two tall bronze horse sculptures flanked a highly polished oak staircase, which led up to a gallery landing. The aroma from fresh lilies in an enormous Chinese vase permeated the air. It sat elegantly on a polished walnut oval table with turned legs, in the middle of the hallway. Alice McKenna may have lacked warmth but she had impeccable taste.

'Do you still have staff?'

'Sure. Mrs Penrose, the housekeeper, and her husband live in the cottage on the edge of the estate. She's a good cook but the biggest battleaxe since the days of the Vikings,' Jem said humorously. 'Baker still works for Dad.' Baker was the butler. He seemed old and crusty when they were teenagers. He must be ancient now, Suzy thought.

'And we have a chef for evening meals. Not bad, huh? Still worried about coming here?'

'Jem? Is that you?' There was an electric whine and a movement in her peripheral vision. Then, 'Jesus Christ!' And it was gone again. Baker appeared silently, to pick up Suzy's battered old Head bag.

'I'd better see Dad. Tell him what's going on,' Jem said.

'You mean you haven't talked to him about this?'

But Jem had disappeared through a doorway like the

White Rabbit. Baker led her upstairs to her room, which was huge and light and airy. There was a large bed with a crisp white duvet cover, decorated with green and pink cabbage roses, and matching soft pale curtains hung from a wrought-iron pole. The remaining furniture was antique French, painted oak. The large window led out onto a balcony, from where she could see the whole of the garden, down to a sizeable lake. Directly underneath her window was the huge, ancient wisteria, which hugged the wall with thick, knotty branches. Its pale purple flowers swayed gently in the breeze, its scent mingling with that of the lavender bed below the walls that encompassed the large, York stone patio area. In the distance, a male figure was working in the herbaceous border, broad shouldered and chunky in dirty jeans and a checked shirt. Not bad, she thought, but the man in the wheelchair, the man she had not seen for almost ten years, was the one she really wanted to see.

Jem appeared behind her, making her jump.

'You like the room?'

'It'll do. Who's the bod?'

'The gardener. He's a traveller I've hired for the summer. Old Mr Penrose is on his last legs, bless him.'

She arched one eyebrow. 'A traveller? You mean you've been consorting with the enemy? Your mother will have your guts when she finds out.'

The gypsies came every year in the Spring, like an annoying attack of thrush on anyone who disliked them. Through Alice's connections with someone high up in the District Council she sometimes managed to get them moved on, even though the land they were on wasn't even hers. Alice McKenna could be very persuasive when she wanted to be, and because of her exalted position in the community, and the generous financial contributions made to the church and other local good causes, nobody dared to ask many questions.

And sometimes the gypsies were successfully moved on. Sometimes they weren't. It had become something of an event, rather like annual cheese-rolling. Suzy wondered which side would win this year.

Jem shrugged. 'Whatever. Sorry about that, by the way. Dad looked like shit. That's why he was upset.'

'I'm flattered.'

'He's a proud man. That's why he won't go out. He thinks people will either laugh at him or pity him.'

'I won't do either. Can I see him?'

'Leave it for a couple of days. I want us to spend some time together before I have to get back to work. Then you can see him as often as you want.'

They ate in the dining room, served by Baker. Salmon steaks on fennel rosti, baby carrots and a delicate horseradish sauce, followed by the first fresh strawberries from the huge greenhouse down by the Victorian kitchen garden. The conversation was mainly of Clifton's accident, because Suzy couldn't get her head around how such a man could collapse so dramatically into mental ruin.

'If the injuries aren't permanent, can't he channel some of that energy into getting himself fit?'

Jem shrugged. 'He does some kind of physio workout with his doctor, but he just seems to love wallowing in self-pity. I can't hack it, to be honest.'

'But you came home.'

Jem rolled his eyes. 'Call me a wimp, but that was because of mother. She was in a terrible state. Saying she couldn't cope, that he was making her life hell. I couldn't really catch waves and enjoy it knowing she was going through that. But when I got home she and Dad were at each other's throats. It's like Armageddon with Villeroy and Boch.'

'You could go back to Australia. No one can stop you.'

Jem seemed to find his strawberries incredibly interesting. 'I could . . .'

'But?'

'It's more complicated than that.'

'You've got a woman!'

Jem pulled a face. 'Yeah,' he said slowly.

'It's about bloody time. Don't tell me it's Jade Donkey-Face Fenchurch?'

Jem grimaced. 'God, no!'

'So? Who is she?'

Her name was Bonny, and she was a traveller, as Jem primly called her. Suzy saw why he had been so coy, and how messy it could get.

'You sure do pick them, don't you?'

'Yeah. Not that it matters, of course.'

It looked to Suzy as if it mattered some.

'And her folks? What do they say?'

'Oh, they're great. Took it really well, considering who I am.'

Suzy watched him. Surely, surely, he couldn't be that naïve.

'How long have you been seeing each other?' She asked curiously.

'Just over a month, but I've known her for longer than that,' he added quickly. 'We kind of had a thing about two years ago, and then . . .' he shrugged, 'just got it together for real this time. She came to the door asking if I could give her brother a job, and I said yes, but only if she had dinner with me. She said yes.'

Of course she would, Suzy thought to herself. Any fly girl, hard-up, traveller or whatever, was hardly going to turn down the advances of the son of a millionaire, even if he looked like Freddy Krueger. And Jem was seriously cute, under those tortoiseshell Calvin Klein specs. She bet Bonny's eyes lit up like cash registers.

'I'm sure it was your gorgeous personality that persuaded her,' she said dryly.

Jem caught the sarcasm in her voice. 'I know what you're thinking,' he said irritably. 'But she's a lovely girl. If you pushed aside your prejudices for a moment –'

'Hold on, I don't have any prejudices!' Suzy rarely lied to him, but it wasn't the right time yet to elaborate on her uneasiness. He was still star-struck and therefore totally unreasonable. It would be up to her to keep an eye on Bonny. 'I think it's cool,' she said, shrugging. 'Go and enjoy it while it lasts.'

'But you think I'm crazy.'

'Everyone is crazy when they're in love,' Suzy muttered, assuming it was true. It hadn't actually happened to her yet, though. Not really. When she had found her boyfriend in bed with another woman she had been hurt by the betrayal, but she couldn't honestly say she had ever been in love with him.

Jem's story troubled her though. It was a gut instinct that warned her he was being made a fool of, and that some time in the near future, he would get knocked back harder than a street fighter.

'I bet she's got a Harry Potter fetish,' she grinned. 'Those cute glasses and floppy fringe and serious good looks. I can see it, I really can.'

'Stow it, will you? Have another strawberry.'

'Cute, dim millionaires must be the most eligible men on earth.'

'Suzy, read my lips. Go fuck.' He stuffed a fat strawberry into her open mouth. She ate it and grinned again.

'Hope you've got your clingfilm handy.' Referring to

the first time he tried to lose his virginity, when he was fourteen. She had never let him live it down.

'That's it. You're going to end up in the lake, Miss No Boyfriend, No Career, No Life.'

Suzy held up her hands. 'Touché. Harry.'

3

Days usually started early in the McKenna house, but as it was a Saturday the atmosphere was a lot more relaxed. Suzy felt as if she were in an exclusive hotel as she joined Jem in the conservatory. The dining table there had been laid with white linen and silver, and the aroma of fresh coffee and bacon made her mouth water.

'Didn't you miss all this in Australia?' she asked.

'Sometimes, but at least I was free.'

Afterwards he showed her the pool and gym, which had been added since she was last there. The pool was set under tinted glass and surrounded by lush palms set in large, honey-coloured terracotta pots. The water was a deep, oily blue, still as night, so the Springfield name could clearly be seen, picked out in darker blue mosaic. It looked very inviting, especially with the wide doors out to the garden flung open to let in the early summer aromas of cut grass and orange blossom. To one side was a large Jacuzzi, and beyond that a bar which took up most of the width of the room.

'Mother has pool parties every month for her friends,' Jem said, rather disdainfully. 'They do it for charity.'

'How nice,' Suzy said politely, and they shared an evil grin.

The gym led from the pool, through a wide changing area with two showers and large mirrors. It was well equipped with barbaric-looking equipment, including a weights rack, running machine and mini-gym. Clifton came here every day for his workout with Dr Maloney, a former GP who specialised in getting wealthy clients back on their feet. Apparently Clifton was healing well. His ribs had mended and his spine was looking healthy, but months of inactivity had atrophied the muscles in his legs and they needed to get stronger before he could walk again. Suzy thought about it as they walked back through the house. What he needed was an incentive to get back on his feet. What incentive could a man have to do that? Money? He had plenty of that. Pride? He had too much of that as well, by the sound of it. What about sex, the most ancient of incentives that motivated men on a day to day basis? She bet he hadn't been getting much of that lately.

After the tour they walked down to Springfields Racing Stables, a mile down the road from the house. It seemed to be bathed in a permanent sun trap. The concrete yard was achingly bright in the morning sun and a veritable hive of activity. She immediately saw how difficult Jem's job was, keeping a lid on the staff, the highly strung horses, the temperamental owners, but he did have some help during the week, including a frankly scary young woman with inch-long nails, called Jakki (no 'c'), who dealt with the marketing. She was also Alice's personal assistant, for both her business and personal life. Alice's role was that of 'marketing and customer relations director', which Jem wryly said was a neat way of saying she went on all the jollies without doing a great deal of work. He made them instant coffee in stained mugs and handed her the biscuit barrel, filled with plain chocolate digestives. During the week, he either had to drink the dry-roasted muck that Jakki insisted on, saying that the smell of fresh coffee gave a good impression to visitors, or make his own, which he invariably did, to the incomprehension of everybody except the stable hands.

They wandered around, stroking noses, patting hard, muscular necks. The names were ridiculous: Raw Pole, Cherry Popper, Get Some In, amongst others, but the magnificent beasts seemed oblivious, interested only in the horse nuts Jem held in his hand. The yard was immaculate, with bales of straw in a tidy pile, and all the tack hung neatly on its own hook, the saddles without exception polished until they shone.

In the field at the bottom of the yard a huge black stallion stood waiting, with its head over the fence. It pricked up its ears at their approach and shifted restlessly. It looked too large to be a race horse, and its bones, though graceful, too heavy. Suddenly Suzy realised which horse it was.

'Sentinel!' she said softly, stroking his velvet muzzle. He whickered at his name and looked at Suzy as if to say, 'And you are?'

Suzy stroked his glossy neck. 'I bet you miss your master,' she murmured. 'Do you miss Clifton, old boy?'

The horse backed away from her, whickering softly. Jem gave him a carrot, which appeased the great animal somewhat.

'Still looks good, doesn't he? It's a shame. Since Dad's accident he won't let anyone else up on his back. We have to exercise him in that thing.' He motioned to a barbaric circular structure in which a horse was plodding despondently round, head hung low. The trainer was giving words of encouragement, but it didn't seem like a very interesting way for a horse to pass its time.

'Has Clifton been down here since?'

'No. I think poor Sentinel here is pining for him.'

Suzy looked into the horse's deep, intelligent eyes. She could believe it.

'Mum wants rid of him. She says he's useless and not financially viable.'

'No! Don't say things like that in front of him!' Suzy couldn't bear the thought of it. And she didn't think that Clifton would take too kindly to the idea either.

Walking back to the house, they took a more interesting route that bypassed the village, and went over a hill known as Goblins Mount. In the early summer sun it was delightful. The heath was alive with blue butterflies and somnolent bees, the fragrance of wild herbs and bright patches of yellow rock roses lying snug against the hillside. From the top they could see Springfields House, with the pool house stuck like a tumour on the side of it. As they walked back down the hill towards the house, Suzy wondered how Alice managed to get that piece of planning approved.

'Pimms on the lawn, I think,' Jem said, breaking into her thoughts. They spread out a blanket and lay upon it. It was heavenly, with the fragrance of lavender, the lush, curvaceous borders bursting with waking colour. In the distance Mr Penrose pushed an ancient lawnmower up and down the formal rose garden, its soft drone complementing the song of a blackbird sitting in a nearby lilac tree. Baker duly brought out a tray with a large glass jug full of fruit salad and tinkling ice cubes.

'So where are Clifton's rooms?' Suzy asked, looking back up at the house. In the achingly bright sun it was difficult to see into the neat rows of dark windows.

'Right behind us. He's probably watching us right now and getting smashed on Glenfiddich,' Jem said airily, jumping to his feet. 'Come on. I'm going to thrash you at badminton.'

Suzy followed him. 'You'd better pray for rain.'

Clifton McKenna lit another cigarette and watched her hungrily through glass, unseen. Her light laughter, the way her skirt rose as she scooped up each fallen shuttle-cock, exposing long, toned legs and, very occasionally, a sliver of white panties. All these things awakened in him desire for women that he had spent too long suppressing, hoping it would never resurface.

And he hated her. She was the sort of woman who made a man want to drop his pants and charge. He knew another woman like that as well. One for ever lost to him, for reasons that ripped him apart every time he dwelt on them. Not that she was as obvious as Suzy. The young woman on the lawn was drenched with sexuality. His woman, the one he still loved beyond reason, had not been at first, but he had seen her potential. Seen it and mastered it. Or had she mastered him? He allowed himself a wry smile. Oh yes, she had mastered him, all right. That was why he had allowed himself to become a physical and mental wreck.

Suzy had missed the shuttlecock again. As she leaned down for it, allowing her small skirt to flip up, higher this time, she glanced his way. And he *knew*. Every laugh, every graceful lunge for the elusive shuttlecock, was not just for his benefit. She was as aroused as he was. His groin throbbed in response. He would have her, the sly little minx, and she would be grateful. Yes, she would. Damned grateful.

Suzy didn't see Clifton all weekend. It was as if he didn't exist. She and Jem talked, ate, drank and laughed, catching up on gossip, romances past and present. It was reassuring to know that they got on as well as they had before, especially as they would be living under the same roof.

'Still got the same horde of braying Sloanes after you?' Suzy asked.

'Unfortunately.' Jem grimaced. 'Mother keeps wheeling them out and I keep being nice to them. She doesn't know about Bonny.'

'I kind of guessed that.'

It was Sunday night, and already Suzy felt as if she had been there for ever. It was easy to be seduced by the effortless service, the constant supply of delicious food, the sound of birds instead of traffic waking her up in the morning.

They were enjoying a nightcap in the drawing room. Suzy sank into one of the huge chintz sofas and wondered whether it would ever let her out again. She and Jem were never allowed in the drawing room when they were teenagers. Anyone under the age of twenty-one was banned. Around the room were several display cabinets, with impeccably tasteful china sculptures inside; on the walls, old paintings in heavy gilded frames, of glossy horses and immaculate riders. The whole place screamed of old money, down to the tiny silver snuff and pill boxes neatly arranged on one table, below a vast Ming lampshade. Suzy felt somewhat smothered by all these riches, and even now there was a certain amount of illicit excitement at coming in here uninvited by the mistress of the house.

'I should go into Oxford tomorrow and see what's around,' she said, not really relishing the prospect.

'Give yourself a break,' Jem told her. 'A couple of weeks isn't going to hurt.'

She couldn't do anything until her car was fixed, anyway. She dreaded to think how much that was going to cost.

Baker came in and spoke quietly to Jem, before disappearing again.

Jem grinned at her. 'Dad wants to see you.'

Suzy clambered out of the energy-sapping sofa and picked up her glass. 'Will I need this?'

'I'll come and rescue you in a few minutes,' Jem said, deftly avoiding the question. 'It's the door across the hall, directly opposite this one.'

As she went out into the airy hallway again, Suzy felt nervous. Clifton McKenna had always been so vital, but now she was steeling herself for a bloated wreck of a man, sitting in a dark, smelly room, his hair ratty and skin pasty with lack of sunlight. Six months could do a lot of damage to someone determined not to care.

OK, here goes, she thought, grasping the brass door knob and taking a deep breath to prepare herself for the stench of sickness.

Not so. First there was the aroma of rich cigars, overlaying the more delicate scent of cut grass drifting in from the dark night outside the open window. Clifton McKenna's living space took up nearly a quarter of the house, and was completely at odds with the ostentatious grandeur outside his door. On the Canadian blond wood floor sat a single large white leather sofa and a matching armchair, a clear glass coffee table between them. There were shelves all along one wall, displaying a state-of-the-art music system with surround sound, and filled with books, ancient and modern, CDs and files stuffed with sheet music.

The middle of the room was dominated by a black Steinway grand piano. It looked stark and somehow threatening, a behemoth of an instrument. She remembered that he once played rather well. From the prominence of its presence in the room, it seemed that at least something still interested him. The whole space had been designed so that he could move about with ease, but there was no sign of the man himself.

Hearing a soft noise she turned, and her heart lurched. There seemed to be another woman in the room, but seconds later she realised it was herself, reflected in a vast mirror that had been hung on the remaining wall, stretching from floor to ceiling. Flanking it were more shelves, filled with books and, above them, two pictures of half-naked women, draped seductively on black satin.

A light clicked on, silhouetting a figure sitting at a large desk situated opposite the mirror. He had been watching her, which made her feel slightly annoyed, and not a little freaked out. At once she felt awkward and scruffy in her small denim skirt and snug T-shirt.

'Do you approve?' he asked. His voice was deeper than she remembered, with more than a hint of gravel.

'Um,' Suzy stammered, too startled to think of anything more profound to say.

'I thought that teenagers were supposed to grow more articulate when they grew up. How depressing it is when some don't.'

'I like to know who I'm speaking to first. Then I make the decision as to how much effort they deserve from me,' Suzy replied coolly, her nerve firmly back in place.

'You know who I am.' She still could not see him, sitting in the shadows behind the light.

'Do I? To know someone is far more complex than just learning their name.' She was beginning to enjoy this. It reminded her of the sparring they used to have over fox-hunting.

'True, but first impressions can leave one standing at the first post, if the person they are trying to impress has no inclination to give them the time to prove themselves.'

'That is on the assumption that I was trying to impress you, which, at the risk of sounding redundant, I wasn't.' Her heart was thudding like a bass drum by now. He laughed softly. The wheelchair moved with a soft whine and he glided to a halt in front of her.

He wore black from head to foot, as if in mourning. Maybe he was, for his freedom. But he looked clean and well cared for, to her relief. His fingers were long and finely tapered, resting on the arms of the chair. A musician's fingers.

It was the beard that upset her – a black glossy beard obscuring those fine cheekbones and sculpted lips, slightly scraggy and long as a pirate's. As beards went, it wasn't bad but . . .

'That has got to come off,' she said, before she could stop herself.

'Suzy Whitbread, as forthright as ever. Bane of my wife's life, you were, threatening to lead our son into iniquity.'

With the weight of his stare upon her, all self-confidence shrivelled up inside again.

'Bummer about the accident,' she blurted.

He stared gravely at her, then began to laugh. 'Life's a bitch and then you die.'

'Jem's asked me to stay for a bit. I hope that's OK by you,' she said tentatively, feeling about ten again.

'What the hell can I do about it if it isn't?' He turned away and reached for a packet of cigarettes on his desk, but they were too far away. She went to get them for him.

'I'll do it myself!' he snapped, but she picked them up anyway, opened the packet and took two out, one for him, one for herself. Her brief flash of insecurity had melted away, leaving an inner core of something far more exciting. She was going to get this tricky bastard up on his feet and living again. How, she didn't know, but it had to be done, before she could make any further decisions about her own life.

She walked around his chair, forcing him to look up and follow her with his eyes.

'Don't come that independent bullshit with me, Clifton. It's a cliché and it doesn't wash.' She flicked his silver Mont Blanc lighter and held it to the cigarette dangling from his lips. He held her gaze levelly over the glowing tip, but she had unnerved him.

'Feisty bitch,' he muttered. 'Worse than my fucking wife. You think because I'm in this chair you can say and do what you like to me?'

'No. Just because you're in that chair you think you can say and do what you like to me, and I'm not buying it.'

'Get out of here,' he said. She could see him trembling with anger.

'I will for now. But I'm going to show you how to live again, you self-pitying sonofabitch, whether you like it or not. And that beard has to go.'

As she closed the door behind her there was a solid thud against the thick oak, followed immediately by a soft crash.

'There goes another piece of Waterford,' Jem sighed. He had been hovering behind the door.

'Is he always that volatile?' she asked, as the chintzy sofa sucked her down into it again.

'Pretty much.'

'Must be lonely for him, if he doesn't go out.'

'He isn't exactly helping himself. I know what you're like about lost causes, Suzy. Be careful. He'll chew you up and spit you out if he thinks you're on a mission.'

Suzy cast him a sideways look. 'I thought that's why you invited me here.'

'Or is that why you agreed to come?'

She wanted to throw her glass at him. She had forgotten how easy it was to underestimate his perception.

Suddenly she thought that maybe Bonny was the one that needed to watch out, if she thought she was pulling one over on him.

'Tosser,' she muttered ungraciously.

4

On Monday morning Jem went into her room and nudged her half-awake.

'I've got to go. Come by later. We'll have coffee. I'll need the break.'

Suzy stretched luxuriously. No more getting up at six o'clock, fighting through the Underground, choking on city pollutants. Not for a while, anyway.

'Hey, slug. Did you hear what I said? Come by about eleven, if you're up by then.'

'Will do.' She yawned widely. 'I'll bring buns.'

'Sounds good.' Jem left her alone.

He drove his mother's blue BMW down the road towards the stables, cruising in the fresh sunny morning, when a girl appeared at the side of the road, as if by magic. She had thick blonde hair that shimmered and sparkled, and long loose limbs tanned from a life spent out of doors. As Jem slowed down to admire her, she cheekily hitched up the back of her short shorts to him, exposing two perfectly formed globes untouched by the sun. As she turned around her hair swung out, falling down around her shoulder as she stared boldly at him. Jem felt his knees give way. It was a good job the car was an automatic. He wouldn't have been able to concentrate on a manual with that vision before him. Ahead was a lay-by, with views stretching over the vale towards Oxford. He glanced at his watch. He could be late. He was in charge, after all, in his mother's absence. He passed the sultry blonde girl, slowly, drinking her in with his eyes. She blew him a kiss. Her T-shirt was very tight, and it didn't look as if she was wearing a bra. He felt a tightness in his groin that very soon began to hurt. He pulled into the lay-by and adjusted his erection inside his trousers. It wasn't going to go away until she did. She came sauntering along the road, hips swaying, occasionally lifting her hair up and letting the light breeze cool her neck. Then she was alongside him. She leaned down to talk to him. Her T-shirt was scooped low in front, so Jem could see her breasts, unencumbered and dainty. He could not take his eyes off them.

'What do you want?' she purred.

'Get in the car.' Jem's voice was raspy with desire. The girl obeyed immediately.

Jem drove to a spot nearby where no one would see them. They had not spoken for the whole time. In the dappled sunlight beneath beech trees fresh with acid-green leaves, he climbed into the back of the car with her.

'I can't be long,' he said, as she unzipped him and slipped a small, slim hand into his trousers. His head rolled back as her fingers slipped up his shaft. 'Do me, Bonny. Please. It's been four days!'

'Has it, lover? A little bird told me there's a woman at your house.' She grasped his cock harder, until the threat of pain was real. His breathing quickened.

'She's a friend of mine, that's all. I was going to tell you...'

'Are you fucking her?'

Jem shook his head rapidly. 'No. She's a friend. I'm sorry I didn't –' his breath caught as she began to fellate him '– warn you. God, I've missed you.' His whole body felt weak under her skilful mouth.

'I've missed you too, lover. I'm expecting big treats tonight, especially after this.' Her head dipped and Jem groaned uninhibitedly as her warm tongue swarmed over his cock. He pushed his trousers further down to free his movement and thrust his hips back up at her, forcing her to swallow most of his length. She slapped him lightly on the balls.

'Don't do that.'

'I can't help it, Bonny. I need you.' His hips lifted again. 'I need to fuck, baby. Let me fuck you.'

'No,' Bonny said cruelly. 'Good things come to those who wait. Tonight you're going to take me out for a very expensive meal to make up for not telling me about your little friend. Is that a deal?' Her pointed tongue traced delicately around his shaft, fluttered teasingly around the tip then back down, over and over, until Jem thought he would explode.

'Deal,' he gasped. With her mouth all over his cock he would have given her anything. Her lips closed over his balls and he moaned loudly. Bonny tugged gently at his scrotum, sucked it into her mouth, rolled it around her tongue. When she tired of that she knelt up again and circled his cock with cool fingers. As she shafted him gently she pushed her pretty tits into his face and let him suck on one long nipple. His eyes were drugged with need by the time she had finished with him. All the time, she was whispering about the exotic things they would be doing later that night, on the carpet of his mother's drawing room. How she would sit on his face and eat his cock, and let him take her like a dog in front of the fireplace. In the end it was too much and Jem lost control, his come frothing over Bonny's hand. She dived down and lapped it up, prolonging his hard climax as he grunted and jerked, his mind a car crash of erotic images.

As he sat in the back of the car, his cock slowly deflating, his legs spread wide, he was dimly aware of her sweet, deep kiss and murmured, 'tonight, lover'. He realised she had gone when he went to make himself decent again. Staggering out of the car, he checked for stains. There were none. They were always very careful. Then he took a piss, aiming his stream far into the woods, feeling invincible. When he made it into the office forty minutes late, no one queried why. He was still in a heightened state of erotic bliss, semi-tumescent and glowing inside. Just thinking of Bonny and how she would look spread across the priceless Persian rug that night was enough to keep him hard all afternoon.

Bonny arrived back at the encampment ten minutes later. She went into the caravan, where her brother was just waking, beery and unshaven. She freshened her face and hands at the kitchenette sink as he belched and scratched at his hairy stomach.

'Been banging that posh prick again?'

'Go to hell,' she said easily.

Robin O'Grady staggered to the sink and took the water and headache tablets she offered. He swilled the water around his mouth and spat it into the sink.

'Fuck you, go to hell,' he muttered.

'You need to be at work in ten minutes.'

'I'll be late then, won't I?'

Bonny shrugged. Robby could never hold a job down for long. He was a slob with good pectorals.

'Yeah, but this is good money. He pays way over the odds.'

'His rich *Daddy* pays over the odds,' Robby corrected, with bitterness born of someone who knew they would never be wealthy.

'So what? Money is money.'

Robby blundered around, struggling into his trousers. He peered in the mirror and decided not to bother shaving.

'I'm waiting for his old lady.' He grinned lecherously. 'She must be gagging for it by now, what with him in a wheelchair, unable to get it up.'

'Huh. Just don't get yourself fired before then.' Bonny slammed the door after his retreating backside.

Suzy felt rather strange, being alone in a large, rambling house with only a crippled man for company, bar the discreet staff of course, but the smell of frying bacon was enough to propel her out of bed. Until then breakfast had consisted of toast (usually half-burnt because of her inattentiveness towards it), bloody awful instant coffee, and a dry Danish pastry at mid-morning. Lunch equalled a baguette, whose main ingredient seemed to be lettuce, from a tiny establishment charmingly named Bellybusters. As for supper, she usually ate out, because she didn't exactly have Jamie Oliver's way with herbs and pasta.

Afterwards she felt in need of some company, but it was too early to start walking to the stables. What she really wanted to do was go in to see Clifton, but outside his door she hesitated. Should she just walk in? Well, of course she should. He wasn't going to walk out, was he?

As her fingers curved around the door knob, she felt slightly breathless. Gently she pushed the door open.

He was unaware of her presence, as the music was loud enough to disguise her entrance. The opera was *La Bohème*, the aria sung by Montserrat Caballé. Suzy stood quietly, enjoying watching Clifton McKenna losing himself in the emotional turmoil of the heroine's anguish.

'I saw Sentinel on Saturday. He misses you,' she said, when the aria had ended.

Clifton spun around in his chair to face her.

'Go away.'

'You didn't have to turn around to tell me that. My

hearing is perfectly sound. Rather like your legs would be if you bothered to exercise them.'

His face darkened with anger. She had scored a direct hit on his ultimate point of weakness.

'Piss off.' He tried to turn the chair again but she had jammed the wheel with her foot.

'Piss off, fuck off, cunt and cocksucker. See? I'm unshockable. Now we've got the expletives out the way there's nothing left but for you to be civil to me. And as you've nothing better to do, I suggest you give it a try.'

'Cocksucking bitch,' he hissed, amber eyes vigorous with rage.

'I don't tend to do it on the first date. Even for you.'

'Bugger off, then. You're no use to me.'

He looked truculent, but Suzy wasn't going to let him get away with it. She stuck her tongue rudely out at him, just like an eight-year-old girl.

Clifton suddenly grinned for the first time, showing good white teeth. The beard made him look manic, his unusual eyes flashing like the sunset. Think pirates, thought Suzy. Think peg legs, think not a turn on at all. All that chiselled bone structure, wasted under a carpet of facial fur.

'Please let me shave you,' she said suddenly, her thoughts tripping over her tongue before she had a chance to rein them in.

He laughed incredulously. 'Why are you so desperate to get your hands on my face?'

She stalled. It should have been so easy to say, 'because you look so much better without it,' but for her that was like admitting outright that she had once fancied him. Once? OK, she still did. And there was that image, enduring since two days before, of him jacking off in the bathroom because a teenage girl had licked her lips at him.

'I like you without it,' she stuttered, doing exactly what she hoped she wouldn't do, which was blush outrageously.

With his amber eyes locked on to her face she didn't feel so cocky any more. She looked everywhere around the room in order to avoid his gaze. When she looked back at his face he was still staring at her.

'Stop doing that!'

'Doing what?' He sounded innocently surprised.

'Making me feel like a stupid twelve-year-old! Just forget I said it and put some more music on.' It was her turn to sound testy.

'I'd really like to know why you're here,' he said.

'Jem tempted me back. He said I could get work and somewhere to live in Oxford just as easily as in London. I hated it there anyway. I missed the countryside, so I allowed him to win the argument.'

'So it was nothing to do with me, then?'

'You obviously think more of yourself than I thought you did.'

'And you're avoiding the question.'

'Am I?' Suzy desperately wanted a cigarette. 'Look, you must be tired. I'll go –'

'I'm not fucking tired! That's what everyone says. You must be tired, worn-out, exhausted, like I've spent the whole goddamned day training for the Olympics, when it is patently obvious that they are looking for an excuse to get away from me! Even as a small child I wasn't patronised as much as I am now! Why can't people be honest? Why can't they say, "Sorry, Clifton, I don't know what to say to you any more so I'd rather leave and save us both any more embarrassment!"'

'You were the one making me embarrassed!'

'Why? Because you openly admitted to me that I turn

you on? So what? It was the best thing anyone has said to me in months!'

'So why didn't you say that instead of making me feel like a total idiot?'

'Because I don't know if I can trust you.'

That shook her a little. 'Why?'

Clifton shook his head. 'Forget it. If you don't know already then I'm not going to tell you. We won't speak of it again.'

'Fine! Whatever. Just . . .'

'What? Keep out of your face? You were the one who came in here, remember?'

She wasn't going to win this; it was obvious by the amused way he was looking at her. He had taken up the gauntlet and had thrown it down again for her, and she had tripped over it before she knew it was there.

'I'm going out in the garden. Care to join me?' she asked sarcastically.

'Fuck off.'

'With pleasure.' She walked out, trying not to stomp. Failed.

She went out into the garden and wandered around, losing herself in the white rose garden and the walled Victorian vegetable garden where Mr Penrose worked, somewhat stiffly. The young gardener was nowhere to be seen. Finally she headed for the old lichen-covered wall that surrounded the patio. There was something very naughty about perching on a wall with one's legs dangling over the side. It was only a couple of feet high, and the bed below was filled with lavender plants, sil-ver-leaved and fragrant. The sun was warm and she was out of the wind, so she sat looking towards the lake, trying not to feel guilty that she wasn't at work.

Although it was very pleasant whiling away the

morning, it was soon time to walk to the stables. She turned to swing her legs off the wall, but as she did a sharp movement in her peripheral vision made her start. She lost her balance and rolled back over the wall, landing in the lavender bed with her legs in the air. Hastily she scrambled out of the bed, doing an inelegant backward roll. She straightened the squished lavender plants as best as she could and looked furtively around to see if anyone had seen. No one had, fortunately.

Apart from Clifton McKenna, who was sitting at the conservatory window, laughing his bloody head off.

Ignore him, she thought, gathering her tattered dignity back together and stalking off, nose in the air. But then she tripped over a protruding paving slab and no doubt made his day.

Nursing her injured pride, she walked down to the village to get the promised buns. The bakery formed part of the general store, whereas years ago it was a shop in its own right. Progress being what it was, the Post Office, the bakery and the general groceries stores were all now one, under a garish Spar sign. As she approached, the door opened and a man walked out. It was Jem. He hadn't seen her, and was walking in the opposite direction.

'Hey, I thought I was getting the buns,' she shouted after him. He ignored her. She ran after him. 'Hey, Jem, wait up...'

He turned around.

'Piss off, bitch.'

She braked fast. It wasn't Jem, but it could have been, if he had been wearing glasses. They looked so alike it was startling. She backed away from his intimidating presence.

'Sorry,' she said, and dived into the shop, feeling slightly shaken.

As she checked out the unfamiliar surroundings she listened to the woman behind the Post Office desk talking to an elderly man with a small dog. Her voice faded out when she saw Suzy. Suzy deliberately took her time perusing the counter. The buns looked good; plain bread fingers with white icing slathered on the top. They used to call them 'sticky willies' but she doubted that would go down very well with the magnificently bosomed Mrs Fenchurch, who presided over the store. Suzy was served silently, as if watched by crows waiting for roadkill. She escaped the unwelcoming atmosphere and carried on walking.

The town's configuration centred around the bridge spanning the River Cherwell, on the side of a steep hill. New executive homes had been built on the north side, but the south side was essentially still as it had been for centuries, with honey-coloured stone houses lining a central street that held a butcher's, an upmarket shoe shop, two tea rooms and the village store and Post Office. Suzy had studied at Oxford, five miles down the road, but at Brookes, doing business studies. She had been on the wintry periphery of the academic circle, but had sneaked in via Jem, who was at Christ Church at the same time. Those were the days, she thought wistfully, days when she had no money, poor nutrition and relationships that ended in messy betrayal. Actually, she hadn't moved on as much as she thought she had, she mused.

She thought of the incident outside the store, and at last remembered who he was. Peter Price, resident psychopath, a troublemaker from her schooldays, from a family who lived on the council estate at the south end of the village and ruled it with brick fists. For a while he had worked at the same building yard as Jem, and for some reason hated the sight of him. It may have been because of the old rumours that they were brothers. The last person who had mentioned it lost two of his teeth. No wonder he was so pissed off at her.

The sight of a small, scrappy gypsy encampment distracted her. She counted ten caravans in all, each with a matching Ford truck or van. On the main road up into the village a large lay-by had been cut into the hillside, for what purpose no one knew, as it had been that way since before Suzy was born. The Council owned it, and sometimes people from out of town came and dumped their refrigerators and washing machines there. Other times large heaps of grit were placed along the entrance to deter the gypsies. It didn't work though. They flattened the grit during the night and parked their caravans on top of it. The 'Great Clutton' sign was just before the bend in the road, and the first thing summer visitors saw when they entered the village was the scruffy heap of old trucks and vans. Not the greatest advertisement for a village where the cheapest private property topped a quarter of a million.

Jem had the phone glued to his ear when she arrived. She left the buns on the desk and went outside. In one of the stables a horse was being tended by a figure in tight blue jeans. His shirt was off, and his body was pretty buff. When he stood up, the rest of him wasn't bad either. His skin was honey brown, with dark hair on his arms and chest. Unfortunately he didn't look very friendly.

'What's wrong with her?' Suzy asked, hanging over the stable door. He was feeling the mare's hocks. Every now and then she shifted, whickering as if in pain.

'Run too hard,' he said.

'I'm sorry?'

He turned impatiently towards Suzy. 'They ran her too hard too soon after her last race. Now if you'll excuse me, I'm busy, Miss . . .'

'Whitbread. Suzy.'

'Oh, you're staying at Springfields?'

Boy, she had forgotten how fast news travelled around the village.

'That's right,' she said.

Another grunt, and a scratch of the head. 'Then if I were you, I would watch yourself with Mr McKenna. Don't meddle in matters you don't understand.'

She was thrown by the unexpectedness of it. 'That isn't my intention. What do you mean, "matters I don't understand"?'

He looked as if he had regretted ever speaking out. He stalked off, leaving her to wonder what was the purpose of that little episode. A warning to guard her virtue, or a warning off?

Later she shared the buns with Jem and told him about it. 'I don't get it. Everyone is so unfriendly. It's like I've got this sign on my forehead saying, "Worthless Tart. Be Rude To Me!"'

'Don't mind Alan. He's very loyal to Dad, but he knows him too well. He doesn't want him to get into trouble with Mum because of you, that's all.'

'I see. Nubile female plus randy Squire in wheelchair equals hot gossip. I'm surprised they aren't throwing money at me to create as much trouble as possible, just to give them something to talk about.' She sucked on her cigarette and stubbed it half-smoked in the ashtray. One day, she really would give up.

5

'My god, it's a miracle,' Jem murmured suddenly at breakfast next morning. Suzy looked at what had caught his attention. At the same time she heard Mrs Penrose talking to someone who had entered the room. Clifton McKenna had decided, for the first time in six months, to have breakfast with his son.

Jem didn't comment on it. He moved the dining chairs to accommodate the wheelchair as Mrs Penrose fluffed around, setting another place. When order was restored, they carried on as normal. The main topic of discussion was their prize horse, Double O Seven, which Jem had entered at Doncaster. Clifton thought it too early to send him to such a high profile event. The owner, a sheik who had two other horses at the stables, agreed with Jem. It was a potentially tricky situation, should Clifton decide to get involved.

'He's too young. He'll get overwhelmed by the journey. Better he cuts his teeth at Ascot,' Clifton said, buttering a sliver of toast and cutting it into neat triangles.

'But you haven't seen him run! On exercise he's eager as anything. He doesn't want to be held back.'

'Precisely. You know how stressful it is for these animals to travel long distances in the box. He's too immature to use that stress in a positive way. However, it's up to you. You're the decision maker there now.' Clifton bit decisively into his toast. Suzy didn't look at him. How she hated that beard!

'I really wish you would come out and see him run,' Jem said.

There was a pregnant pause. Suzy remembered the night when he had hurled a very expensive crystal tumbler at her, and Jem's comment about warfare being raged with bone china. Clifton's shaking hand was betrayed by the light tinkle of his cup against the saucer.

'And how are you proposing to fill your time whilst you're here, Suzy?'

The abrupt veering away from the conversation was his way of restoring order. A look to Jem warned him that if he persisted with his insistence that Clifton come out of the house, the calm would be broken, probably violently. Jem threw up his hands in silent exasperation.

'I'm ... looking for work in Oxford.'

'As?'

'A beauty therapist. You know, nails, waxing.'

'I know. My wife uses them to try to stave off the cruel march of time.' He laughed unpleasantly. 'I'm sure there's enough work in this house to keep you employed until retirement.'

'Perhaps. I do men as well.'

He arched one elegant eyebrow, as black as a raven's wing. 'Is that so? What exactly is it that you "do" to them?'

'Pedicures, manicures, facials. Light massage. Back, sack and crack waxing.'

Clifton was caught off-guard. His cup missed the saucer and overbalanced onto the pristine tablecloth. There was a fluster as Mrs Penrose homed in on the stain to mop it up. Suzy saw Jem grinning widely. Clifton wanted Mrs Penrose's ample backside out of the way so he could see Suzy again. When she finally left Suzy was nibbling at her toast.

'I'd forgotten how gorgeous your garden is. I must go

out and explore,' she said. 'Are you having the open weekend again this year?'

She could tell that Clifton wanted to pursue the intriguing subject of men's hair removal, but she wasn't going to let him have too much fun at once. She asked Jem about decent local garages. Getting her car fixed was her number one priority that morning.

Mrs Penrose came in bearing more coffee. Bounding after her was a large, handsome blond man of tangible energy, dressed in brown corduroys and a suspect lemon yellow Pringle sweater, topped with a paisley silk cravat. Dr Maloney, the unlikeliest fitness guru Suzy had ever seen. He shook Clifton's hand and looked appreciatively at Suzy.

'Hello, young lady. Are you here to help this lazy bugger to his feet?'

'He needs a bomb under his arse,' she said archly.

'Damned right. I'll hold him down, you light the blue touchpaper,' Dr Maloney said cheerfully. He shook hands with Suzy and Jem, and they talked for a while before Dr Maloney grabbed the handles of the wheelchair as if they were a bull's horns and steered Clifton into the gym. As he closed the door behind him Suzy heard him say, 'You randy dog, McKenna. We're going to get you fit so you can give that pretty maid a proper seeing to.'

'I wish,' was the curt reply. It kept her grinning for most of the morning.

Two hours later she was out on the patio. Jem had left and she tried to assuage her guilt by swimming thirty lengths. Dr Maloney appeared beside her. He sat down on the lounger next to Suzy's and admired the view of the river. 'Fabulous location here, isn't it? It's a pity he won't get out a bit more.'

'Why won't he?' She asked.

Dr Maloney drew in his breath and let it out again, slowly and thoughtfully.

'It's common for people with these types of injuries to become very demoralised, but he was incredibly strong before the accident. His stamina should have been able to kick-start his recovery. His lack of motivation has been frustrating up until now, but maybe you have the magic touch?' He let his chunky fingers drift softly against her knee before reaching into his jacket pocket. He pulled out an embossed business card, printed on thick cream paper. 'Any time you need advice, and I mean any time, give me a call.' He winked at her. 'Keep it to yourself though. Mr McKenna would not approve.'

Suzy smiled at him. What a ladies man, and what bedroom eyes, the colour of dark chocolate. 'Definitely.'

After having lunch with Jem at the Red Lion she went back to the house. That night she was travelling back to London for a long-standing date to go clubbing with some old friends, but first she wanted to see Clifton. Give a little, take a little; that was her strategy. If he was rude, ignore him until he backed down.

He was doing the *Daily Telegraph* crossword puzzle. Crashing classical music was on in the background. It made her want to plug her ears with cotton wool. Even so, he heard her come in.

'I could be forgiven for assuming that you can't keep away from me,' he said humorously.

'On the contrary. I've been warned away from you,' she replied easily. 'It seems you might be after my virtue. If that's the case, someone has been there first. I'm sorry.'

'I rather doubt you ever had any in the first place.'

'Is that an educated guess or a fantasy?'

Clifton gave her a sardonic smile. 'The music you hear now is Wagner. What do you think?'

'It's awful.'

He picked up the remote control and killed the sound. 'When you say awful, do you mean you like it, or are awed by it?'

'I'm sorry? I meant I hate it.'

'Then it seems the intricacies of the English language are lost on you. I suggest you furnish yourself with a dictionary.' He glided over to the sound system and perused his collection of compact discs.

'Do you know anything about opera, Suzy?'

'They're all about love, and everyone dies at the end. Is that right?'

'I think the word you are looking for is "passion". Love is an ephemeral thing, not to be taken too seriously.'

'I thought it was a many splendoured thing,' Suzy quipped lightly, earning herself a withering look. 'Do you have any Stereophonics? Red Hot Chilli Peppers? Nickleback?'

'*Carmen*, actually. A calculating woman whose only virtues were physical ones.'

'One assumes that is all that matters to you.'

He laughed loudly. 'I like you, Suzy Whitbread, and for that, I'm going to grant you a wish. Take off your dress.'

She scooped her jaw from the floor. 'I'm sorry?'

His strange yellow eyes glittered at her. 'You want to shave me. I want you to do it in your lingerie. Quid pro quo. You are quite safe. I shall not touch you. Not today.'

Suzy recalled what she was wearing underneath the simple cotton Gap dress. Her sheer white bra and panties meant she might as well have nothing on at all, but nothing ventured, nothing gained. Meeting his challenging look, she pulled the dress over her head.

She could feel the heat of his gaze roaming over her body. Her nipples had noticeably tensed with anticipation. Her black pubic bush was flattened and very visible under the gauzy material. Self-conscious and a little nervous, she shivered, raising goosepimples on her arms and legs.

'It is warmer in the bedroom,' he said, turning the chair and propelling himself in through the door.

'Of course it is,' she murmured dryly as she followed him.

His bedroom was very different from the main room, vibrant with texture and deep, rich colours. The four-poster bed was sumptuous, with a crushed velvet, wine-coloured cover and rich brocade drapes edged in gold at the head. The simply carved posts were old mahogany, smooth and warm to the touch. She ran her hand around one of them. It felt like the smooth skin on a lover's arm. It took second place to the many pictures on the walls, and the marble sculptures that invited her fingers to feel how smooth they were. They all had a similar erotic theme. The explicitness of one set of black and white drawings made her do a double-take.

'*The Postures*, first drawn in the sixteenth century, but reproduced here by Count de Waldeck,' he said. 'They caused quite a stir. The artist was thrown into jail.'

In a frame standing on the bedside cabinet there was a sepia print of a woman with upswept hair crowned with flowers. Her dress was early Edwardian, her pose provocative. She sat in a huge, balloon-backed wicker chair, one leg hooked over the arm. The silken folds of her dress were gathered up to reveal silk stockings with lace tops and gartered with more flowers. One could just see the dark shadow between her legs, when attention had been torn away from her breasts, dark nipples peeping out from her décolletage. Although the picture looked as if it had been taken long ago, Suzy wasn't so sure. There was something knowing about the eyes, and the high-heeled shoes looked suspiciously like Lulu Guinness creations.

'No prizes for guessing what interests you,' she said.

Clifton watched her with an amused expression. 'I've always been a sensualist. The infinite variations of erotic joy interest me intensely.' There was a small silence, in which he challenged her to find a witty comment for that. She kept quiet, and he looked slightly disappointed. 'How are you with a razor?'

'I know what to do.'

'With one of these?' With a flourish he produced a cutthroat razor, so sharp it made Suzy wince. The handle was ivory, delicately carved, and the lethal edge had been lovingly honed by an affectionate owner.

'I've ... never actually used one of those,' she admitted.

'Now is your chance. This was my grandfather's. He used it in the trenches. If you look carefully, you'll still see some Ypres mud engrained in the carving.' He held the razor out to her. She took it, carefully, holding it gingerly by the tip of the handle.

'I hope you won't be holding it like that when you start on me,' he grumbled. 'Though if you cut my throat it wouldn't really matter.'

Suzy ignored that and went into his bathroom to gather the equipment she needed, again feeling rather self-conscious, knowing he was watching her every move.

First she trimmed his beard. When it was very short she could see the line of his jaw. Now he looked like an ex-convict. She took a warm towel from the rail in the bathroom and positioned him so that his head was almost resting in her lap. His chair was one of the latest models on which the back could be lowered and the feet lifted, as in a recliner. A cushion slid up to support his head.

'My wife isn't going to like this one little bit,' he said, gazing up between her breasts.

'Do you want me to carry on?'

Clifton suddenly gave her a full wattage smile, his eyes gleaming like old gold. 'Of course. I may get into serious trouble.'

She wasn't sure what he was getting at. 'You may,' she conceded warily.

'And I may be punished for my sins,' he murmured, letting his eyes close again, 'but mine will be the greater pleasure.'

As Suzy wrapped the hot towel around his face she did it tightly to discourage any more talk, thinking it fortunate that he would not be able to speak again for a while. With her tools around her, she took a deep breath and began.

It was very peaceful, with Maria Callas in the background. The heat from the towel relaxed Clifton's facial muscles and opened the pores. His eyes drifted shut, and she almost forgot that she was half-naked.

The cream went on next, lathered up with a soft badger-hair brush and then massaged in with her fingertips to raise the bristles. He sighed deeply, and Suzy guessed it had been a long time since he had been pampered in any way. The razor did the job for her. She hardly had to work at it as the blade glided over his taut skin. It was immensely exciting to see the face of the man she had lusted after emerge under all that damned hair. His jaw, so angular and strong, was gradually restored to full glory under her fingertips. As the result of his fall it was slightly misshapen, giving him a more angular appearance than she remembered from before.

She removed the final offending vestiges of hair but did not want to look properly at the result yet. She turned his face side to side, looking for stray hairs. There were none. His skin was slightly reddened, until cool water closed the pores.

'And a facial massage to finish with,' she said, but did not say why, because at that moment she couldn't think of a feasible reason, other than she didn't want to stop touching him. She squeezed sandalwood fragranced moisturising cream into the palm of her hand and began to massage it into his skin, taking her time to work it in, her fingers gaining as much pleasure from touching him as he was feeling from the sensuous pleasure of being touched. He seemed to melt into the chair as she worked the cream down his throat. The open shirt revealed silky tufts of dark hair and pectorals still hard and toned. As her fingers slid inside the shirt of their own volition he seemed almost to lift towards her touch, as a cat does when it approves of being stroked. She heard the slight catching of his breath as her breasts brushed against his cheek. Her fingertips drifted over his nipples before trailing back up his neck to his jaw line, making tiny little circling movements, moving up to his temples, around his eyes, his high, smooth forehead. Glancing further down, she saw a ridge obvious enough to make Mrs Penrose blush. No problems there, then. He must have known it was obvious but it didn't seem to bother him. Maybe he was reacting as she was to the sensual turn the afternoon had taken in that brothel of a bedroom. She sometimes went into a trance whilst administering massage, especially with someone she found extremely attractive, and it was happening again now. She could feel herself going, her fingers communicating pleasure whilst her mind was on matters more sexual than healing. Her sex was moist and her nipples hard as nuts.

Then she saw him, watching her. She flushed scarlet, and the mood was broken.

'Sometimes I get a bit carried away,' she gabbled, backing away and pushing the chair back into a sitting position. She removed the towel and the bowl of hairy water in order to compose herself in the bathroom. When she had cleaned up he was staring in the dressing table mirror, touching his face.

She tried to keep her voice brisk. 'So how does it feel?'

'It doesn't look that bad.' He smiled lopsidedly at Suzy and her insides did a back flip. She snatched the opportunity to feel his face one last time, running her fingers over his smooth jaw and top lip.

'It might tingle for an hour or so, but that will pass.' The last word was more of a breath as his hand gripped her wrist in a vice-like grip. Contrary to the fierceness of his grasp he kissed her palm with a warm, velvet touch, then let her go.

'Thank you,' he said. 'You may get dressed and go.'

Suzy did as she was told, but she felt irritatingly confused. She was usually very good at being flirty. So good in fact, that most men didn't actually know they were being targeted until it was too late. She hadn't yet met one who could play her at her own game. But it seemed she had now. He might be hungry for sex, but he was also an intelligent man whose interests extended far beyond those of the average, gagging-for-it, 18–30 Cro-Magnon she encountered with depressing frequency up in London on a Saturday night. The question was, how was she going to get under his skin?

Jem called her as she was fighting rush hour traffic on the M25. He had let her borrow his Audi TT whilst the Golf was being fixed.

'How was your day?'

'Great. I bummed around, saw your Dad. His bedroom's a piece of work, isn't it?'

'Yeah. We only found out about it after the accident. Until then he wouldn't allow anyone in there.'

'Even your mother?'

'Oh, especially her.' There was a delicate pause. 'What were you doing in his bedroom anyway?'

'Oh, I gave him a shave,' she said casually.

'And you've still got your fingers?'

'He gave me the razor. I just did my thing. It's what I'm good at, you know,' she added primly.

'Yeah, as well as the other thing.'

'What other thing?' Her eyes went wide with curiosity.

'The pretty, innocent maid with the heart of Linda Lovelace thing.'

Suzy laughed. 'I might have changed since you went away.' Or maybe not, as she winked at the businessman in the BMW next to her.

'Leopards don't change spots. I'm finding this all very interesting, you know.'

'I have no idea what "this" is supposed to be.'

'You and my dad. It's like . . . destiny fulfilling itself.'

'Oh please, concentrate on your own love life, would you?' But she was grinning. Just thinking about the possibility of her and Clifton . . . it was weird, but ever since she had moved down to Great Clutton she had been in a heightened state of anticipation.

'Bonny's giving me a hard time at the moment,' Jem was saying. 'I don't think she likes us spending so much time together.'

Bonny hadn't taken the news that he had a female friend staying at the house terribly well. Suzy could have told him that she wouldn't, but she had vowed not to interfere in Jem's love life.

'Oh, like we've been joined at the hip since I got here. I've hardly seen you!'

'I think she's jealous.'

'You're too soft. Don't let her bully you.'

'I won't. See you tomorrow.' He rang off. Suzy crawled at a snail's pace around the North Circular. This, as much as any other, was a good reason to have moved into the country.

Within the hour she was sipping Chardonnay and catching up with the gossip. She had plenty of her own, but it would keep. She painted toenails and fingernails and listened to stories of conquests and one-night stands, and it seemed so far away and so bleak and pointless now that she was out of it. Finally it was her turn.

'You're plum crazy,' Sacha said when she had finished. Suzy painted top coat on her new, leopard-spotted talons.

'Tell it like it is, Sach,' she murmured.

'I mean, how old is this guy?'

'Forty-six,' Suzy replied shortly.

'And crippled,' Annie said.

'In a wheelchair. There's a difference.'

'How big is his dick?' Sharon asked.

'That's kind of academic, isn't it?' Annie said, witheringly.

'See what I mean? Cra-azeee,' Sacha said, tapping her temple with her porcelain nail extensions.

Suzy had had enough. 'Look. I'm staying rent-free, with waitress service at every meal. I can get pissed every night and not have to get up in the morning. I have access to a pool, a gym, and as many men in tight jodhpurs as I could wish for. On top of that my host is an incredibly good-looking, horny man who hasn't had sex for over six months. Now what is so crazy about that?'

There was a small silence.

'He can't get it up,' Sharon said flatly. 'I mean, there's no point if the guy can't get hard, is there?'

'That's right! I remember when you had that biker guy. Man, he was like a jackhammer, you said. Couldn't think how any man would match him, you said.'

'I also said he was a dickhead who dealt coke. And I dumped him,' Suzy reminded her. 'Anyway, Clifton has no concerns in that area.'

'Talk properly, girl. You saying he can get a boner? How would you know if you haven't fucked him?'

Suzy critically examined Sacha's nails and left them alone. 'Sometimes, all you need to use is your eyes.'

There was a collective whoop from the girls.

'What's his wife like?'

'Yeah, isn't she, like, kind of noticing all this going on?'

Suzy grinned wickedly. 'She's on vacation. And she thinks her shit doesn't stink, so I have no intention of feeling guilty.'

'Huh. I thought you said you'd never mess around with a married guy,' Sacha growled.

'If you're serious about me coming with you tonight, I would drop the subject right now.'

The evening went as they usually did. Two clubs, the second one noisier than the first. A cocktail of Bacardi Breezers, followed by vodka slammers, plenty of groping on the dance floor and unintelligible conversations shouted over clubbed-up renditions of 90s classics. Suzy ended up being cornered by a drunken computer salesman, on the loose from his family up in Lancashire. He was quite sweet so she snogged him for quite a while, giving him a stiffy on the dance floor. Over his shoulder she could see Sacha with two male friends, each trying to fondle her round backside. Annie and Sharon had disappeared altogether. Same shit, different night.

Before the salesman decided he wanted her back in his hotel room she left him and the girls to it and went back to her flat. She slept long and deep, and took her time getting up, getting fed and driving back to Great Clutton. It would be interesting to discover Clifton's reaction to why she wasn't at breakfast.

Jem was grateful to Suzy for staying away that night. He and Bonny ate at Browns in Oxford before going back to the house. At the front door she moulded herself against him and put her arms around his neck, pressing her lips to his. He dragged her inside and closed the door behind them.

There was no privacy in the camp. Whilst Robby had no qualms about bringing various women home to test the pull-down bed to the limit, Bonny preferred to keep her trysts with Jem private, although everyone knew about them. Their favourite place was the drawing room, where there was little chance of Clifton hearing them. As Jem spread her out on the Persian rug and contentedly lapped at her sweet, shaven pussy she looked around at the silver, the valuable china, the trinkets, and she smiled to herself. Most of all, she liked the painting above the fireplace. The horse was glossy black, the rider standing beside it in full hunting regalia, scarlet top coat and high leather boots, a supercilious smile on his aristocratic features. And Bonny fantasised that he was eating her out with exquisite finesse, before riding her hard like he rode his horse, his face contorted with lust.

Jem hit the spot, and Bonny's soft cries became genuinely needy. She kept eye contact with the huntsman on the wall, and she tugged at her nipples, making them huge and long, and the image of him striding towards her, intent on taking her any which way, his erection starkly visible in his cream jodhpurs, sent her over the edge. Her inner muscles contracted against Jem's tongue, sucking it in as he kept her pulsing with pleasure.

When it became unbearable she pushed him away. His face was awash with her juices, his eyes narrow with lust. As he kneeled up to remove his clothing, she swooped down on his cock so suddenly that he lost his balance and sprawled out on the floor. She continued to suck him. His size was impressive, there was no doubt about that, and he was responsive too, leaping up at her every time her tongue trailed across him. She smiled up at the man on the wall, teasingly, all the while inching Jem's cock into her mouth, so far that he groaned when she reached the root. Her lips closed and she drew them back, letting him feel the whole of the inside of her mouth. He trembled wildly.

'I'm going to shoot,' he whispered. She didn't mind. He could get it up again faster than any man she had had before. She did it again, and he was right. He bolted deep in her throat, so deep she could hardly taste it. He hissed loudly with pleasure, his hips lifting with just the one, deeply felt spasm.

As they lay together on the rug Jem looked around, thinking how horrified his mother would be if she knew what he had been doing in her favourite room. Then his eyes alighted on her collection of jade. At the back, lurking furtively as hidden there, was an exquisitely carved chunk with a rounded end. He would not have seen it if he had been standing up, or even sitting in one of the armchairs, and it was immediately obvious why. It looked for all the world like a sex toy for a prized Oriental empress. As he looked closer, he saw that the tiny figures carved into the stone were all copulating in outrageously athletic positions. He laughed in disbelief. What on earth would his mother want with something like that?

He took it out of the cabinet and turned it over in his hands. It was cool and heavy, and as he glanced at Bonny, languishing on the rug, his juices began to flow again.

'How does that feel?' he asked, trailing the jade dildo over her nipple. At its cold touch the nipple sprang to life, crinkling the dark skin around it. He flicked at it with his tongue and Bonny moaned softly. Then the other nipple, followed by a heated flick, and her eyes began to grow hazy. Her legs fell apart as he teased her with the tool, stroking the soft skin between hip and thigh, down the insides of her thighs and behind her knees. It was big, bigger than him, and as he teased her pussy lips open with its blunt round tip her eyes widened. But Jem wasn't fooled. Inside she was as slick and pulpy as an overripe mango, and the hard tool slipped in without argument. She gasped at the cool heaviness of it, spreading her legs wider, the tip of her tongue pressed against her top lip as she watched Jem push it in further. He knelt over her, letting his balls hang over her face as he continued to fuck her with the priceless instrument. It was his turn to moan when he felt her tongue sweep around his balls. His penis began to thicken again, and in a few moments he knew he would not disappoint her. His head dipped and he carefully strummed her clitoris. Bonny shrieked softly, her hips jerking up so hard that a couple more inches of jade impaled her. Her moan was one of abandon as Jem began to fuck her rhythmically with it, his mouth gently but relentlessly attached to her clitoris. Her legs were spread as wide as they could go. He plunged into her mouth as her moment of orgasm approached, and he felt every single jolt of her body. Bonny, enslaved totally by cock and tongue and jade dildo, could do nothing but moan and buck and claw at Jem's back, leaving long scratches that he would feel later. Afterwards, he turned her over onto her front, her backside stuck high in the air, and he fucked her for real, his fingers digging into her hips. Bonny revelled in this kind of rough, tough fucking, and the added spice of having this son of a genteel family behaving like a farm animal was, to her, the best aphrodisiac of all.

She left him two hours later, replete and fucked-out, and walked back to the camp. Despite the lateness of the hour there were people still up, huddled in a little group around the dying fire. They had been playing poker, and drinking Bell's scotch. Her stepfather looked up as she approached, and the group fell silent.

'Well? What did you find?'

'Nothing,' she said sullenly.

'What? You were with him all evening!'

'We were banging on the floor!' She stepped back as Seamus stood up, his fists bunched.

'If you don't get some decent goods next time, I'll beat the shit out of you.'

Bonny ran to her caravan before he hit her anyway. Robby was snoring loudly, an empty beer can on the floor beside his dangling fingers. She quickly undressed and slipped into her narrow bed, shivering violently.

6

When Suzy arrived back the following afternoon there was no one around. She thought about visiting Clifton, but she didn't want him thinking that she actively needed to seek him out. With the rain lashing against the window and no one to disturb her, the ideal opportunity to go exploring had presented itself.

She started upstairs. Each room was sumptuous, swathed in Jacquard, damask and carved mahogany, but not very interesting. Most of it she knew about already, but there was one place she had never gone before.

The door to Alice and Clifton's suite beckoned, although it was forbiddingly shut. She knew that directly below lay Clifton's rooms, so she would have to be very quiet.

The door creaked softly as she opened it, but there were no alarm bells, no sirens. The room was actually two large bedrooms, the first one being Alice's, which was romantic and filled with powder blue and cream toile de Jouy. There was a bathroom leading off to one side, and a huge walk-in closet filled with designer garments and row upon row of shoes, all with notes about what they should be worn with. Suzy took it all in for a moment, but it was the other door that had caught her interest.

This bedroom had to be Clifton's, as it was before the accident. The furnishings were undoubtedly masculine, with dark oak panelling on the walls. Two Indian sabres crossed over a large white marble fireplace. There were silver frames with old photographs, presumably of blood relations long gone, some with improbable moustaches and white uniforms covered with medals.

When she opened the door to his closet, it smelled of his aftershave, very faint, like a ghost lingering in the corner. Leather riding boots, buffed to an army-standard shine, sober business suits, all of them bespoke tailoring, and handmade shirts folded and pressed. There was a faint smell of mothballs, but it was as if he had just gone downstairs for a moment. A Jeffrey Archer novel was sitting on the bedside cabinet. In his bathroom, cedar soap, bath foam, all Molton Brown, brand new, as if awaiting his return. She wandered out again and sat on the vast bed, leaning down to open the drawer in the small cabinet. No secrets there. Nail file, clippers, some Olbas oil.

Realising now that she was hunting for something more, something to get into his psyche, she went to the tallboy opposite the bed and knelt down by the bottom drawer. It glided out on well-lubricated runners. She had chosen that one rather than any of the others because by tradition secrets, if there were any, did tend to lurk in bottom drawers.

Boxer shorts, silk and cotton, silk socks, still with the Saks label on them, two new pairs of silk pyjamas. Car keys. She remembered the XKR, languishing in the garage. She put them back, vowing to remember them. Then her fingers brushed against something hard. She drew it out carefully, so as not to dislodge anything else.

It was paydirt, in the form of a silver frame. In it was a photograph of a woman surrounded by vivid azalea blossoms. It definitely wasn't Alice. She was attractive rather than beautiful, in a crisp white shirt and modest denim skirt, a delicate gold chain around her throat. Her features were small and her hair an ordinary light brown, but it was the eyes and the smile that made Suzy understand. The eyes held knowledge of the man behind the lens that no other had, and the half-smile was of someone destined to be unfaithful that very day.

Underneath that was a cream envelope. Knowing she shouldn't, she opened it and drew out several photographs. It took several moments for Suzy to realise that it was the same woman, this time in a bitch-queen-from-hell basque with pointy cups, tall shiny boots laced all the way up the sides, and a riding crop.

'No shit!' Suzy breathed, struggling to take it in. Clifton was bare-chested, in his jodhpurs and riding boots, crawling around on the floor at the woman's feet. On his back, Suzy could just make out long marks, presumably where she had hit him. Even then, he could not pretend to be cowed by the humiliation. He was almost smiling, wanting the lash across his back. Suzy felt at once turned on, confused and jealous of the unknown woman. She forced the jealousy back to where it belonged and enjoyed the pumping of her heart as she stared at the photos again. They had been taken in Clifton's room. She recognised the marble fireplace and the crossed swords.

The last photograph was totally different. This time the woman was on all-fours on the bed. Suzy looked around. Yes, it was the same bed, and that mirror was the one that Clifton had taken the photo into. His partner had a shagged-out, lewd smile playing around her lips. Clifton was kneeling up behind her, holding the camera up to his face, taking the photograph as they screwed. God, he looked so fit! All muscle and sinew and fearful pile-driving energy. Suzy felt her sex quiver. She wanted him as he had been then, but in any other given situation, would he have still wanted her? With the photographs was a letter, written in a delicate, presumably female hand, and dated December 2002. It had been stored in its envelope, and when she pulled it out she felt how soft the paper was, as if it had been held and read many times.

Feeling that she really shouldn't be doing it, but knowing she was hardly going to put it back without having a look first, Suzy put the photographs back where they belonged and started to read.

C

I cannot forgive you for what you have done to me. You have ruined my life, changed me irrevocably. I cannot sustain the façade for much longer. I wear the scars of what you did to me and will wear them all my life. My husband wonders why I come to bed clothed, and turn out the light before I get into bed. He fumbles in the dark, opening my legs, entering me, hearing my gasp, thinking it is for him. But it is not. In the velvet dark it is you, coming to me like a thief in the night, your hair slick with the same sweat I can smell and feel on your body. I can taste its salt, feeling the burning heat of you as you plunder me, over and over. My lips are raw from your kisses, and the effort of not screaming your name as he spends his seed into me. You have broken me, and for that you must pay.

How? I have it worked out. I am ready for you now, my nails sharpened like talons to score across your back. For a whole day you will wait on me, cleaning my boots, making my coffee, cleaning my house. You are wearing nothing but jodhpurs and riding boots, and a collar that I have placed around your neck for later use. If you are insubordinate I will lash you with the crop. If you attempt to look up my short skirt and snatch a glimpse of my shaven cunt you will get five lashes. You will be able to smell me, mingling with the animal scent of the short leather skirt I am wearing, but if you try to touch me you will be kicked to the ground and made to lick my shoes clean. I will ride on your back, and you will be able to feel my sex burning into your vertebrae, and smell my musk. You will carry me to the garage, the stones on the path making your hands raw. From there I will drive us to the barn, where it is warm and private and there are many thick, strong beams from which I have rigged a special piece of equipment designed to render you totally accessible and in my power. But before I do that you may wash me with your tongue, licking away the juices from between my legs and down my thighs. Your own excitement is reined in hard, painfully so, but prominent and very visible. I can smell your need. You're like an animal, waiting to be set free, but I am not going to set you free. Instead I string you up with leather straps on your arms and legs, and you cannot move, cannot do anything. I undress in front of you, slowly, and slap your face when you turn away to escape the exquisite torture. Underneath my micro skirt and the white silk blouse I am wearing a boned bodice made of leather and lace, my nipples just resting above the shallow cups. It is laced tightly, so my breathing is somewhat restricted. This makes my bosom heave and swell, but as you greedily stare at them you earn another lash, this time across the massive bulge in your jodhpurs. My boots come halfway up my thighs, buckled and laced, the toes as sharp as the heels. Earlier I made you polish them whilst I was wearing them.

The outline of your cock is obscenely visible. I can see the head, the indentation below it, and I can smell you as well. Smell your feral need to fuck. Slowly I unzip you, peeling the jodhpurs away, commanding you not to make a sound, but you do. The relief of being out in the open is too much. I hear you gasp as your cock falls out and hangs heavily in front of me, inches from my lips.

By this time, Suzy was sprawled on the bed, breathless, her sex tingling as she envisaged Clifton, trussed and erect, awaiting his lady love to do her thing. She could almost hear his groan as she eased her mouth over his cock, stroking his dangling balls with the other hand, and see the cords on his neck stand out as he fought not to shoot too soon, turned on beyond reason by the woman's tiny waist and rounded hips, and her plump, naked sex pouting out of reach. But now she was making him suffer even more. Suzy read on.

I am wearing long, black gloves, snug and silky. You can feel them running over your backside as I press my cunt against your cock, tormenting you by refusing to fuck you. I stroll around behind you and suddenly thrust one finger deep between your buttocks. You've never had that done before, have you? That tight, virgin hole, so unwilling to submit to my advances. But it will now, because I lubricate and ease and persevere, my other hand on your cock. You cannot escape it, but then it is gone. You think I have given up, but you are wrong. You cannot see me, or guess what I am doing. You have no idea until you feel the blunt head of another cock pressing against your backside. Then you start to curse, but I am merciless. The strap-on dildo has imparted a sense of power that I could never have imagined. I palm it as if it is an intrinsic part of me, before guiding it into that secret place. You are protesting, swearing, pleading with me, but my other hand is on your cock, gliding up and down, a ceaseless rhythm that makes you want to thrust hard. As you do the backward motion impales you onto my rubber cock. You are being buggered senseless, my fingers deep in your hips, just as you did to me last night. I protested, and screamed, but you wouldn't listen, and despite myself I was overwhelmed with a deep and terrible joy. Now you are feeling the same, hating me, loving me, a slave to your own depravity. You waste your seed on the straw, sobbing and cursing, and for that you have to stay there and watch as I sprawl before you and make myself come. The dildo has gone and you can see right into my lubricious pussy, see my hands and how they give me pleasure.

So you can see what you've done to me. I am a depraved woman, a sensual being whose life lurches from one decadent experience to the next. You have made me this way, and for that you will pay.

Yours

K

'Phew,' Suzy muttered, putting the letter to one side. That was quite a woman. She could see the attraction now. The enduring image of Clifton in his jodhpurs and riding boots, submitting to the lash of her riding crop, would not go away.

But where was she now, this lady he was obviously smitten by? It had been more than a one-night stand, or even a heated three-week affair. Suzy could tell by the tenderness between the lines of the letter, and the intimacy in the photographs that had nothing to do with the physical dynamics of their crude love-making. She read the letter again, entranced by the scenario. When she slipped her hand between her legs she was shocked at how wet she was.

Voices downstairs made her heart lurch. Hurriedly she replaced the letter and slipped back out into the corridor. Jem and Clifton were having a heated debate directly below her. She tiptoed back down the stairs and into the drawing room. Too psyched up to sit and read her book, she wandered around, waiting for Jem to finish.

She came to rest where the family photographs were displayed in an artful cluster on one table in the corner of the room. There were the usual suspects. Jem, moon-faced and six months old, in a white dress and looking very pissed-off about it, Jem in mortarboard at his graduation. And Alice in white chiffon dress and white gloves, with a corsage of freesias, looking sweet and smug, posing for her coming-out portrait. There were none of Clifton, Suzy noted, except one rather grand one of him and Alice on their wedding day, flanked by two sets of tense, well-dressed parents. Alice's smile was professional, rather than radiant, and Clifton looked as if he would rather be somewhere else.

But it was a photograph right at the back of the collection, almost as if it had been hidden, that caught Suzy's eye. She picked it up, and stared. Two young men, their arms slung lazily around each other's shoulders, wearing the insolent grins of those who knew they had the world at their feet. One of them was Clifton. Black hair, fine bone structure, piercing eyes that could undress a woman at fifty paces. God, he was a fine-looking man in his twenties, Suzy thought. And he still was.

The other man was identical.

A door slammed, and Jem came into the drawing room. He was in jodhpurs and an old Lacoste polo shirt, both smeared with mud. His hair was sticking to his head from where he had been out in the rain all afternoon.

'Who's this?' Suzy tapped the photograph.

'Uncle Clayton. I can never tell them apart.' He didn't seem that interested.

'Where is he now?'

'In Cape Town, exporting wine. Mother calls him "that drunken rogue" when they talk about him, which isn't often. He's *persona non grata* in this house.'

'Which is why you still have a picture of him,' Suzy pointed out.

Jem grinned slyly. 'Ah well, the rumour goes that Mother had to choose between the two of them, and she chose Dad, because he had the better prospects, but secretly she would have preferred Uncle Clayton.'

'Where did you hear that?' Suzy laughed at his conspiratorial tone.

'It's called keeping an ear to the ground. My nanny liked to gossip with the housekeeper. I learned all sorts of things about my family that I would never have heard about otherwise.'

'Anything else?' What could be juicier than Alice lusting after her husband's brother?

'Nothing that interesting,' Jem sighed. 'But the wrong man might have shelled out for my expensive education. I've always wondered.'

'And this doesn't bother you?'

'Why should it? My life hasn't exactly been underprivileged, has it?' He took the photograph from her and put it back. 'I need a drink. Let's go to the pub.'

They went into the White Hart, a bastion of faded splendour that didn't mind muddy boots, as long as they had been engaged in the worthy sports of hunting, shooting or fishing.

'I have a bone to pick with you,' Jem said, as they sat down with glasses of cider. Their order for toasted cheese sandwiches was on its way. 'This morning the first thing Dad did was ask after you. When I said you had gone to

73

pick up a merchant banker for the night he wasn't impressed.' He sipped his cider and grinned. 'Can't imagine why.'

'Nor can I,' Suzy said primly.

'Let's just say his mood hasn't improved. Now he's blaming me for Seagrass's injury. It was the owner who was at fault. He insisted on the horse racing last week. Now he wants to speak to Dad because he thinks I'm the incompetent, but Dad's having none of it. Maybe you could speak to him?'

'And risk getting hospitalised by a piece of flying crystal? I don't think so.'

'Come on, you wanted the challenge, remember?'

'That was to get him walking again.'

'To get him living again,' he corrected her. 'Go and see him tonight, for God's sake. He's waiting for you.'

'I hardly think so.'

'Go on. He likes you, Suzy. He'll listen to you.'

'When did you work that out?'

'I didn't. It's a desperate attempt at flattery to get you to do what I want.'

'Thanks a lot,' she said.

'You're very welcome,' he said, grinning widely.

Suzy went back to the house but did not go to see Clifton immediately, although he would have known if he had been watching the windows that she had come back. It wouldn't do him any harm to wait. She lay on her bed and thought about the photographs and the letter. The woman had to be the reason for his bottled-up aggression, but he was also a sensual being who thrived on the delights of the flesh. He had to channel that frustrated energy into something useful. Maybe then he would find the gut determination to get back on his feet.

After a few moments she knew what to do. She

stripped and put on pale pink gauze panties and matching brassiere, a white blouse tied at her midriff, undone so that every time she moved, one saw what was inside it, and a very short denim skirt that she only wore when she wanted to get laid. It was time to up the ante. If he wasn't ready, that was tough. She damned well was.

She knocked softly on his door and went in.

'So? Where were you last night?' he asked by way of greeting. He did not look at her.

'I'm fine, Clifton. How are you?'

He spun the chair around to face her. 'Don't get insolent with me, girl. You're a guest in this house.'

Suzy drew in a patient breath. 'I went out with some friends last night, up in London.'

'My company not good enough for you, then?'

'If you want my company, you only have to ask. To expect it and not tell me is impolite. With your upbringing surely you should know that.'

The whisky bottle rattled against the glass. 'What did you do up there?'

'Had a laugh, got drunk, danced. The usual stuff.'

'Meet anyone?'

'That isn't your business.'

'The hell it isn't!' He smashed the glass on the floor, sending splinters of glass shooting around her stiletto heels.

'You need to learn some manners,' Suzy said mildly.

'I hardly think you're the right one to teach me.'

'I didn't say I was.' She leaned on the arms of his wheelchair and looked deep into his angry eyes. 'Soon I'm going to ply you with single malt and make you tell me what the hell is going on inside your head, and you can't stop me.'

'I can refuse to drink.'

'Clifton, I doubt if you've ever refused a drink.' Their faces were very close. She could smell him, warm and male, lightly fragranced with sandalwood.

'Go to hell,' he said.

'That isn't very nice,' she chided gently. She captured his wrists and pinned them to the chair arms, using her weight to keep them there, and pushed the chair around until he was facing the large mirror. Then she altered her position so that her skirt would subtly ride further up her hips. In the mirror behind her she hoped he would be able to see her long, taut thighs and tightly encased sex pouting out between them.

He swallowed hard, all composure gone, raw anticipation in his eyes, and she knew he could. Was he thinking of K teasing him in a similar way? She still had his arms pinned down, but Clifton seemed too transfixed by her mirror image to fight her off. Glancing back, she saw that her reflection looked even better than she expected. The heels made her legs look endless, and the pale pink panties gave the illusion that she was naked, shaved bare, her sex lips slightly parted to reveal a hint of the molten core inside. He couldn't take his eyes off them. She gave him a lick from jaw to eyebrow with a moist, pointed tongue, and he gasped.

'What do you want from me?' he asked hoarsely.

'I want you to give one hundred per cent effort to get on your feet, or you won't get your candy,' she said regretfully.

'What are you talking about?' His breathing had turned shallow, and a creeping flush spread up his neck as she moved closer.

'Ever been greyhound racing?' she asked, shifting so he could see inside her blouse. The small bra was doing its bit, barely restraining her full breasts.

'Once or twice.' He coughed to disguise the gravel in his voice.

'Then you'll know that the dog that catches the rabbit loses his incentive to win. You'll need to do a lot of work before you get your reward. Do you understand?'

'Who the fuck do you think you are?' His voice shook with anger and desire.

'That depends on you. I can be your maid or your mistress.'

One nipple had escaped her pink chiffon bra and was the sole focus of his attention. His tongue passed over his lips. She let that raspberry pink nipple drift closer for the briefest of tantalising moments. His eyes were vivid with lust, a small vein in his temple throbbing as hard as the other, far larger veins were undoubtedly throbbing further down.

'You're hurting, aren't you? I can tell. Well, whilst you're hurting, you might as well work to get back on your feet. Then you might be able to catch me and give me the punishment you think I deserve for tormenting you. That's what you really want, isn't it, Squire? To give his maid a spanking?'

'Get away from me, woman,' he said huskily. He tore his attention away from her chest but the back view offered even more temptation. He switched his attention back to her breasts, so alluringly displayed. He reached out one trembling hand, but she caught his wrist again and sucked one finger into her mouth. His attempts to pull away from her failed. Mercilessly she continued, trailing her tongue up the length of his finger and swirling it around the tip. His breathing became distinctly unsteady, his attention lurching crazily from her breasts to her reflected backside to her lips, enclosing the tip of his finger. Suddenly he uttered a strangled sound

77

and shuddered violently, moisture breaking out on his smooth forehead. He tore his hand away from her and sagged back in his chair, his eyes blank. When they cleared again she was smiling at him.

'Oh dear, Clifton, did you have an accident? I'll get you some tissues.'

'You'll pay for that,' he whispered. His need had been so fierce that his voice had faded.

She retrieved the toilet roll from the bathroom and put it on the coffee table, just out of his reach. She patted it lightly. 'I won't tell anyone about your lack of control, but you do need to get yourself together a bit more before you become a viable proposition for a lusty young maid such as myself.' She walked out, leaving him to clean himself up.

7

She thought about the photograph of Clifton and his twin brother constantly. It had affected her more than the discovery of him and his mystery woman had. What a powerhouse that would have been, with the two of them together in the same room. The possibility of having them both at the same time, together with the enduring image of Clifton's desperate face as he came in his trousers the previous evening, had given her a luxurious morning of self-pleasure that she was still glowing from, even in the smoky innards of the Red Lion.

Jem pointed at her glass, which had been holding gin and tonic. 'Same again?'

The bar had become busier since their arrival. A group of men about the same age as Jem were in the corner, talking loudly. Peter Price, Jem's old enemy, was amongst them. They had been looking at Suzy since their arrival, and making funny comments that she had pretended not to hear.

'Got yourself another pikey bitch, McKenna?'

'Just ignore them,' Jem said to Suzy. He went up to the bar and ordered their drinks.

'Nah, that's Suzy Whitbread, the village bike.'

That was unfair. She had had her fair share of boy-friends, but Peter Price had not been one of them. That was his problem, she guessed.

'You're just jealous,' she said easily. 'Even if I shagged the whole of Oxfordshire, what business is it of yours?'

Jem took her arm. 'Let's go,' he said. 'We don't need this.'

'No, and we don't need no gypsy scum in our village,' Price jeered. 'Tell that to your girlfriend.'

'Is that the one with no teeth?'

'She had them taken out so she could get her gums round his plums!'

There was coarse laughter. Jem placed his beer glass on the counter. The landlord continued polishing glasses. Unlike the man at the other pub, he hadn't tried to crawl up Jem's backside when they had arrived.

'I don't have trouble in my pub,' he said to Jem, which Suzy thought was grossly unfair.

'Then don't have arseholes in your pub,' Jem replied quietly.

'Hey, fancy pretty boy McKenna pulling a pikey chick. She must go for your little dick and your big wallet!'

'Yeah, just like his father.'

'Oh yeah, the crippled cocksman.'

Jem walked over to the grinning group. Peter Price stood up and widened his shoulders, tucking his thumbs aggressively into his too-tight jeans. He leered at his mates.

'Come on, you weedy little shi –'

Jem head-butted him. It happened so fast that Price had no time to defend himself. He collapsed in a heavy heap on the floor. His friends stared, open-mouthed. Suzy stared, frozen with disbelief. The landlord elbowed past her into the bar, grabbing Jem by the collar as he was picking up his glasses.

'Out.'

'But it wasn't his fault!' Suzy protested as Jem was led to the door. She looked around at the other customers. They stared back unhelpfully.

'You too,' the barman said. 'You're both banned. I don't tolerate behaviour like that.'

'But bigotry and insulting women is OK, is it?' Suzy yelled back at him.

The man advanced on her. 'And tell your gypsy friends they're not welcome in here. We don't have riff-raff on our doorstep.'

'Just cowards and dickheads,' Suzy retorted. She followed Jem outside. He was rubbing his forehead.

'Come on, let's get out of here before they decide to follow us,' he said.

Too late. The door opened and three hefty farmers' boys came lumbering towards them.

'Oh shit,' Suzy muttered. They had walked from the house, so there was no hefty Landrover to retreat to. They began to leg it down the road towards the gypsy camp. Heavy footsteps pounded after them and grew closer. Jem was flagging. The crack on the head had cost him. He stumbled and the first man reached him, landing him a punch to the chin that floored him. Then the others waded in with feet and fists, whilst Suzy tried to kidney punch them, screaming at them to leave him alone.

It was the loneliest feeling in the world, until a passing truck screeched to a halt and four men piled out. One lifted her out the way, legs flailing, and the others joined in the scrum. Miraculously, Jem appeared from under the heaving mass, bloodied but grinning. The three men who had attacked them were now outnumbered. As the horde broke up they were on the ground, one of them insensible.

'Come on,' someone said, pulling her hand. Dazedly she followed and was bundled into the cab. They pulled away in a cloud of exhaust fumes, spitting gravel at the thugs' faces, and drove back to the encampment.

Jem collapsed on an old sofa that someone had help-fully dumped a few days before. Beers were quickly produced. Bonny did not fuss around Jem, but slung her arm carelessly around him, pushing her breasts into his face. She didn't seem that pleased to see Suzy. Jem nuzzled her contentedly. Robby laughed at him.

'Hey, titman, you fight like a pussy.'

Jem lifted his beer at the insult and drank deeply. The talk turned to the trouble brewing in the village. Price was spoiling for a fight. So were the Fisher boys. If they decided to bury their differences just to turn against the gypsies, the result would be bloody.

Suzy watched Jem. He obviously felt right at home and content with Bonny, who kept giving Suzy spiky glances. Suzy decided she didn't actually like her very much. She was too sly, too quiet and too possessive of Jem when she really didn't need to be.

Instead she talked to Lena, a full-bodied wild woman of indeterminate age, with long, dyed black hair. After a while she was invited back to Lena's caravan, to get away from the fighting talk.

Lena had a dirty cackle of a laugh, and delicate fingers just perfect for the intricate wire jewellery she made to hawk at the fairs they visited. She was also an excellent saleswoman. Suzy had bought a silver and jet beaded toe ring with matching anklet within the first five minutes of entering Lena's chaotic, patchouli-fragranced den.

'You want another beer?' Lena asked as soon as Suzy had drained her first bottle.

Suzy grimaced. 'No thanks. I'm a vodka girl really.'

'After my own heart then.' Lena grinned, producing a full bottle of Stolichnaya. The jewellery business, it seemed, wasn't doing that badly.

Outside, people were already dancing and singing around the fire. The air was thick with the smell of barbecue, but Suzy was quite happy with Lena in her tiny living-space. She curled her legs up on an old fringed throw and fussed Lena's old ginger cat, Nibble.

'Got any piercings?' Lena asked. 'I do that, too.'

'No thanks. I nearly fainted when I had my ears done. And no amount of this stuff will persuade me to have any more.' Suzy held up her vodka and sipped some. It was going down very nicely, but she didn't want to wake up in the morning with a clit ring.

'So you don't fancy these, then?' Lena suddenly pulled her blouse open, revealing two large, very firm breasts, no brassiere, but each enormous brown nipple had a small silver bar running through it.

'Take a good look, lovely,' she said, pushing them closer to Suzy's face.

Suzy gave Lena's nipples close inspection. They were fat and long, forced to be by the silver bars running through them. The thought made her shiver with excitement. To be permanently aroused was a state she had gotten used to recently – since her meeting with one crippled man with an attitude. She thought of Clifton, feasting visually on her nipple, and realised she was doing the same to Lena's. Her mouth watered with the desire to reach out and suck, but her attention was also drawn to a fine silver chain leading from each erect point in a vee down to ... where? Not the navel. That had a dainty black stud all of its own. Lena's skirt, slightly straining over a soft stomach, hid where the chain was headed.

'Is that going where I think it's going?' Suzy asked, keeping her voice light so as not to betray her confused thoughts.

'I'll show you, if you like.' Lena stood up. Suzy wasn't sure she wanted to see, but the woman was already easing her skirt down to her ankles. She was very curvy, her panties so small they just covered her pubic bush, hiding the final destination of the silver chain. She dropped the panties as well and stood in front of Suzy.

The chain didn't go to her clitoris, as Suzy had supposed, but to two matching silver bars, one on each labial lip. Every time she moved, the chains tugged slightly on those fleshly lips, opening them to expose her clitoris and inner core. Lena stretched luxuriously and her sex lips opened even wider.

'You see? Open all hours.' She chuckled lewdly.

Suzy swallowed carefully. This was the first time she had ever been this close to another woman's private parts. She had been scared that she wouldn't like what was there, but seeing them, so pink and frilly and soft, half hidden in silky black hair, she was pleasantly surprised. She even felt the urge to touch, knowing how much pleasure it could give. Lena was watching her, her arms behind her head, a Venus-like pose that accentuated her lush curves, pale in the dimming light.

Why she did it, she had no idea. Maybe it was the vodka, but Suzy blew gently on the proffered nub of flesh. Lena sighed contentedly and stroked her hair.

'Have you ever had a woman, sweetheart?'

Suzy mutely shook her head. She didn't want to stop looking at that open, juicy pussy. She leaned forward and ran her tongue gently around the swollen clitoris. It tasted musky and sweet, not quite as she had expected, but very pleasant, and oh-so-soft, like a warm marble. She could feel Lena's hand on the back of her head, stroking, not guiding, but encouraging more exploration. Another lick, bolder this time, feeling hair catch slightly on her tongue as it went around. Lena stretched up again and held onto the low ceiling of the caravan. Her sex lips opened up. Emboldened, Suzy probed deeper, hearing the woman sigh, feeling the reaction of it in her own body, her own pussy getting wet as she cupped the woman's buttocks and began to lavishly lick her out as though she were doing it to herself. She took another mouthful of icy vodka and ran her cold tongue around Lena's clitoris, eliciting a soft wail of pleasure. The tip of her finger slipped inside the woman's moist sex and pushed in, then more and more. Lena was moaning loudly, her legs wide apart, a slave to Suzy's wicked tongue and punishing hand inside her.

The door opened and Robby O'Grady came blundering in.

'Hey, when are you two girls coming . . .' He stopped and stared at Lena, who gave him a hazy look.

'Beat it, hairy. We're busy.'

Suzy closed her eyes, not caring if Robby stayed or went, as her tongue fluttered with increasing urgency against Lena's turgid bud. She felt the wave come, deep and voluptuous, and a deep moan that could have been either of the two women. Her own legs widened, and her free hand moved urgently against her own clitoris as Lena's hips churned in an erotic dance partnered perfectly by Suzy's compliant tongue. Robby's hand was on his cock. He wasn't going to pass up an opportunity to witness something like this. Suzy was dimly aware of him slumped in a chair nearby, wanking slowly, his face corpulent with lust. In a daze she let Lena lay her down on the narrow bed and kneel between her legs. Her velvet tongue fluttered against her pussy and she sighed contentedly, gathering up her breasts and playing with her nipples, knowing that Robby was watching, but not caring. As she came she heard him grunt hard and saw the juice spurt over his hairy stomach. He lay there, replete, letting his cock deflate, before Lena's harsh command sent him packing again.

* * *

The next morning she left before Lena woke up. It was hard to get herself together with a hovering hangover, but she didn't want to face Robby after what he had seen the night before. All she really wanted was a decent-sized bed and close access to a bathroom. Her stomach was feeling decidedly queasy.

She vaguely remembered the end of the evening, when a fight had broken out and someone's nose had been broken. Everyone either got fucked or knocked unconscious eventually. It was the normal way to end an evening. But she had been in the safe haven of Lena's caravan, being subjected to a tongue bath at the time. When she felt better she would go over what exactly they had done together, but for now all she could think about was the ominous rumblings in her lower regions.

Jem staggered out of a green caravan into the grey light. He hadn't seen Suzy. He went to the bank of the hill and urinated, really revelling in it. His stream arced wide and he sighed loudly with relief. As he was zipping up again Suzy walked delicately towards him.

'You could piss for England,' she said.

He took her hand. 'Come on, Floozy Suzy. Let's go home.'

The nice thing about no responsibilities is that one can get hammered and indulge in recovery without inconvenient things like work and commuting getting in the way. Suzy spewed up twice on the walk home, probably as the result of some suspect sausages, and Jem pissed like a racehorse at least twice more. They made an unsavoury sight, lurching back up to Springfields House, their hair ratty and smelling of beer and God only knew what else, but by the time they got there, they had at least sobered up a bit. She was getting used to this, she thought wryly, throwing another round of painkillers down her throat before collapsing back onto her comfortable bed.

She didn't feel right until the next morning, and even then she felt light and delicate, as if a puff of wind would blow her to oblivion. She went for a swim, spent some time in the Jacuzzi, and spied on Clifton in the gym. His body still looked pretty good, she thought, as he lay on his back lifting weights. Dr Maloney was walking around him, counting off. He looked up and she dived for cover, then went back to her room for a long, hot shower. She felt quite exhausted, so she collapsed back on the bed thinking unfocused erotic thoughts before drifting into sleep again.

She awoke when the door opened. Dr Maloney was there, and he looked as surprised as she. He probably had not been expecting to see her sprawled on the bed, her pubic hair slightly sticky from her hot shower an hour before.

'You are the sexiest little minx,' he said softly. 'No wonder Clifton is working like a dog to get on his feet.'

She hastily grabbed a pillow to hide herself and sat up. 'How is he?'

'He worked hard today. As I said, you obviously have the magic touch.'

There was a tiny silence, in which the good doctor closed the door. He coughed to clear his throat. 'I don't suppose,' he said carefully, 'that you require my help, whilst I'm here?'

Suzy shivered slightly. She knew what he was offering. In his wholesome, ruddy, upper class way he was actually quite handsome. His eyes were the softest, kindest eyes she had ever seen.

'I don't think Clifton would appreciate you being up here,' she said.

'He doesn't have to know.'

Suzy had never accepted immediate sex from a stranger before Lena. It usually took her a few hours and a couple of glasses of Chardonnay. But this house and everywhere surrounding it seemed steeped in sensual possibilities. Here she could be as bad, as wanton, as wicked as she liked, without reproach. She lay back on the bed, suddenly fired up yet again. What was happening to her?

'I do have an ache,' she murmured. The doctor sat on the bed beside her.

'Oh? Where?'

'Deep inside me. As deep as you could get.' Now she had made the decision to be bad she was going to make it good. She ran the tip of her tongue around her lips, moistening them, and saw the doctor swallow deeply in response.

'Really?' He lay one large hand on her stomach. It was very warm and heavy, but his fingers were smooth as silk. He let them trail lightly down, glossing over her neat bush of black hair. Down, down, tickling her inner thighs, opening them slightly. His breathing had become slightly uneven, and her practised eye could see a definite shifting under his soft corduroy trousers. His middle finger was probing between her pussy lips now. They were engorged, closing around his finger like a sweet clam as he pushed it inside her.

'Then I'd say you need a thorough internal examination,' he murmured. Her eyes never left his face as it changed, becoming flushed and greedy. She loved this game, this slow-burn of desire, the fact that he was so hard, yet holding back, wanting to savour this snatched opportunity. Her nipples stiffened and stood proud as he thrust his finger in all the way.

'You're very wet,' he said huskily.

'Is that bad?'

88

'Very bad. You're a very bad little witch.' He pushed deeper, bending his head to take her nipple between his lips. A sigh escaped her, along with more moisture that made the insides of her thighs slick. He did it again and her back arched against his lips, her eyes drifting closed. He slavered her breasts with his tongue, making them glisten, the tips now super-sensitive and slippery beneath her fingers as he pressed kisses down her stomach and alighted on her clitoris. She gave a wavering cry as he fluttered gently against it, his finger still deep inside her. Drowsy from the swim, languorous in the sunlight streaming in through the window, she succumbed to the burgeoning pleasure. It was too soon, but her body was so ready to accept the doctor's tongue there was no stopping it. And as she came he licked along her folds, always returning back to her clitoris, keeping it singing. Her inner muscles worked around his fingers as her cries became low, intense moans. His other hand clamped over her mouth, keeping her quiet, and the intensity of not being able to make a sound forced more sensation into her lower body, prolonging the exquisite agony until she had to push him away and roll over, presenting herself to him. She looked back over her shoulder as he unzipped. His cock stood upright, unencumbered by underwear. It was a very serviceable cock. Nothing outrageous, but nothing to be ashamed of.

'Oh doctor, you've forgotten something,' she chided him. 'I hope you're not that forgetful when it comes to practising medicine.' She crawled over to take the plum purple head in her mouth, just the head, and sucked it gently. Above her the doctor shuddered, and sweet juice coated her tongue. She continued to wash him, up and down, around his balls, covered in a soft nest of golden hair. They seemed very tight and full. It was his turn to moan as she gently sucked on one of them.

'Why don't you lie down?' he murmured. She lay on her back before him, and he lifted her legs, resting them on his shoulders. In this position he pushed gratefully into her, deeper than she would have imagined. She felt helpless, exposed and sexy, especially when he took her ankles and widened her legs even more. In the mirror she could see them, his pink cock sticking out of his brown corduroys, pumping her solidly, his fingers digging into her buttocks, keeping her up. His blond hair flopped all over his flushed face, his cravat was slightly askew. She caught his eye in the mirror and licked her lips at him. It sent him into overdrive. He rammed into her for a few heated seconds and pulsed hard, his back bent like a bow. Another thrust, another pulse, and he was through, his jaw clenched to keep any sound from escaping him. After a few seconds to recover he pulled away and zipped up, his cock still hard in his trousers, lying to one side. Suzy sank comfortably back onto the bed. It had been a very pleasant interlude.

He kissed her and left very shortly afterwards. Suzy slipped her fingers between her legs and felt his seed, dribbling out of her. She rubbed some of it over her breasts and the rest over her clit and made herself come once more, revelling in how dirty she was becoming in such a short space of time.

She spent the next four days at the stables, shovelling muck, or working out in the gym, or at the gypsy camp. When she saw Lena again they hugged affectionately. 'Any time,' Lena whispered, and Suzy knew it was true.

In fact, she did anything to avoid Clifton, albeit subtly, and he did not appear at the breakfast table, although Dr Maloney did comment that his strength was improving. No more was said about their interlude. She didn't want to compromise her relationship with Clifton for the sake of a convenient screw, and he seemed quite content with what he had received.

On Friday evening Clifton called to her just as she was leaving to meet Jem. He wheeled out into the hallway, as far as he could go before the rug made it too difficult to continue.

'Would you care to join me for dinner tomorrow night?'

The charm with which the invitation was delivered surprised her. She was due to meet some friends in London, but on this occasion, she was happy to turn them down.

'I should be delighted to,' she said with equal politeness.

When she spoke to Jem that night he was amused by the whole thing.

'It's great you're getting on so well again,' he enthused.

'Sure we are. I'm going to seduce him and get him walking by dawn tomorrow.'

'You know, when you say it like that it almost seems possible. Maybe you should start doing it for a living?'

'What, bullying crippled men into walking again by withholding sexual favours? I don't think even my mother would approve of that.'

As she towelled her body dry after her shower she felt almost sick with anticipation. Calm down, she told herself sternly. She smoothed Crabtree & Evelyn rose body lotion into her skin, and took care over her make-up. Her Agent Provocateur lingerie had pink roses on a cream silk background, the panties mere wisps of satin. She had no intention of letting Clifton see them, but just to have the gorgeous garments on made her feel sexy and in control. The white wraparound top fastened with a bow at the back, and left a deep vee at the front, but nothing too obvious. The jersey was just thin enough to capture a hint of what she was wearing underneath. Coral linen trousers made her legs look endless, and with her pale skin and simple gold jewellery she felt elegant and graceful. A light spray of Hot Couture and she was ready.

The game was in play, and she needed to exercise strict self-control. She sat on the bed and breathed deeply ten times, telling herself to relax. Piano music floated up from downstairs. The timbre of it told her that it was not from the music centre. He was actually playing.

It was music she did not recognise, but each piece segued so effortlessly into the next it was obvious that a master was at work. Some of it was hard and angry, but the next piece would be as soft and delicate as a butterfly's wings. She went downstairs and looked at him. His eyes were closed, his hands guided only by the shifting mood patterns in his head. There were no theatrics, no tossing of the head and grimacing with pain. It was as if the music gave him licence to be calm, to project his anger outside himself whilst making it something beautiful.

'Come closer,' he said, still playing. 'What kind of music do you like, Suzy?'

'I like what you're playing now.'

His body was gently rocking back and forth, his fingers slender and oh-so-deft over the ivory keys. His nostrils flared at her light, spicy scent. His eyes opened and flickered over her. If he had expected her to dress like a King's Cross hooker, she had disappointed him. His fingers left the keys.

'What else? What was that noise I heard you playing in your car this afternoon, for example?'

'That was Nirvana.'

He laughed contemptuously. 'I hardly think so.' He gestured to the table, where a fat glass jug was filled with a tropical pink juice, garnished with fruit and ice cubes. 'Have a drink. I had it made especially for you.'

She regarded the innocent looking cocktail suspiciously. 'What is it?'

He handed her the first of two long glasses, tinkling with ice. 'It's called a Key West Cooler. Totally non-alcoholic and detoxifying, according to my doctor. Tell me what you think.'

'You think I need detoxifying?' she asked playfully.

'Most women do,' was his acid response.

Suzy took a tentative sip. There was cranberry, and mango, a hint of coconut, and something else she could not put her finger on, but it was very smooth and luscious.

'Are you sure there's no alcohol in it?'

He laughed. 'You are suspicious! No, there isn't the smallest quantity of alcohol in it. My doctor doesn't approve of my drinking habits. Do you like it?'

Her glass was two-thirds full, and she hadn't noticed. Just as well it wasn't alcoholic.

'It's wonderful,' Suzy admitted, sitting opposite him on the couch.

'Don't drink it all too soon. Monsieur Rossi will be most offended if he knew I was serving you cocktails before dinner. I have had a very decent bottle of Chateau Lafite Rothschild brought from the cellar.' He turned back to the piano and began to play Beethoven's *Moonlight Sonata*. Suzy nestled back into the leathery folds of the couch. It was very pleasant in the darkening night, sipping a Key West Cooler and listening to the hands of a disabled man she found sexually incredibly stimulating.

'What moves you, Suzy? What reaches down into your soul and tears your guts out? What makes you cry?'

The question threw her. 'That's private. Why would I want to tell you?'

'That's a better answer than telling me you don't know, but if you want me to talk then the least I can expect is the same from you,' he said, still playing.

'All right. The truth is that I don't know. It depends on the nature of my mood. I can't really remember the last time I cried and it's probably just as well. What about you? Can you answer that question?'

Clifton abruptly stopped playing. He scooped up his packet of Dunhills and lit up.

'What do you know about me?'

Suzy took a deep breath, remembering the pictures in his bedroom upstairs, the letter, the things Jem had said, and she chose her words carefully.

'Only that I know things have been ... difficult between you and Alice for some time.'

He watched her closely. 'Alice?'

'Your wife?' she prompted him. It was almost as if he had forgotten about Alice altogether.

But then he smiled grimly. 'Oh yes, my wife.' He glided over to his desk, and from there threw a manilla file in Suzy's lap, nearly spilling her drink.

'You might as well see this. It'll bring you up to speed on the dynamics of our marriage and get all those bloody awkward questions you want to ask out of the way before we have dinner. Read it and weep.'

There was a single document, headed up with a solicitors name. At the bottom were four signatures: Alice McKenna's, the solicitor's, a doctor's name that wasn't Maloney's and, finally, Clifton's. Suzy read the middle bit with growing disbelief. Amongst the legal jargon were the words, 'if I should ever indulge in further extra-marital liaisons', and further down, 'sole ownership of the property known as Springfield House, plus the holding share of Springfields Racing Stables, will be handed over to my wife'.

Suzy stared incredulously at him. 'And you actually signed this?'

'I was depressed, drugged up. They said it was a temporary document handing over responsibility for the running of the stables until I was fit enough to take full charge again. To be honest, I didn't care at the time. She was at me, yammer, yammer, saying how could I be so careless as to fall off my bloody horse and saddle her with all these problems. I wanted her to go away.' Another sour smile. 'Guess I screwed up, didn't I?'

'Big time,' Suzy said, handing the folder back to him. 'There must be a way of getting round it. Why don't you get divorced?'

He gave her a pitying look. 'Because, my dear, she would clean me out. You have heard of my reputation?'

'Why don't you tell me?'

'What does it matter now? I'm not worth anything to anybody. Put some music on, will you?' He reached for his cigarettes again. He let her light one for him, cupping his hands around hers as it held the tiny flame to the tip. She went over to the music system and pressed 'Play'. This time it was Brahms, soothing but slightly edgy.

'I don't think,' she said carefully, 'that you really believe that.'

'You know nothing,' he said bitterly, staring into the distance as if he saw something he loathed.

Through dinner, consisting of butterfly of lamb, with redcurrant jus, baby potatoes and green beans, he drank the Lafite Rothschild and talked of horses, and of the stables, both of which seemed to be playing on his mind. She kept his glass topped up and her own half-empty, keeping to the delicious non-alcoholic cocktail. When she suggested that Jem had let the horse that was injured run its races too close together because he was inexperienced, with no one either interested enough to guide him or brave enough to tell him he was wrong, she didn't get any china thrown at her. Instead Clifton conceded mildly that she might have a point.

'Everyone's afraid of you,' she ventured boldly, encouraged by his reaction. 'I don't know what you were like as a boss before, but now you've got this reputation for being crazy and liable to attack people with Ming vases if they dare to cross you. Either that or you'll plunder the village virgins and eat their girl-children for breakfast.'

Clifton picked up his wine goblet and gave her a sensual stare over the rim.

'Let's talk about you,' he said, deftly changing the subject.

As she talked about her life over the last five years it occurred to her that he was the first person who had actually asked. Jem had assumed he already knew, and was too wrapped up in Bonny and the stables to give it any extra thought. Her friends just saw who she was day to day and judged her on that, without probing any deeper into the reasons why she might just want to leave London and go back to her roots. Clifton seemed to understand why she had done it. At least he didn't think she was crazy.

'But you think I'm foolish?' she suggested.

'When I was your age I was married, with a small son I never saw, a wife who was patently only interested in my money, and my father's reputation to uphold. And that was only the start of it. Live your life, Suzy. When you do take on responsibilities, make sure you are ready to face them.'

'That's a bit rich, coming from you.'

His eyes narrowed. 'What do you mean?'

'I mean making Jem struggle with the stables on his own without the support of your superior knowledge. He's going through hell. If you gave him some guidance it could only help both him and the stables, and wouldn't cost you anything at all. You wouldn't even have to leave the house.' She paused. It was difficult to tell what he was thinking, because his features were so still, almost as if they were frozen.

'Everyone still thinks of you as the boss,' she continued. 'Jem just hasn't got the same credibility. He knows that, the owners know that, and your rivals must know that. You're doing far more damage than good by being such a stubborn, proud bastard than you would be if you forgot for a while what you think people are saying about you. Surely it's all been said by now anyway. Old news. Time to move on.' She picked up her glass and sucked at the straw, watching the pink juice disappear around the ice cubes. Clifton still hadn't spoken.

'If you're going to throw something at me, do it now, because I'll be gone in ten seconds,' she said.

He picked up the jug of fruit cocktail. For a split second she thought it was going to come hurtling her way, but he reached for her glass instead and filled it to the brim.

'Drink. Enjoy my company, but please do not speak of this again. Not tonight.'

She flipped him a salute. 'Yes sir.'

'Insubordinate bitch,' he growled, and flashed an unexpected grin at her.

She wheeled him back into his room for dessert and coffee. A bottle of Talisker was waiting on the coffee table, along with a wooden humidor. Clifton levered himself onto the sofa, with some difficulty. She took his legs and helped him, and for once he didn't snap at her for doing so. She was surprised at how heavy he was. He reached for his glass and the Scotch bottle and poured himself a triple.

'So much for abstinence,' she laughed. She had stuck with the cocktail that evening. It had been so delicious, sliding effortlessly down her throat like cool water after a prolonged workout. Now the jug was almost empty. It was the rich red wine that had made her slightly light-headed, even though she had only drunk a glass and a half. It must have been pretty strong stuff, she thought, as she checked her make-up in Clifton's bathroom.

When she went back into the living room, he was reclining on the sofa like a Roman emperor, his eyes closed, his hands conducting the invisible musicians with fluid grace. When the piece ended he opened his eyes.

'*Turandot*. The whole opera is over eight hours long, which is rather self-indulgent for such a thin story line.' He picked up his full whisky glass and held it to the light. 'Look at that colour, Suzy. Straight from the peat bogs of Skye. Exquisite.' And he drank deeply, leaving the glass half full.

'You're going to suffer in the morning,' Suzy warned him. 'Never mix grape and grain, remember?'

'I'm suffering now. What's the fucking difference?'

It didn't appear as if he were suffering much. On the coffee table a feast had been laid out. Parma ham, a dripping Brie, Muscadet grapes and assorted crackers, together with succulent olives and slices of Canteloupe melon. He breathed in the flavour of his cigar with obvious relish, watching her through the creamy smoke. She suddenly remembered an old boyfriend with a pen-chant for Havanas. He had taught her to smoke them, because watching her do it turned him on. She sent a mental thank you to wherever he was right then.

'Do you mind if I have one?'

'Feel free.' Clifton looked rather amused. She clipped the end, gave it a sniff and felt along its length. It felt plump and firm, not too moist, not too dry. She picked up his lighter and held the small flame to the tip, drawing in the heat, feeling the first smoke hit the back of her throat. She gathered the thick smoke in her mouth and let it linger there for a moment, before parting her lips and letting it trickle out in a slow drifting stream. Clifton didn't look amused any more. He looked almost hungry.

'Well,' he said evenly, 'the lady is full of surprises.'

'Most ladies are. Most gentlemen don't have the patience to wait for them.' She drew on the cigar again. The flavour was very strong and made her feel rather dizzy. She laid the cigar to rest on the marble ashtray and sipped at her cocktail to freshen her mouth.

'I'm a very patient man,' he said.

Laughter exploded from her. 'Bullshit! You don't know the meaning of the word!' She was feeling very relaxed, her legs slung over the arm of the chair she was slouched in. Her shoes had disappeared long ago. She took another pull on the cigar and watched the smoke coil leisurely up to the ceiling. When she looked at Clifton again, she realised that the mood in the room had changed. When he spoke his voice was a low whisper.

'I could be so dirty with you right now.'

She could not move. Her heart felt like a bass drum in her chest, so loud she was surprised he could not hear it. Stay cool, she warned herself. It would be so easy to launch herself at him and ravish him to death. And now there was the contract, hanging like the Sword of Damocles over his head.

'This conversation is very risky for you,' she said.

'Don't be such a frigging prude. You've been prick-teasing me ever since you arrived in this house. I could argue that you took advantage of me. I cannot move from this chair, so what was I supposed to do? I've been left in a weakened state, unable to fend off any healthy female that might seek to ravage my poor, broken body.' His eyes held a spark of mischief as well as desire. 'You could take me right now. Abuse me. You've wanted to since you hit puberty, so why don't you do it?'

Suzy watched his long middle finger trace along the entire ridge of his erection, distending the crisp cotton trousers. The need to lick her lips was as tempting as if she were in one of those doughnut-eating competitions, but she wouldn't, not this time. To do so would be to admit her salacious thoughts out loud.

'Come on, Suzy. I haven't had an erection for months. Then you appear and my cock doesn't know which end is up. What am I supposed to do about it?'

Her heart was calming down now. She was back in control. 'You're a grown man. Surely you know by now.'

'It isn't a lot of fun though,' he said sulkily.

'But what about the contract?'

'Fuck the contract. I'm a man with needs, you know.'

'That's your dick talking.'

'I'm a good listener. And so are you.' He looked speculatively at her. 'I know how desperate you are to get into my trousers, Suzy Whitbread. Why waste time?'

'You're the expert on desperation, not me.'

A hard laugh. 'Ouch. You'll pay for that.'

'How? You're hardly in a position to put me over your knee, are you?' she said cruelly. He shook his head and smiled benignly.

'I know you think you have the advantage over me. You're young, beautiful, and you can walk out of the room any time you like if I offend you.'

'Tell me something I don't know,' she said arrogantly, giving him a narrow-eyed look through the cigar smoke.

The cigar made her feel empowered and invincible, like cocaine in her brain.

'OK, I will. The reason you keep seeking my company lies in some insult I inflicted upon you in the distant past.'

'You've never offended me in the distant past, except by killing foxes. That's pretty offensive.'

He smiled indulgently. 'I'm not talking about foxes, Suzy. I'm talking about idealistic virgins with over-active hormones. You've never forgiven me for not seducing you, have you?'

'That's a wild shot in the dark. I lost my virginity when I was thirteen.'

Clifton laughed softly. 'When was the last time you had a fuck? Was it last night? Two days ago? When?'

'Oh no, you're not getting any cheap titillation by making me talk about my sex life.'

'You're wrong about me. I have very expensive tastes.'

She didn't like the way he was looking at her. Or rather, she did, but it seemed as if he knew something she didn't. She poured the remains of the cocktail into her glass. For a non-alcoholic drink it really was the business.

'Do you really want to know?'

'Yes.'

She watched him, assessing how he would take the news that she had been screwing his good friend the doctor, and decided to give that one a miss. She leant back in her chair and gave him a smoldering look.

'A week ago. It was the first time I had ever been with another woman.'

He wasn't expecting that. She could tell by the way his lips opened and his chest rose and fell, almost as if he had been hit in the solar plexus.

'Was it good?' he asked steadily.

She nodded. 'I'll always prefer a man, given the choice. I like being taken hard. Is that what you wanted to hear? How hard I like it? How often, what position?'

He stared levelly at her. 'Ever wonder what it's like to be stuck in that wheelchair?'

It took her a moment to think about it. 'It must be very frustrating.'

A sly smile. 'But it can have its advantages.'

'How come?'

'When certain young ladies insist on seeking out my company, I have no choice but entertain them. In these situations, I must take whatever they choose to give me, whether it be pleasure or pain.'

Suzy laughed. 'And what would your pleasure be?'

'Is that a question or an offer?'

His suggestive smile sent a dull throb through Suzy's lower body. She returned the smile.

'You answer my question and I'll answer yours.'

He stroked the leather sofa beside him. 'Come here and I'll tell you.'

As soon as Suzy stood up, she knew she was drunk, but couldn't quite understand why. The space she occupied seemed at odds with everything else in the room. She swayed and tripped on the rug, landing in his outstretched arms. She found herself lying beside him, full length on the couch.

'Oh dear,' she breathed, before being silenced by his tongue.

It was totally unexpected. In her shock she did not move as he pulled one of his legs over to trap her underneath him. His weight was deliciously heavy on top of her. Even so, she knew he was taking advantage. She tried to push him away and failed.

'I am the Great Clutton Cocksman,' he said lasciviously. 'And I'm coming after you, my little vixen. Oh yes,

I'm coming.' He kissed her again, a moist, open kiss tasting of wine and rich tobacco. This time she did not protest, but when his hand found her breast and began to knead it, she pushed it away.

'What's the matter? If you don't like it you can always walk away.'

In the few seconds he gave her to do just that she didn't have the energy and his hand was soon back where it had been. She let it stay, too intoxicated to fight him off.

'I haven't felt this randy for months,' he growled. He eased the top of her blouse down, past her shoulder, revealing her breasts swelling out of the small rose-printed brassiere. Realising she had little choice in the matter, Suzy let him push the blouse down to her waist. Clifton licked his lips and dipped his head, going straight for her nipple. She stroked his hair, woozily thinking that this was the type of thing she had fantasised about as a teenager. He suckled her for a while, she lying content on the fat sofa cushions, her sex throbbing lazily in response to the pull of his lips. Lower down, he had unzipped her trousers. Again she tried to stop him, but the overwhelming depth of his kiss was enough to stall any protest. As if it were happening to someone else she could feel him easing them down past her hips, and then his fingers were sliding up into her knickers, searching for her sex. Their breath caught simultaneously as he found her, wet and wanting, her soft folds sucking at his fingers as they pushed past into her very core. She tried to wriggle away, but his hand was too deeply entrenched between her thighs to shift easily. She knew it was wrong. He was leeching her of the power to seduce him in return for working to walk, but by now all she could think of was her vivid fantasy of him in the hayloft, and how familiar the soft sounds emanating from the back of his throat sounded as he explored her. He brought his fingers up to his lips and tasted them, then made her do the same. His eyelids drooped as she sucked his finger into her mouth, answered by a strong throb in his groin. He took her hand and showed her how wet, how slippery and open she was, and as he licked her fingers clean again he found her clitoris and applied an exquisite amount of pressure, so much so that her legs opened wider for him and the need for something more became almost unbearable.

'Fuck me,' she whispered languorously. She could feel him, erect and insistent beside her, but she was too inebriated to take control, to unzip his trousers and force his cock inside her yearning body. 'Fuck me,' she pleaded again. 'Clifton, please. I want your cock so badly.'

'I know you do, my little maid, but you're not going to get it.' His touch became insistent, denying her the right to argue. She thrashed against his hand, frustrated, wanton, cursing at him, feeling a building orgasm rise like fast-moving bubbles in a deep ocean. Skilfully he found the spot and held her moaning and writhing there, whilst his own breath came fast and hot and his cock throbbed pitilessly inside his trousers, out of reach.

After her climax peaked he unfastened his trousers and finished himself off, his other hand holding hers out of reach. He spent his seed over her stomach and breasts and then massaged it in, his mouth on her throat, sucking at the pulsing vein just under her skin. It moved down to her breast again, and she fell asleep to the rhythmic pulling on her nipple.

Three hours later she woke up, dizzy and nauseous. Clifton was snoring softly beside her. She extricated herself from his dead man's grip and staggered to the bathroom. The mirror seemed set at a crazy angle as she peered into it. Her hair was like a bird's nest and her face was white. She looked like Heathcliff's nemesis, back from the grave. Her mouth was foul and dry, and her eyes felt as if they had been blasted with a blowtorch.

She tried to remember what had happened earlier that evening, but that small action prompted a hasty inspection of the bottom of the toilet. She held onto the lid as if to prevent herself from slipping down waiting for the wave of nausea to pass. He had done something to that cocktail, she was sure of it. The amount of wine she had consumed wasn't enough to make her feel this wretched.

When she felt able to she got to her feet and tottered out into the living room. He was settled comfortably on the sofa, snoozing away as if he had not a care in the world. She even imagined a self-satisfied smirk on his face as he shifted and sunk down again into deep sleep. Groping for her shoes, she knocked over the whisky bottle. It clattered deafeningly on the glass table but even that didn't wake him. She stumbled out of the room and aimed for the stairs. She reached the bathroom just in time.

8

The next morning her hangover was complete. She groped for the painkillers she always kept handy and glugged them down with tepid tap water. Then she lay for an hour watching the ceiling until it stopped spinning. After that, her stomach felt that maybe it could cope with a piece of dry toast.

Clifton smiled broadly when he saw her.

'Did you sleep well?'

'Did you?' she asked bitterly.

'I got off without any problem at all,' he said airily. 'A couple of times, actually, thanks to you.'

'Fuck off,' she muttered.

'I'll put your churlishness down to mixing your drinks last night. Wine and spirits really don't mix well, you know.' He said it in a fatherly tone, but his eyes glittered wolfishly.

'You spiked my drink, you bastard,' she croaked.

He licked butter off his thumb with relish and winked lecherously at her. 'Oldest trick in the book, and you fell for it.' He grabbed her wrist, so hard she heard the bones creak. 'You want to play games with me, girly, you need to know how to win. Understood?' He let her go, giving her hand a comforting pat. 'Nice tits, by the way. You were very obliging last night, which was most interesting after you informing me that I was the expert in desperation.'

She wanted to crawl under the table. Her cheeks burned as she chewed her toast carefully, so that the noise wouldn't set off the burgeoning headache waiting for any excuse to come bursting out of the wings.

Jem crashed in, smashing her carefully balanced bubble of silence. He had the cheerful look of a man who had been fucking royally for hours the night before.

'What's the matter with you then?' he asked Suzy with depressing joviality.

'She's got a hangover,' Clifton explained helpfully.

'That's great!' Jem bellowed, making her wince. 'What was it, sex, drugs and rock and roll night, last night?'

'Shut up, Jem,' Suzy said sickly. Jem kissed her heartily on the cheek and began slathering butter on his toast. Clifton raised his coffee cup at her and looked smug. Suzy realised that the whole breakfast thing had been a bad idea. She staggered without excuses back up to her room and spent the next hour with her head down the toilet.

It was the following morning before she felt human again. He had done a real number on her, the cunning bastard. In future she wouldn't accept any drinks from him unless she saw him opening the bottle first.

'Do you feel better today?' Clifton asked slyly over an exquisitely served breakfast of fresh figs and roasted Java coffee. This time, she was able to do it justice.

'Yes, thank you.' She had decided to be cool with him, but inside she was burning up. Ever since her headache had subsided she had been thinking of ways to get back at him. The possibilities were endless, but it wasn't until she saw him heading towards the gym with Dr Maloney that she hit upon the revenge that suited his crime.

She waited until they had nearly finished the routine. He could lift the weights well, his toned upper body was testament to his stamina, but his legs were still as weak as a baby's. When she looked again, he was sitting at a mini gym doing lateral pull-downs. He clung to the trapeze bar, his back to her, and slowly hauled down sixty pounds of solid metal. He was at the limit of his endurance, judging by the wide dark patch of sweat staining his small grey singlet, and the explosive breath out as he let the bar go. The weights crashed down, making the floor shake, and Dr Maloney caught him as he was about to fall backwards.

'Remember your control, Clifton,' he said.

'Bastard sonofabitch,' Clifton gasped, leaning against the doctor and breathing great gulps of air.

'You think you can do one more?'

'You think you can go fuck yourself?'

Suzy saw her chance. 'He'll do one for me,' she said, walking into the room. The doctor gaped, looking her up and down. She had changed into tight cream jodhpurs and a white blouse knotted at the midriff. She had borrowed Alice's riding boots, and they gleamed in the dull sodium light of the gym. She had also borrowed the riding crop from Clifton's wardrobe that morning, suspecting it was the same one that the mysterious woman had used on him previously.

Clifton could see her reflection in the mirrored wall running the length of the gym. His smile was slightly supercilious, as if he knew what was to come and found it rather predictable. He motioned for the doctor to hand him the trapeze bar again. As he did, Suzy took the key out of the weight block and moved it down to one hundred and fifty. Clifton was stuck, unless he let go and ended up an ignominious heap on the floor.

'I would appreciate it if you would leave us alone for . . .' she paused and glanced at her watch, 'fifteen minutes? I doubt it will take that long, but he may surprise me.'

Dr Maloney looked at Clifton, who nodded silently.

'Well, I wouldn't dare to oppose a lady with a whip in

her hand,' the doctor said in a jocular tone. 'Don't be too hard on him.'

'Hard? I think that's up to him.'

Dr Maloney smirked and winked at Clifton as he left.

'Hope that hand-job grip is up to par,' she said, as realisation dawned on Clifton's face.

'Cunt,' he hissed, his eyes burning with fury.

'I don't think you're in a position to be impolite now, do you? I thought we could have a civil conversation, seeing as we got on so well the other night.' She stood to one side so that he could see her from head to toe, and slapped the crop against her thigh. 'That was before you got me trashed, of course. Now that wasn't a very gentlemanly thing to do, was it?'

'Just let me down from here, there's a good girl.' He was trying his best to sound benevolent and reasonable, but his eyes burned with impotent fury. She shifted so that he could see right into her white blouse, and the deep cleavage her movement had created. Her scent wreathed headily around them, together with the subtler aromas of sweat and rubber.

'Anyone who falls asleep sucking on my breast like a baby has no right to call me a good girl. And you, Squire, have been a very bad boy.' She placed the crop under his chin and forced him to look at her. 'This is for you, good sir, for thinking you can mess with me and get away with it.' She stood behind him, and with scissors that she had been hiding in her back pocket she cut the bottom hem of the singlet. She took the cut ends and pulled them violently apart, ripping the garment right up the back. His bare back was slick and glistening. Suzy waited, and his shoulder blades tensed even more. He was expecting the crop to land across his back or his buttocks, but instead he felt her tongue, rippling up his back bone. She licked her lips at his deliciously salty taste and did it again. His back arched as he let out a strange, wavering cry. She saw his hands tighten on the padded bar as she slipped her hand underneath and felt for his balls. They felt big and packed tight in his black Lycra trunks. Her other hand felt around his front. He was hard, rigidly so, pulsing against her hand as she briefly palmed his cock.

'Just checking,' she said, drawing her hands away. Around to his back again, and she pressed her velvet breasts against his back, sliding her hands around his legs. The frustration of not being able to guide her hands radiated menacingly from him as she continued to rub her body lazily against his, her tongue flickering around his neck, under his earlobes, nipping gently along his shoulders. She was abusing him, using his helplessness to heighten her own pleasure.

'Keep holding on,' she warned him, as if he had any choice. The tendons in his neck stood out as the pressure to keep from falling grew. She fondled the enormous bulge in his shorts again, her other hand idling between his buttocks. His jaw tightened, but he refused to look at her, or her reflection in the mirror.

'See if you can ignore me now,' she said, slipping her hand down into her own panties. She was molten with lust, her fingers coming away almost dripping with female honey. She ran them past his nose and pressed them between his lips, careful not to let him capture her between his teeth. Then, because she couldn't help it and he felt so wonderful, she went back to his cock, fighting the urge to thrust her hands into his shorts and pull it out and suck on him. Instead she worked her other hand into the back of his shorts and probed, teased, found his tense, tight hole.

'No,' he muttered, his eyes closing. She pressed lightly against it.

'Sorry, Clifton, what was that?' She pushed further and felt him resist.

'No,' he said again, through tightly clenched teeth. 'Don't do that. It –'

'Feels good, doesn't it?' She pressed further, and this time, the tip of her finger was sucked coyly inside. Clifton bucked weakly against her other hand.

'Please,' he muttered. She could see his arms tensing, shaking with the effort of supporting his weight.

'Was that a request? You spiked my drink then sexed me up when I was too drunk to fight you off. I don't need to do that to a man to make him want to throw me on the floor and fuck me. So tell me, who is the more desperate one between us?' She pushed her finger mercilessly inside him, frotting him more forcefully from the front. Clifton's lips were pulled back in a feral grimace. Fresh sweat had broken out on his forehead. His body was twisting, jerking against her hand, trying to escape it, unable to. He let out a roar of orgiastic anger as Suzy let go with cruelly accurate timing, sending his climax crashing into nowhere, leaving him spitting and cursing at her. She gave him a light kiss on his snarling lips and pushed her hand down the front of his shorts. He had ejaculated, briefly. She saw the humiliation on his face as she drew out the pitiful vestiges of his truncated orgasm and smeared it over his cheek.

'Here endeth the lesson,' she whispered, licking his other cheek.

Right on time, the doctor came in. He looked somewhat flushed. Suzy wouldn't have been surprised if he had watched the whole thing.

'You can let him down now,' she said as she walked out. It was on her mind to offer him a little time in her room. Her clitoris felt like it needed licking very badly.

But she didn't, because the game was now exclusively between her and Clifton, and another man would only get in the way. She went upstairs, to relive what she had just done to him and to enjoy a little self-stimulation.

As she was on her way to meet Jem for supper later she heard her name mentioned. Mrs Penrose was in the kitchen, talking to another woman with thick legs. She was collecting the bed linen for laundering, and picking up a few juicy bits of information on the way.

'It's disgraceful. John said he saw them walking back here as he was going to work. Drunk as skunks, heading back from that gypsy camp.' Suzy recognised Mrs Penrose's tight-lipped tones, her fussy mouth no doubt puckered like a disapproving rosebud. Yeah, and she was enjoying every damned minute, Suzy thought sourly.

'He was always such a quiet boy,' the other woman said.

'It's the quiet ones you have to watch for, I always say. He's been hanging around with those gypsies ever since they arrived here.'

'So where does the Whitbread girl come into it?'

'Oh, she's homeless now. No job, no place to go. She spends her time with Mr McKenna. Every time I see them together he's drunk.' That was Mrs Penrose again, the lying old cow.

'Poor Alice! She isn't going to be pleased with that!'

'She's such a good woman. Doesn't deserve all this nonsense. And he's no help.' Suzy presumed Mrs Penrose was referring to Clifton. 'Right old misery he's becoming. Won't do a thing to help himself. Since that girl came he's been nothing but trouble!'

'Do you think they're . . .?' But no one dared say the words. There was a shocked gasp.

'Poor Alice.'

Suzy had had enough of poor Alice. She slunk out of the house, wishing she hadn't heard any of it. It was no fun, being cast as a villainess. How many other people thought that way about her?

'Who cares what those old witches think?' Jem said breezily when she told him what was obviously going around the village. 'You've never leeched off anybody. When have you ever worried about anyone else's opinion? Cheer up and get your laughing gear around that,' he said, slamming a pint glass of cider in front of her.

She was halfway through it when Bonny came in, flanked by two men from the camp. One of them had a bloody nose. They bought pints and sat with them. There were looks and hushed voices, but they ignored them.

'These three guys went past in their van earlier, calling names. Rob shouted something back and they stopped. There was a bit of a punch-up.'

'Couldn't you call the police?' Suzy asked. They looked at her pityingly.

'And risk being turned off for causing a disturbance?'

'They'll be back,' Bonny said grimly. 'And there'll be more of them.'

Jem took her hand. 'I'll stay with you tonight,' he said, missing the sardonic looks of the men behind him. But Suzy didn't. They were thinking the same thing she was. He couldn't fight for shit, which made him an expensive liability they could well do without. Nobody wanted Alice storming down on them with the police in tow and trumped-up allegations of assault. She vowed to have a word with him when he wasn't drunk or too stressed to listen, whenever that might be.

9

The following afternoon was the hottest yet, a record for
May, according to the weather bores. The bluebells in
Lickfold wood suffused the whole area with a delicately
fragranced hazy glow, and on the heath, small butterflies
seemed almost too lazy to flap their brightly coloured
wings.

Suzy could hear Clifton playing the piano as she
sunned herself on the grass outside his window that
afternoon. The lilting tune was from *The Godfather*, and
it was so beautiful that she found herself lured towards
the cool room so that she could observe him playing.

He did not look up as she entered. His eyes were
closed, his fingers able to feel their way around the
keyboard by instinct. His arms were very taut and sin-
ewy, something she had not fully appreciated the day
before, she thought, watching the veins glow slightly
through his pale skin. She thought very suddenly that
she should like to feel the strength of those arms holding
her down onto his bed. Her ancient teenage fantasy of
being deflowered by him in a heated moment of passion,
brought on by many months of teasing on her part,
didn't seem that dated after all. She could still see him,
his black hair spiking his forehead, his face angry and
triumphant, as he ripped her cotton panties away and
spanked her raw for teasing him, before flipping her over
and pushing, forcing, thrusting hard into her reluctant,
terrified pussy. She could hear her hot little cry of pain,
followed by the voluptuous realisation that his cock felt

so damned good, deep inside her, and that her tightness was making him lose control in a way she had never dreamed of in her wildest fantasies. As he withdrew and lunged into her again she realised for the first time that she was in control, and that he was the slave to her steaming, tight pussy, her pert breasts with their long, rosy nipples, and that when she tugged at them with her fingers and stared boldly into his eyes he was lost, drowning in the pleasures of her flesh. He was –

His deep voice broke into her reverie and she jumped guiltily, hoping that her thoughts weren't being betrayed by the look on her face. The moisture between her thighs felt so obvious that she prayed that he could not smell her.

But he looked serene and unsuspecting enough. 'I want to play something for you. Sit.' He patted the wheelchair next to the piano stool. She sat on it, trying not to squelch. Her panties were sodden.

'My brain sometimes still plays tricks with my electrical impulses,' he continued calmly. 'If I sound like a donkey playing with its hind feet, that is why.'

'You were playing perfectly just now.'

'Thank you, but this is special. I like to get it right. Ever been to Manhattan?'

'Only in my dreams. Why?'

'If you ever have a chance, go in August. The heat is so thick it chokes you, leaves you wringing with pollution-stained sweat. It's hot, dirty, and uncontrollable.'

'Like you then,' Suzy said.

Clifton smiled slightly. 'Perhaps.' He aimed the remote control of the CD player back over his shoulder with lazy nonchalance. There was a moment of complete silence, before the opening bars to *Rhapsody In Blue* oozed through the speakers. Then he began to play.

Suzy was so awed that she forgot her previous lust.

Clifton's fingers rippled over the keys as if wedded to them, faultlessly in time with the pianist on the sound system. His talent was prodigious, humbling and exciting her at the same time. She walked around the piano, watching him from every angle. The music spoke eloquently of the hedonistic 20s, and of Gershwin's manic desire to prove himself. She could almost see the chalk-stripe suited men and glamorous women, smell their Chanel No. 5 and Chesterfields, hear the shady deals being done in New York blues clubs. It was playful, searing and violent. As the tempo swooped and dived, she could tell it was exhausting him. His hair had flopped into his eyes, and a thin sheen of perspiration covered his brow, but still he played, for fifteen exhilarating minutes, until the music slid to a sated halt.

At the end, Suzy was breathless enough to need to sit down again. She stumbled for the wheelchair, but before she had the chance to reach it, Clifton captured her wrist. When he pulled her into his lap she did not have the strength or the willpower to stop him. His kiss was warm, almost chaste, allowing her to savour the cruelty of his lips as his tongue snaked its way between hers. It was like being kissed for the first time all over again, as uncertainly her tongue found and curled around his. In that instant, something broke in both of them and they were kissing as passionately as long-standing lovers. She drank down his taste of fine wine and expensive cigars, inhaled his spicy, woody fragrance, hungrily, as if it were a drug. Then he smiled and said two words that confirmed the honey-trap he had set for her.

'Got you.'

She could have easily escaped him, probably, possibly. She didn't do it. All she was aware of was his hot breath, his masculine scent, his insistent throbbing desire. One hand curved around her throat, the other arm hard around her waist. She tried to move out of his grasp and found she could not.

'Where do you think you're going?' he asked.

She didn't know, so he answered the question for her, positioning her so she sat facing him. It felt incredibly intimate, her sex pressed close against his, despite the layers of clothing between them. She could smell her own excitement from earlier, and so could he, it seemed, as he smiled knowingly and slipped his hand between her legs, bringing it back up soaking wet. He licked her essence off his fingers and growled softly in his throat as his tongue thrust deep into her mouth. She could feel a bruising force against the cleft of her sex.

'I haven't had a woman for months,' he whispered, 'so you had better watch out.'

In the kiss that followed his shirt was ripped off his back, and her blouse was a tattered scrap flung over the piano. Skin against skin, he ravished her throat, her breasts as she leaned back, her elbows connecting with the ivory keys with a tuneless thud. She grabbed at his hair and forced him up so that she could kiss him again. In doing so they toppled from the stool and ended up on the floor, Suzy on top of him. His chest was heaving, sweat sticking his hair to his brow in dark spikes. He pulled her down and kissed her so violently it hurt, but she welcomed his overwhelming need. Their combined breath was turning to steam, adding to the slickness of their bodies. He gasped silently as she palmed his cock under his trousers and squeezed it. There was something incredibly erotic about a man's erection straining against good cloth, in this case, fine wool. She ran her finger down it, feeling it lift in supplication. She wanted to see it. She had been waiting years to see it and finally realise the fantasy she had held in her head since her early teenage years. His need was written all over his face, naked, wanton and raw.

It occurred to her that he had seduced her by playing that wonderful piece of music. He thought he had her in his power, but she could walk away now, and he wouldn't be able to stop her. The realisation made her wetter than ever.

'Don't you dare,' he said, pulling her down to him again. He manoeuvred her on to her back, and he was the one calling the shots. 'Don't fuck with my head any more, Suzy. You want me as much as I want you.' He thrust his hand rudely up her skirt and into her soaking panties. His fingers came away glistening wet. 'You see? The game is over, my little maid. The Squire is calling in all debts.' His kiss crushed the argument out of her. He tore his lips away and glared down at her, like a hawk with cornered prey. 'You want me to walk. I want you at my bidding, night and day. Quid pro quo. You don't like it, you leave. Yes?'

Suzy felt a fearful excitement burning in her chest.

'Yes,' she gasped.

'Say, "yes, Squire".'

'Yes, Squire.'

'Good. Now get us out of here. If I'm going to fuck you, it isn't going to be on the goddamned floor.'

A light breeze, puffy clouds, gentle sun on freshly cut grass – all were a world away from the velvet red depths of his bedroom. He lay on his back, watching her slowly teasing his zip down over the prodigious erection he had been nursing. She had stripped for him and given him a shave, so that his elegant jaw was smooth as silk. The spicy fragrance of candles scattered around the room created a mood of Eastern sensuality in a room far removed from the reality of the outside world.

She eased his trousers off and cast them aside. A small wet patch near the top of his black silk boxers gave away his need. He smelled musky, with a hint of sandalwood. His breathing was unsteady as she slowly peeled the boxers away. His cock was so hard it hovered above his belly, lifting at the cool breath she played over it. He was exactly as she had envisaged, heavy, and thick, with pendulous balls. She gathered his shaft into the palm of her hand and kissed it lovingly, like a long-lost friend. He hissed with pleasure as she wetted her lips and let them glide over the bulging wine-coloured head, making it glisten with saliva. His hand was in her hair, stroking it, as she let her throat relax and take in his whole length. It was a party trick of hers that she was still very proud of. Clifton sobbed with joy as she sucked him long and slow.

She removed the boxers and let them drift over his stomach, as thin and light as gossamer. A clear drop of dew appeared at the top of his cock. She wanted to lick it away, but he was so tense that the risk of him coming too soon was very real. She slipped her hands under his buttocks and lifted him slightly, and ran the tip of her tongue around the base of his balls. His cock slapped audibly against his stomach, and he uttered a quietly aggressive grunt. She did it again.

'Fuck, that's good,' he said tightly. Then he couldn't speak as she continued the stealthy attack, swirling around and around, nibbling, sucking, eliciting curse after guttural curse from his tightly drawn lips. Then, when he was least expecting it, her tongue trailed up his shaft, to the tip of his cock. Down and up, spiralling round and round, helter-skelter around his shaft, a white-knuckle ride that made him groan in wild abandon, clutching the sheets with fierce fingers.

'I'm losing it,' he said at one point. Suzy squeezed the base of his cock tightly and the urge to explode subsided enough for him to take the sustained assault her mouth muscles wrought on him. Eventually he slapped her rump.

'Sit on my face, wench,' he whispered. His exclamation at how wet she still was was lost as his tongue flickered over her swollen bud. As he teased and probed and explored each fold with consummate skill she began panting, becoming breathless. When he began to probe deep with his tongue she felt her mind going. This was Clifton McKenna slavering at her pussy! The knowledge released a fresh oozing of moisture, which he realised, responding with even more enthusiasm. She felt weaker as the sensation built, making her thighs quiver and her breath become shallow. The image of him in the hayloft, peeling away his jodhpurs so she could see him naked for the very first time, tilted her over the edge. She took him deep into her mouth so that he could feel as well as hear every moan. He found the focus of her pleasure and relentlessly worked it as her body shuddered in a seemingly endless series of overblown spasms, her juices drenching his face. As the first waves ebbed she sucked on him so lavishly that he began to make strangled noises of his own. He pushed her away and told her to sit on him. Still weak from her shattering orgasm she manoeuvred on top of him. He was flushed, breathing heavily, and so deliciously disarrayed that she felt another post-orgasmic quiver shoot through her body. Trembling with anticipation, she impaled herself onto him, right up to the hilt.

'Oh-my-God.' Gagging the words, overcome by the unexpectedness of it, she sat, fully stuffed, dizzily waiting for that stretched sensation to diminish. It didn't; it was replaced by a swollen desperation as his cock pulsed mercilessly, punishing her inner muscles. She swayed backwards, to be caught by his hands on her wrists. She blasphemed softly again, and said with absolute truthfulness, 'Oh Squire, you're fucking *massive*'.

Another brutal pulse. She was glad he could not move, could not thrust. He would half-kill her with that thing at full speed. She felt his hands on her buttocks, lifting her up off his cock, but not all the way. She got the message and undulated slowly, rotating her hips, performing a very personal pole dance, her hands toying with her breasts. He let her do all the work because he had to, but she could tell he wasn't happy about it, and in a perverse way it added to his pleasure. He pulled her down to face him in the end, so she crouched over him like a wild animal.

'Do me, girl,' he snarled. 'Look at me!'

Flashbacks of every fantasy she had entertained about him came crashing back. The hayloft, the piercing joy of being painfully initiated on his bed, the domination she briefly had over him. All these images raced through her head as she fucked him relentlessly, like a wild animal, her hair tossing all over her face. It didn't take long. His focus slid and became vacant, whispered obscenities falling from his lips. Then a look of utter savagery and a hard jolt, which sent her over the edge, plummeting into oblivion for several sweet seconds. Several smaller ones followed before peace fell over his features. She collapsed beside him, breathless and joyful.

They had breakfast the next morning in the dining room as usual, all dignity preserved. She had gone back to her own bed sometime in the night, just in case Baker chose to walk in with an early morning cup of tea before she had the chance to escape. There was a calmness about him that she had not noticed before, an unwillingness to talk, but when she asked if anything was wrong he smiled and took her hand, kissing it and telling her she had nothing to fear.

Not that she was afraid of anything. There was no guilt, no complicated agonising over what would happen if Alice found out. They both knew the risk they were running, and Clifton seemed happy to take it. No, Suzy guessed the real reason lay in the bottom drawer upstairs. At the end of the day, however good Suzy was in bed, however successfully he managed to lose his reason in the delights of her flesh, she was a substitute for the real thing. This was unspoken, but it would not be for long. Very soon she would attempt to get him to talk about the mysterious K.

But first, that afternoon she found the keys to his Jaguar and went out to the garage. She had had the idea long before, but had put it away to be aired at the appropriate time. Now it had come, a glorious warm afternoon with the bluebells at their full glory. She had seen them through the trees the day before and had stopped to breathe in their heady fragrance. Nothing excited her more than nature asserting itself, whether it be in man or beast or the flora all around her.

Dr Maloney had come just before lunch and was enjoying a very civilised cigar with Clifton out on the patio. The doctor came into the hallway as she was heading out the door. He opened his mouth to speak, but she put her finger to her lips. Obligingly silent, he let her explain what she had in mind.

A few minutes later the double garage door opened swiftly and silently, revealing the sensuous rounded rump of the spanking new XKR in harlot red livery. Suzy's mouth watered, with both anticipation and fear.

She had never driven anything more powerful than her old Golf. This machine seemed to have muscles built into its shapely hind quarters. Inside the car the smell was new and leathery. She carefully backed the car out into the sunlight and saw the thin film of dust covering every surface. That would have to go before Clifton saw it. She spent some time cleaning and polishing, then pointed the car forwards and drove carefully around the central rose bed, getting a feel for it. There was a definite sense of power waiting to be unleashed.

She turned the engine off and climbed out, and then spent a while ogling the lozenge-shaped exterior. Dr Maloney appeared beside her.

'I don't think he's going to like this. Not one little bit.'

'I shouldn't think he will, especially with me driving it.' They went back inside the house to find Clifton.

'I didn't work him too hard today. He'll need his energy now,' Dr Maloney said cheerfully. 'Anyway, by the end of next week you'll be limping around the garden.'

Clifton grunted rudely. 'What's happening now?'

Suzy didn't reply. She nodded to Dr Maloney, who steered the chair out into the hallway.

'This has absolutely nothing to do with me,' he said over Clifton's shoulder. 'She's a force of nature, that girl.'

When Clifton saw the red Jaguar with the roof down his face paled. Suzy could see his jaw tighten and a small tic appear in his temple. He was enraged, but couldn't find the words to say so.

Dr Maloney opened his mouth, but Suzy hushed him. Finally Clifton spoke, through tightly gritted teeth.

'Take me back inside.'

She knew he would be angry. The Jaguar was a painful reminder of how his life had changed. Still, it was a hurdle he had to overcome, sooner or later.

'You're coming out with me,' Suzy said firmly. 'We're going to hack down the motorway listening to Nirvana at top volume and you're going to start living again.'

Clifton's knuckles were white on the arms of the chair. Suzy could see him trembling.

'This isn't funny,' he said bitterly. 'Even by your low standards, this stinks.'

'There's some hideous Royal Doulton poodles inside. Shall I fetch them?' She asked calmly, unfazed by his insult.

Dr Maloney stared uncomprehendingly at her. Clifton said nothing. It seemed he had run out of expletives, and as there was nothing to kick, smash or rip up within his grasp, the only option was to give in. Suddenly he looked defeated, sagging back in the chair.

'Oh for God's sake, I'm offering you a ride in the country, not a one-way ticket to a concentration camp,' Suzy said crossly. She nodded to Dr Maloney, who wheeled the chair down the ramp. Suzy opened the door. Clifton's face was still stony as Dr Maloney let down the sides of the chair.

'You can get in yourself, or I can throw you in,' he said sternly.

There was a long pause. Then Clifton heaved himself out of the chair and swung down into the Jaguar's low seats. Dr Maloney slammed the door with the air of a job well done.

Clifton sat there, unmoving. Suzy reached over and fastened his seatbelt. The doctor would keep his mobile on if they needed help, but Suzy doubted they would. With a little wave she gunned the engine, and they set off.

She turned towards the long Roman road heading out of the village, and put her foot down.

The wind whipped through their hair and flicked it out behind them in black tangles.

She didn't look at him or speak to him. It was enough just to let him get used to the idea of being out and enjoying freedom, away from the oppressive confines of the house.

'Dent it and you're dead,' he shouted above the music. She flashed a grin at him.

For half an hour she drove, the two of them alone on roads empty because it was during the week, when everyone else was at work. She headed North up the M40, keeping the car ticking over at ninety in the fast lane. They played Nirvana and Manic Street Preachers, and Clifton drank in the soft blue sky, the sparkling white sheep on rain-washed rolling fields, the small golden-bricked villages tucked under the lee of undulating hills.

Eventually they found a wood, where through the trees there was a mass of bluebells, even denser than the ones Suzy had admired. She stopped the car in a lay-by so they could admire them.

'Hungry?' she asked.

'I would be,' Clifton replied carefully, 'if I didn't think you were going to say "I told you so".'

'I wouldn't dream of it,' Suzy replied. 'Wait here.'

She went to get the rug and the picnic hamper. There was a patch of grass bathed in warm sunlight not ten feet from the car, so she spread the waterproof rug out and opened the hamper. By the time she looked back, Clifton had climbed out of the car and was hanging grimly on to the door.

'I can't move,' he complained.

'It's OK.' Suzy retrieved his crutches from the back seat, extended them and painstakingly helped him over the short distance. Luckily there was a handy tree that he could pull himself up to his feet on later. He leaned up against it and lit a cigarette, closing his eyes to listen to the sound of birds high up in the trees.

'Fucking heaven,' he murmured.

'Not such a bad idea of mine then,' Suzy retorted.

He opened his eyes, smiled, and closed them again. 'I hate you.'

They feasted on smoked chicken, ciabatta and sun-ripened tomatoes and mozzarella salad, drank elder-flower cordial and finished with fresh pineapple, papaya and mango salad. It was a wonderful, peaceful meal, and afterwards, when Suzy had put the hamper back in the car, Clifton lay back and let his face be warmed by the sun.

Suzy lay next to him, enjoying his closeness and the blissful peace of the place. She could feel herself dozing off, lulled into sleep by good food and warmth and comfort, and the fragrance of a thousand bluebells.

Something was stroking her face, soft and petal-like, moving down to her throat, down between her breasts. The touch became indistinct as it drifted over her nipples, making them tingle. Sly fingers tugged at the satin laces that held her blouse together, loosening them and nudging the material apart. She breathed deeply, pretending she was still asleep. The material was peeled away from her breasts, the front fastener of her bra dealt with efficiently. She sighed and moved, thrusting out her breasts, seemingly still asleep. She sensed his fingers hovering, waiting for her to settle again. When she had he stealthily moved her bra away from her breasts and continued to stroke her with the soft petals. A bluebell, she could tell from the delicate fragrance. Around her nipple, stiffening it, making her back arch for more.

'Clifton,' she whispered, and there was an answering rumble, before lips pressed against her own and a hard tongue thrust deep into her mouth. His other hand dropped down to her warm thigh, thrust underneath the minuscule skirt and quested for her sex. He tutted at her when he felt how slick she was.

'The Squire is shocked,' he said huskily. 'Has his little maid been having bad thoughts?' His fingers probed deeper. She shifted so that he could get underneath her panties and delve into her succulent centre. He withdrew his fingers and brought them to his lips, sensuously sucking her glistening juices from them. Against her thigh she could feel his arousal, very hard, very ready. He broke the kiss and took her hand and placed it over his cock.

'You did that. Now you can damned well get rid of it.'

'We might be seen,' she whispered.

'I don't give a fuck,' he replied roughly, covering her lips with his again. She squeezed him gently and felt him throb heavily in her palm, setting off an answering moisture between her thighs. Another throb, his eyes heavy-lidded, breath hot on her cheek, and the moisture turned to steam. Their tongues were wet and slippery, joined in a sinuous dance of sensual pleasure. He hardened further, settling to a turgid pulsing urged along by her hand, squeezing him gently in response.

A car went past. She could not see it but had the occupants seen them? She wasn't sure she cared. Clifton didn't seem to. He lay back as she unzipped his trousers and set him free. Glancing back, they were just out of sight from the road. Although it was only twelve feet away they were in a slight dip in the land and surrounded by trees in full leaf.

'Fuck me, Kate,' he whispered, so low that not even the curious wildlife would be alarmed.

Suzy coughed delicately. 'It's Suzy.'

'Sorry ... whatever ... just fuck me.' He was too needy

to be bothered by this crashing *faux pas*. That told Suzy a lot about their relationship. She sat up and drank in the vision of him. He was a beautiful sight, his clothes all disarranged, his black hair in spiky strands over his forehead and on the blanket. And his cock, livid red against his pale stomach, so heavy and powerful yet totally defenceless against her. She climbed atop him and eased him inside her. For a while all they were aware of was each other, and the searing need that kept them locked together.

His voice woke her up a while later.

'It's started to rain,' he was saying, shaking her shoulder.

It was, too. Where had all the blue sky gone? A distant rumble woke her up completely. Big fat drops had started to penetrate the dense beech canopy and land with a patter on the leaves around them.

'What about my car?'

She looked at the Jaguar. With the top still down.

She sprinted over to it, keys in hand, climbed in and looked around. The black leather seats were spattered with raindrops.

'Where's the button for the roof?' she asked him.

'How the hell should I know? You were the one who put it down, remember?' Clifton looked as if he wanted to crawl over to the car and do it himself. Suzy leafed frantically through the manual as its pages started to turn soggy, and, at last, the roof glided into place. She climbed out again. Clifton was getting wetter and wetter, clawing his way up the tree trunk, muttering about whose bloody idea was this, and other very ungrateful observations. She shoe-horned him back into the pass-enger seat with impressive speed, but it still wasn't enough to avoid getting soaked. This rain was actually seeking them out, Suzy thought. Maybe Alice had sent it all the way over from Cannes.

She packed up the boot and collapsed beside him, slamming the door after her. The inside of the car was already steamed up. They looked at each other and laughed.

'Check the weather next time,' he said mildly.

'Oh, so there is going to be a next time?'

He cupped the back of her head in his hand and drew her towards him for a final kiss. 'What the fuck do you think?'

A week passed, then two. Suzy began to forget which day was which. Clifton had progressed to the treadmill and by the end of the fortnight had walked five faltering steps that left him an exhausted, triumphant, sobbing mess. When he wasn't trying to walk, he was with Suzy. She was in an altered state, not quite in touch with reality. It couldn't last, but she intended to enjoy every hour, even though he was still rude and demanding at times. She had her own way of dealing with him then. She would tease him with her body, then refuse to carry through until he apologised. Sometimes he did, and sometimes he didn't. When he didn't she would find some way of getting revenge. She would spike his drinks, get him worked up and hot but unable to perform, or whip him lightly with the riding crop. Her thoughts were dominated by what she could do to heighten their pleasure. He especially liked the array of toys she pro-cured. These included a leather ring, tight around the thick base of his shaft, keeping him hard all day, and love beads, inserted into his rectum and slowly pulled out as he came. He liked her to do it when they were in the pool, her legs around his waist, welded to him by the heat of his cock. She tormented him, not allowing him the pleasure of spanking her, as he often wished to do. Sometimes she stood in front of him, lewdly gathering up her skirts to reveal her lack of panties, and almost made herself come whilst he watched. Then she would wheel him to the bed, chain him up when he was on it, and sit on his face whilst she sucked him dry.

But not once did he talk about the two subjects that intrigued her most. That of his twin brother, and of Kate, the woman he was still obsessed with. And even in their most intimate moments, she couldn't find the courage to ask him.

It was a stormy Sunday night, after a hazy, humid day filled with innuendo and suggestive small talk. At eight o'clock Baker brought in a selection of creamy cheeses, grapes, water biscuits and olives, and a 1997 Chablis to wash it all down.

Suzy opened the conservatory windows and they listened to the full brutal power of the storm. There was still no rain, not even a hint. The heat of the night was saturating, permeating the old house, making their clothes stick to their bodies. Clifton beckoned to her and pulled her onto his lap. He had removed the sides to the chair and she pressed close as they kissed feverishly, sharing their body heat. Sweat dripped between her shoulder blades. Clifton's shirt was damp, and beads of sweat lay on his forehead, both from the stifling air and the need to have her.

'Sit on my cock,' he said.

'No.' She continued the torture, brushing fingers flavoured with pussy juice to his lips. Another crash of electricity rocked the room. Clifton uttered a gasp as Suzy suddenly complied, sinking down onto his cock because she couldn't wait a moment longer. Clifton was muttering, nonsensical stuff, hissing words that had no meaning, out of his mind with bliss, yet still cruelly frustrated. He wanted to fuck, to thrust, to give her a hammering, but he couldn't. He was at her mercy. The knowledge exhausted him, made him ragged with need. And angry. So angry.

Suddenly he pushed her away. Suzy landed on the floor.

'What's the matter?'

Clifton beat his fists uselessly on his thighs. 'Don't you get it? I want to fuck you. *I* want to fuck *you*. Christ, I want to ...' He lashed out at the first thing that was in reach, which was his wine glass. It smashed into wicked shards on the conservatory floor. He was sobbing, great heaving cries of rage. She rushed to him and held his head against her breast.

'Don't lose it now,' she whispered. 'You're working so hard and it's paying off. Don't give up. Please.' She had never pleaded with anyone in her life before but now it was fundamentally important to her. As if he sensed it he calmed down and squeezed her, as if trying to impart some comfort of his own.

'I'll be right back,' she said. She galloped upstairs, into Jem's bedroom. She knew he still had some weed hidden in a horrid Chinese urn containing pot pourri on the dressing table. She rummaged around and found it. Jem was very neat and tidy, and all his joints were ready rolled in a plastic sandwich bag. She took four and resealed the bag, tucking it under the pot pourri again, and went into her room to get the duvet cover and two pillows.

Downstairs, Clifton looked defeated, his head in his hands. The storm outside was abating, and now she could smell refreshing rain, beating down on stirred earth.

'Come on,' she said, kissing him on the mouth, 'it's time we chilled out a little bit.' She moved the table to one side and threw the duvet down underneath the mirror, dropping the pillows on top. He looked quizzically at her as she sat down and patted the duvet beside her.

'Come on down. I won't bite.' Nirvana began to filter through the speakers. Soft, soft, but building. Clifton shrugged and lifted himself out of the chair. Between them they got him comfortable on the duvet beside her.

She turned the music up and handed him a joint. He laughed at it.

'Where the hell . . .?'

'Jem's room. You won't give him a hard time, will you?'

'Depends on the quality.' He flicked his Mont Blanc lighter and held it to the squashed end of the joint. 'And get me some vodka. I need something to take my mind off sex.'

She poured double shots of vodka, thinking she was so going to regret this in the morning. Clifton rolled to one side, supporting his head on his elbow, and grinned up at her.

'OK, so what are we supposed to talk about now?' he asked. 'Deep meaningful shit, like the meaning of life, or poetry, or –'

'Kate,' she said. 'Why don't we talk about her?'

Clifton drew on the joint. 'How did you find out about her?'

'I found a photograph in your room when I was looking for the keys to the Jag. There's also the very small matter of you getting my name wrong at a rather crucial time on more than one occasion, so I think you owe me an explanation.'

Clifton passed the weed to her and lay on his back staring up at the ornate plaster ceiling, his hands behind his head. He didn't seem inclined to say anything. Suzy didn't hurry him. If he wouldn't tell her now, then he probably never would.

'It started on our wedding day. The rot, that is. Clayton tried to warn me but I wouldn't listen. He wanted her as well, you see. Alice, not Kate. I didn't know her then.' He took a drag on the joint.

'Go on.' She rested her head against the crook of his shoulder and listened.

Clifton had been delighted when Alice fell pregnant soon after they were married, but Alice wasn't. She loathed the whole trauma of childbirth and she wasn't a natural mother. The baby was thrust into the arms of a nanny from day one, whilst Alice continued to be a professional wife and social organiser for their increasingly successful business. It was left to Clifton to nurture his son, and he did so admirably, much to the surprise of those around him. Men simply weren't meant to show affection, to play with small children, to read to them. He bucked the trend, and a few people began to look at him with new eyes, especially women.

He had his first affair when he was in his thirties. Afterwards, he wondered why it had taken him so long. He was very discreet, as was the woman, who was married also. The relationship reached a natural conclusion after six weeks and both parted happy.

The next one came a year later. He was fussy, because he didn't want to be roped into any heavy emotional issues, and he knew that Alice would sharpen her claws on his back if she found out. Again, it lasted a mere three weeks.

By now, Jem was at Eton and reaching puberty. Clifton found that there were rich pickings amongst the wealthy mothers of other boys at the school. Alice had persuaded him to buy an apartment in Cannes, which he had never visited, and she spent her summers there. That was when he felt safest indulging the sensual side to his nature, and this side to him was growing with every heated liaison, becoming dangerous and essential to his continuing happiness. It wasn't any particular woman, but the excitement of the chase, rather like the thrill he had when chasing a fox. In the winter, fox hunting replaced his affairs, until he met his nemesis, and then he knew he was in trouble.

Kate Palmer was the wife of the local builder, Alfie. He was known for his evil temper and love of beer. The two didn't usually mix very well. Fridays he was in the pub for the duration, straight after work, not rolling home until well after midnight, when he had lost a sizeable amount of his earnings on the poker table. Kate used to wait for him in bed and pray that he was too drunk to demand his conjugal rights that night. She hated the smell of beer and stale cigarettes on him, and the snorting coupling he enjoyed so much.

Then came Clifton, who opened her up like an exotic flower and she found it within herself to blossom. He would visit her at around coffee time. At first he would just sit at the kitchen table and drink her flavourful vanilla coffee. Soon he would drink the coffee and eat the cookies she had made for him before taking her up to bed. He would be gone by two o'clock, back to the stables, leaving her in bed to spend the next hour drowsily reliving their lovemaking before she had to get up and prepare supper for her husband.

Of course, the women of the village noticed first. The new dusky blonde highlights, the soft pink glow to her cheeks. It was enough to arouse suspicions in those whose interest in other people's lives surpassed interest in their own. And it didn't take long to figure out who the other man might be.

When Clifton was around she no longer spoke to him. Indeed, to a stranger it might have seemed that she could not bear the sight of him. They were very careful not to be seen together at any social functions, but it only took one smouldering glance across the village hall at the Harvest Cheese and Wine party, witnessed by the village's most notorious gossip-monger, and their cover was blown. Clifton knew he had to make a choice. What was it he really wanted? Was his relationship with Kate a summer fling, like the others he had had before, or did he have to admit that this time, this woman was the one he had been searching for?

He talked to Kate. At first she insisted they dismiss their liaison as a foolish summer fling, but she could not keep away from him. Finally she admitted that she loved him, perhaps hoping it would scare him away. It did not. He wanted her just as much. They made plans to leave together the day after Boxing Day. Alice was holding a dinner for some of her friends and Alfie would be in the pub. That way they could avoid any messy confrontations.

'She hasn't been to see me since the accident. She and her husband moved to Norfolk. They were going to set up a bed and breakfast.' He laughed hollowly. When Suzy laid a hand on his shoulder he grasped at it like a lifeline. 'I guess Alice began to panic before it happened. She suddenly saw what she could lose if I left her. Of course, she had been clever. No-one suspected her of playing away from home, yet by then I had gained something of a reputation. It is to my discredit that I actually enjoyed the notoriety for a while.'

'So you fall off your horse and the rest is history.'

Clifton nodded. 'Although I think the word "fall" is open to interpretation. It was Kate's husband who found me and raised the alarm. I don't remember anything other than his big, fat, stupid face above mine, and he was laughing his fucking head off.' He reached for the heavy lead-crystal ashtray. 'I'm no use to her now. That's why she decided to stay with him. I thought we had something, but the accident fucked that up, didn't it?'

Suzy hoped he wasn't going to sink into melancholy. 'Let's not dwell on that now,' she said, as briskly as she could after a load of vodka and a head full of marijuana. 'Tell me about Clayton.'

Clifton practically shuddered. 'No! Anything but him.'

'Why? What's he like?'

'My dark side. You'd love him, which is why I'm glad he's six thousand miles away.' He drained the last of his vodka and poured another, spilling some on the table.

Suzy groped for the remote control and turned the music up. As the razor-sharp guitar of 'Heart-shaped Box' filled the room Clifton's eyes closed and he smiled. The riff was doing its stuff, searing his brain clean of gloomy thoughts, at least in the short term. They would keep coming back, like a bloodstain on a carpet, but for now the pain could be eased by hard liquor and soft drugs and savage rock and roll. Suzy just enjoyed watching him. She cupped her hand over his crotch. Solid as granite. She took him in her mouth and sucked hard on the sweet-tasting head. His penis seemed to swell before her very eyes, a massive priapic vision luring her to engulf him and drown in his essence. It felt tight to bursting but he only came once clean silence had filled the room. She massaged the pearly pools into his skin.

'Shit, that was raw,' he said. 'Who is that guy?'

'Kurt Cobain. He's dead. He killed himself.'

Clifton nodded as if he understood why. He lit another joint and took a long toke before handing it to Suzy. She felt his hand drifting over her leg, just under the short skirt, but it turned out he was looking for the remote control. He found 'Come As You Are' and cranked up the volume.

Time ceased to have meaning. They were truly mellowed out, the vodka and wine bottles empty on the floor, the food eaten. Clifton had undone his shirt and asked Suzy to remove her dress, because he wanted to feel her skin next to his. She wore a diaphanous pale blue bra and panties set from Coco de Mer, held together with white silk bows. It looked very sweet but it didn't hide her dark bush or her nipples, which showed through like bullets.

'I feel like getting lasted and waid,' Clifton said, nuzzling his face between them.

Suzy laughed, and her laugh sounded like honey dripping from a wooden spoon into a metal bowl. 'You're half-way there already.'

Clifton rolled towards her and put a heavy hand on her stomach.

'But I don't do things by halves, so what do you want to do about it?' He was watching her with a blurred, lascivious expression.

Suzy sighed regretfully. 'You couldn't get it up anyway right now, Clifton. Otherwise I'd ball your brains out.'

He unzipped his trousers and felt around inside. 'Fuck, you're right.'

She crawled heavily around and took him in her mouth again.

'That feels good,' he sighed, 'but I think the Squire is all shagged out tonight.'

Too languid to try any more, she lay by his side and they started to sing 'All Apologies' really, really badly.

He played a pretty mean air guitar, Suzy thought, considering he was on his back. She started to giggle, watching his slender hands pluck and strum the invisible strings. He flipped a middle finger at her and continued, the soggy end of the joint dangling from his lips.

It took them both a few seconds to realise that the music had stopped, sooner than it should have done.

'Clifton! What on earth do you think you're doing?'

They both looked towards the direction of the appalled voice. Alice stood in the doorway, her jaw sagging in disbelief.

10

'What does it look like I'm doing, you dumb cow?' Clifton drawled, stubbing out the ragged remains of the joint. He had meant to do it in the ashtray, but missed and found the coffee table instead. 'I'm reliving my youth. The one I should have had without you.' He struggled to a sitting position. Suzy saw the focus of Alice's gaze and threw a pillow into Clifton's lap.

Alice's mouth tightened into a grim line. 'I shall be on to my lawyer first thing in the morning!'

'Like you were on to him in Cannes?'

Alice bridled under the jibe. 'How dare you lecture me when you're looking ... like that!'

'I will not,' Clifton paused, his stoned brain groping for the words, 'be chastised by my own wife.' He made a complete mess of 'chastised'. Suzy bit her lip, trying desperately not to laugh. Alice glared at her.

'And where is my son?'

Clifton laughed crazily. 'He's fucking a –' Suzy clamped her hand over his mouth and held it there.

'He's out for the night. He'll be back in the morning.'

'He had better be, and he had better have a very good reason for allowing you in this house again. I'll see you in the morning to discuss this unfortunate situation. Now please leave so that I may assist my husband to bed.'

Suzy gave Alice a 'gee, sorry' shrug and stumbled from the room. Up the stairs, swaying dangerously, she knew she needed the time that night to think about her next move, but she was just too stoned and drunk to do it.

She fell asleep dreaming of Clifton, destitute and home-less, begging on the streets of Oxford.

The riding crop landed on the tender part of Clifton's buttocks just as he was drifting off into a drug and alcohol-ridden sleep. Somehow he was on his bed, on his front, naked. He couldn't remember how he got there, but Alice was now standing by the side of the bed. She brought the crop down hard again and he gasped, hauled reluctantly out of his daze. Even so, the warm stripe of pain across his backside wasn't totally unpleasurable. There was a shifting in his groin that always came when he was being punished like this.

'You're going to regret ever laying hands on that slut,' Alice said coldly, striking him again and again.

'Never,' he said hoarsely. His erection had grown and was pressing uncomfortably into the mattress. He tried to move, but his limbs had been tied to the posts at either end of the bed. There was a snapping sound. Alice was pulling on latex rubber gloves.

'You really don't quite understand the position you've put yourself in, do you?' she said. He turned his head and looked at her. She had in her hand a large, green dildo, which she was liberally slathering with KY Jelly. 'You'd better start walking tomorrow, dear husband, because you're going to find it very difficult to sit down after this.'

He gritted his teeth as she thrust his buttocks apart and stuck her finger between them, finding his rectum and probing against it. His groan was base and needy as her finger past the first muscular barrier and went deeper. The first woman to do that to him was Kate, after he had asked her if she would. She had been reluctant at first, but then . . .

Oh God, now he was hard. That woman had been so

mean to him, in ways only they understood. Under her sweet exterior she knew how to flick his switches, how much pain to inflict. As Alice buggered him with her finger he could not help thrusting into the bed, picturing that wicked woman beneath him. Without even realising it, he moaned her name.

Alice stopped and began raining wild blows on him with the riding crop.

'I hate you!' she said viciously, over and over, raising welts all over his back. The pain merged into hot, desperate pleasure and he started to come, shooting urgently into his bedcovers. Alice gave him one final, vicious lash in pure frustration and stalked out, leaving him tied up and laughing hysterically.

Mrs Penrose found him like that the next morning, but she made no comment. After releasing him and averting her eyes from the stained bedcovers and his battered nakedness, she asked him whether he would prefer tea or coffee with his breakfast.

Alice called Suzy to the drawing room before breakfast the following morning. Jem hadn't arrived yet, so Suzy was going to have to do it alone.

She knew that Alice was going to tell her to leave. That she had expected, but the tongue-lashing before the final blow she really couldn't cope with at all, not with another crashing hangover. She braced herself and knocked on the door.

Alice smiled as she bade Suzy to sit down. Suzy perched on the edge of one of the huge sofas, ready for flight, but Alice's clear features were filled with pity.

'I know how you feel about my husband,' she said sweetly. 'I believe he's made great progress under your care in the last few weeks.'

'It really hasn't been anything to do with me,' Suzy

said. She knew she had to apologise for the night before but the thought of having to eat humble pie before Alice made her stomach churn.

'I've heard differently. Mrs Penrose says you have been very attentive. Anyway, I've brought you in here to say that you shouldn't worry about last night. I want you to stay, for Clifton's benefit, of course. If I sent you away because of a little foolishness he would never forgive me, and, as you are aware, I am concerned for his welfare as you are. Unfortunately, I don't seem to have the magic touch.' She injected a crestfallen tone into her voice. 'We've been having our problems, you see, and the accident hasn't helped. He can be such a difficult man.'

Suzy stared at her in disbelief.

'Of course, you have my permission to do whatever you deem necessary to expedite his full recovery, but this conversation must not leave this room. There are others who will not understand the arrangement. If it should ever become public,' she paused dramatically, 'then your position here will be rendered untenable. Do I make myself clear?'

'Of course,' Suzy said, nodding professionally. Alice was watching her like a cobra tasting the air before a small mouse.

'Now you may go,' Alice said graciously. 'I'm sure Clifton will be delighted to see you.'

Jem saw her as she left the room. 'What the hell is going on?'

She told him and held her breath. She wasn't sure how he would take it, having her turn his father into Oxfordshire's answer to Ozzy Osborne over the course of one night.

'I'm really sorry, Jem. I didn't mean it to turn out like this!'

Alice appeared at the door. 'A word, Jeremy, if you please.'

Jem grimaced at Suzy and meekly followed his mother into the drawing room.

Clifton was awake but still in bed when she went in. Propped against the pillows, draped half-naked in sumptuous wine-red silk sheets, his black hair long and silky against his pale skin, he resembled a character from another time. He looked hunted and lost.

'I suppose this is a goodbye?'

'On the contrary, she wants me to stay. The damage has been done, hasn't it?'

Clifton's lips twitched. 'You're a bad influence on me.'

'That's my role in life,' Suzy said lightly.

Clifton put down his tea cup and reached for her. She climbed onto the bed and slipped her arms around him and stroked his back. One of her nails caught on something raised on his skin, making him wince.

'What's wrong?' She looked at where she had caught him. When she saw his damaged back she made a sharp sound of dismay.

'What the hell happened to you?'

He smiled wryly at Suzy's horrified expression. 'You should see my arse.' He lay back down and turned over. She ran her hands lightly over the marks. They felt slightly raised and very hot.

'I'm really sorry,' she said. 'This is all my fault.'

He turned his head on the pillow to look at her. 'Don't be. I'm not.'

She fetched a pot of aloe vera cream, usually used for rough, cracked skin. She smoothed the cream over his back and gently massaged it in.

'Why did she do it?'

'She thinks she's punishing me,' he said, 'but she isn't really. It turns me on.'

'Does she know that?'

He laughed lightly. 'She does now.'

The sound of Alice's voice put them on red alert. Suzy kissed him and slipped out of the room.

As soon as Jem closed the door Alice turned on him.

'You idiot! I leave you in charge and this is what happens! And Mrs Penrose has just informed me whom you've been seeing the past few weeks. Some gypsy girl! Is this true?'

Jem sighed heavily. 'Before you start –'

'How could you! With all the decent girls you know and you're dallying with some strumpet who doesn't know any better?'

'You can't judge her if you haven't met her,' he said calmly.

'What about the neighbours? I'm probably the laughing stock of the village! My own son ... dabbling with a traveller! I hope you haven't brought her here,' she said warningly.

'Once or twice.'

'Oh, for goodness sake, she's probably helping herself to the family silver! I cannot believe you would do such a thing, Jeremy, I really cannot! I will have to speak to your father about this. You will not be allowed to spend our money on a tramp! Do you hear me?'

'Loud and clear,' Jem sighed, as if bored with the whole thing.

'And insolence will not be tolerated in this house either! Just remember what you will be inheriting in the future. You won't get a penny of it if you see that girl again!'

Jem walked out, slamming the door. Suzy was waiting for him.

'Oops,' she said.

Jem shrugged. 'Whatever. I can live with it.'

'You mean live without it. Potentially.'

'Dad wouldn't let her get away with it.'

'I guess you don't know about the contract, then.'

'What contract?'

His grin gradually faded as Suzy explained.

'That's great! Why the hell did you get him in such a state if you knew what it would mean?'

'It was his choice! How were we to know that she'd come back so soon?'

Jem stabbed his finger at her. 'This is your bloody fault. If you hadn't been so desperate to get into his pants none of this would have happened!'

He stumped off up the stairs. Suzy was tempted to run after him, but she couldn't help feeling that his outburst had been somewhat justified.

Now that Alice had returned, it seemed that she had brought half of Oxfordshire with her. Women friends arrived for visits that had been arranged weeks ahead of time. There was no such thing as a spontaneous cup of tea. Alice's life was far too organised for that. When she wasn't in residence she played tennis and chaired committee meetings. Just listening to her itinerary was enervating. And she talked non-stop, mostly about the cocktail party that had long been arranged for the middle of June. Most of the wealthier villagers would be there, together with the owners from Springfields and a few carefully chosen people Alice had invited for business purposes. Jakki was by her side, in her power suit and neat little BMW X3, ready to run off on whatever errands Alice had planned for her.

'Why are we having this bloody party anyway?' Clifton

grumbled as they were eating breakfast, two days after her return. Alice was in a fearfully triumphant mood.

'It's about time everybody knew we were back on track. It's been a very stressful few months for the stables. I've heard all sorts of rumours that we're going downhill, and that is simply not the case!'

'It may have escaped your notice, but it's been rather stressful for me, too,' Clifton said tightly.

Alice studiously ignored her husband as Mrs Penrose served them with toast and tea, and Jem hoovered up eggs and bacon as if he would not be eating for the following week. Alice tutted at him.

'Really, Jeremy, when are you going to show some restraint?'

'I need the carbohydrates, Ma, especially now I'm working.'

'Is that so? Please don't call me Ma. And when are you going to start speaking properly again?'

Suzy smiled into her bone china cup. Jem's Australian accent always seemed to be a lot more pronounced when his mother was in the room. Clifton was staring out of the window. He reminded Suzy of a captured hawk, longing for the freedom of the open skies.

'I've told Bonny it's over,' Jem said casually.

Alice's smile was satisfied. 'Good,' she said. She dabbed at her mouth with her linen napkin. 'I need to talk to Mrs Penrose about refreshments for Friday morning.' She stopped suddenly, her attention drawn to the garden. 'Who is that?'

Suzy looked outside and saw Robin O'Grady. He was shirtless, hacking manfully at a stubborn tree stump with a large axe. As if realising he was being watched he stopped, stretched, displaying muscles that were impressive even at that distance, then picked up the axe and slung it over his shoulder. The pitchfork went over the other shoulder, and he stood there for a moment, Oxfordshire's answer to Vinnie Jones, broad chest radiating hirsute masculinity, before he swaggered off down towards the greenhouse.

She glanced worriedly at Jem, but he was still refusing to look at or speak to her.

'That's Robin O'Grady. I hired him for the summer to help John Penrose. His arthritis is getting so bad now, we should think of retiring him...'

But Alice wasn't listening. 'That's fine, Jem,' she murmured, dabbing her lips again with her napkin, as if she had forgotten that she had already done it. 'I'll go and introduce myself.'

'That was a lucky escape, my boy,' Clifton said humorously when she had gone. It seemed as if the whole room heaved a sigh of relief. Jem started to eat politely again, and Clifton turned his attention away from the patch of blue sky outside the window. Outside, Alice was making her way purposefully down the garden, where Robby was now digging in one of the flower beds.

'I don't suppose my son explained to you the problems we've been having with the badgers, Mr O'Grady,' Alice said as they walked down the garden. He really was a fine specimen, she thought, taking in his thick, sensual lips, matted black hair on his chest and arms, and the bulging bicep muscles. The temptation to run her finger over one of them was just too much.

He braked sharply as she did it and looked at her. It wasn't a look of shock, but pure insolence. She knew she was panting slightly in the heat, her small breasts rising and falling in a pale pink Janet Reger brassiere. And the matching knickers were damp, too, but from the reaction of her body to his. He gave her a frankly sexual glance that took in everything, from her Cartier heels to the string of pearls that Boris Hicks had given her whilst they were away. A very generous man he was, and an excellent lawyer.

'Mr O'Grady, you are very fit,' she murmured. Her suntanned cheeks felt very hot, but the heat in his eyes was hotter. He passed his tongue over his lips, moistening them, and inflated his chest.

'Is there anything else I can do for you, Mrs McKenna?'

'Maybe,' she said. 'It depends how much you think you are worth.'

'Name my price, like? For extra services?'

'Perhaps,' she said, with a ladylike nod of the head.

Robby speculatively looked at her slender ankles, long legs and firm breasts, almost as if her clothes were no longer there. Then he took in her wispy pale blonde bob, expensive pearl earrings and clear blue eyes. Finally he nodded, as if approving of a particularly fine mare. 'I think I can give you what you need.'

He led Alice into the large shed and shut the door, trapping them in the warm, musty room. As soon as they were behind closed doors, Alice's frosty demeanour changed. She fell on him like a ravenous tiger, thrusting her hands into the waistband of his trousers and pulling him towards her. She ran her fingers through the thick curly hair on his chest, plucking greedily at his nipples as he pawed roughly at her expensive silk blouse. There was a small ripping sound, almost inaudible underneath their steamy breathing, but Alice suddenly stopped, pushed him away and looked down. One of the tiny bone buttons had been torn off. She looked at it, scandalised, and then at him, her eyes blazing. The crack as she slapped his face reverberated around the room.

'You fool! Look what you've done!'

Robby's lip curled contemptuously. He gathered the silky folds of fabric in his spade-like hands and rent the material violently, spraying buttons in a shower around their feet. He mashed her tiny breast in his hand, at the same time stalling her outraged squeal with his thick lips, his muscular tongue working its way deep into her throat. Alice quivered and melted, instinctively opening her legs as his hand left her breast and shoved rudely up her linen skirt, rustling the lining. She could feel his grubby fingers groping around, soiling her expensive silk panties. Her slim hand felt for his crotch, and on finding what was there, she whimpered against his mouth. He was built like a bull. She clawed at his zip, hungry, needful. His cock reared out of his jeans, but it was still trapped in very small briefs, so the head was being strangled by the tight elastic. He made a sound of release as she freed him, pushing his trousers and briefs down past his buttocks. He was still kissing her. Actually, not a kiss, but an invasion. No tenderness, just raw lust. She grabbed his scrotum and squeezed hard.

His balls were huge, hanging heavily downwards. He grunted in pain and tore his mouth away from hers. Her lips were swollen. He grasped her wrists so fast she had no time to defend herself.

'I'm going to have to tie you up,' he said. He found a length of thick twine and fastened it around her wrists. Then he pulled her arms up above her head and fastened the twine over a hook in the ceiling. He prowled around her, cock and balls swaying heavily. Alice could feel her nipples tingle and her sex grow moist. Robby removed her skirt and fingered the scrap of satin that was left, demurely covering her crotch. He evidently decided they weren't worth the £45 she had paid for them and they were dispatched with a rip, landing somewhere behind a heap of flowerpots. The smell of warm compost, fertiliser and fresh grass clippings assaulted her senses, adding to the heady aromas of sex and sweat.

Robby nudged her legs apart and rubbed himself against her. Slowly, deliberately, teasing her. He slipped it between her legs so she could feel it all along her pussy lips. They yearned to enfold it, but he cruelly denied her. Then he went around behind her and did the same, his hands playing over her breasts. Looking down, she could see the tip of his cock peeping out from between her legs. She tried to close them, to trap him, but he was wise to that. He moved away and around to her front again.

This time, he sank to his knees and buried his face in her neatly trimmed fur. She sighed sharply and pushed against him. He breathed her in, and suddenly she felt his tongue dart out and flick against her clitoris. She yelped sharply, and he got to his feet.

'You're making too much noise.' He opened her mouth and popped his briefs in, gagging her. She could hardly breathe, let alone make a sound. He knelt down again and tasted her. This time she squealed, but the sound came out as a soft sigh. Not being able to scream and shout had suddenly intensified the feeling of his mouth. She started to squirm like a caught fish, until he held her in a hard grip and started to lick her for real. The restricted air running to her brain, and the delightful skill he had, brought her to orgasm so intensely she nearly blacked out. When he released her legs they widened wantonly, her hips thrusting aggressively out at him. He lifted her, impaling her on his erection. She groaned and bucked, but he just stood there, watching her give herself pleasure. She was trying to say, 'fuck me, fuck me', but it came out as an infuriated mumble. He stood with his hands on his hips, buried in her, her legs scrambling up his.

As Alice thought the pressure would make her faint he walked away and let her loose. But not for long. This time he laid her on the sun lounger, arms above her head and attached to a hook in the wall. He played with her some more, making her squeal again. Then he stood over her and rubbed himself, one hand fondling his balls, the other on his dick. His face suffused with lust and he came, spurting over her body and between her legs. As it ended he still stood, his penis semi-erect. She was wide open, silently screaming for him to give her what she so desperately needed, but his smile was cruel.

'I know what you want, lady, but you're going to have to pay me first.' He removed the gag. Alice was red-faced and spluttering; her perfectly coiffed hair now a nest of expensive frosted highlights.

'What do you want?' Her voice was different. Lower, more guttural, like a woman from the street.

He leaned over the sun lounger, so that the tip of his cock just grazed her overheated sex.

'You want a raise out of me? I want a raise out of you.' He plucked a figure out of the air, expecting her to tell him to go to hell.

She didn't. She nodded silently, and reached for his dick. He moved out of reach. 'Money up front, sweet-heart. Then you can have all the pounding your posh little pussy can take.' He began to pull on his jeans, leaving his soggy briefs on the floor. He paused just before zipping them up, accentuating his heavy balls and cock hanging over the dirty denim. Her eyes were bright and greedy, visually feasting on him. He knew she would pay.

That evening Alice held a dinner party for sixteen, to which Suzy was inexplicably invited. She was introduced as Clifton's nurse, and she was put at his end of the table, next to a florid banker who kept looking down her dress. The conversation was of people and places Suzy had never been to, and therefore could not talk about, which she presumed was the whole idea. Clifton fielded Alice's subtle but poisonous barbs with quiet dignity, though his restraint was barely noticed by the occupants of the table, who seemed to be more interested in point-scoring against each other. Clifton weathered it all, until the talk turned to a familiar name.

'Whatever happened to Kate Palmer?' one of the women asked. She sounded too innocent. Suzy knew she had been primed.

'Oh, she and Alfred went to Norfolk. They wanted to start a family,' Alice replied.

'At her age?'

'She was only thirty-five,' someone else said.

'I'm surprised their marriage is stable enough for children,' the first woman said. 'After her behaviour.'

'She did get around a bit.' A woman called Cecily looked disapproving.

'But how? She was never much to look at.'

'Some men don't care, if it's on offer.'

'I say, that's a bit unfair,' the lecherous banker protested, leering at Suzy.

Suzy could feel Clifton's blood pressure rising from across the table.

'Are you feeling well, dear?' Alice asked.

'Kate Palmer is a good woman. Everyone knows that,' he said tightly.

'It seems that they do. Especially the men,' Alice said archly. 'The fit ones, that is. She was never interested in damaged goods. Anyway, changing the subject, we've had this wonderful new chair fitted in the bathroom. Clifton can now take a bath all by himself. Another little step towards independence, isn't it, dear?'

It was too much. Clifton threw his coffee cup at the wall with a violence that shocked even Suzy.

'Steady on, old boy,' one of the men muttered, looking uncomfortable. Everyone else wore appalled or disapproving expressions.

'I'm sorry, he has these little fits. It's the medication.' Alice smiled sadly at her husband. 'Suzy, take him out, would you? It's obvious I've expected too much from him this evening.'

Suzy nervously approached Clifton, thinking that he might strike her if she attempted to touch the chair. But he nodded calmly and allowed her to steer him out of the room.

'I rue the day I married that bitch,' he muttered, staring disconsolately into the triple Scotch that Suzy had poured for him.

'If you've always been so unhappy, why didn't you get a divorce years ago?'

'Because she would have had custody of Jem, which meant she would have packed him off to boarding school as soon as she could and carried on living exactly as she pleased.' Clifton abandoned the Scotch and lit up a Dunhill with trembling fingers. 'Actually, the arrangement suited both of us. She went up to London and did God knows what, and I satisfied my appetites closer to home. It was only when it got serious that she began to resent it.'

'When you say serious, you mean Kate.'

He gave her a terse look. He was jittery, on edge, sucking ferociously on the cigarette as if he hated it.

'Did you have to mention her again?'

'Why aren't you fighting to get back on your feet so you can go to her? Maybe there's a reason she can't see you.'

'There's only one reason. She doesn't think I'm a proper man anymore.'

'I don't believe you really think of her like that. If you

did you wouldn't have fallen in love with her, would you?'

'What the hell would you know about falling in love?'

Suzy finally lost patience with him. 'She's probably going through hell right now and all you can think of is yourself! Any more self-pitying crap like that and I'll jam the spokes in your wheels and leave you to piss yourself!'

His jaw dropped. 'Jesus, you're a hard-nosed bitch!'

'When I want to be, yes. All your whining makes me want to vomit!'

Cold liquid splashed on to her face. It took a couple of seconds before she realised that he had thrown his whisky in her face. She wiped it away from her eyes before they began to sting. He was watching, waiting for her reaction.

'I'm going to find this woman,' she said calmly, and I'm going tell her to get down here and sort you out herself.'

The colour drained from Clifton's face. 'You wouldn't do that!'

'Just try to stop me.'

'No!' Without warning he lashed out at a tall wrought-iron plant stand and sent it toppling. It landed on the coffee table with a splintering crash, breaking the glass table top. Earth and ferny plants spilled everywhere. Suzy stared at the wreckage in amazement.

'You don't do things by halves, do you?'

'Don't you dare go anywhere near her! You hear me, you lousy cunt-eating bitch? Don't you dare!' His eyes were murderous and his face was white. A drop of spittle had escaped with his furious words and landed on his lower lip. He dashed it away and glared up at Suzy.

Mrs Penrose came bustling in and exclaimed at the mess on the floor.

'I'll get Mr Baker to deal with this,' she said, with an

accusing look at Suzy. 'I think you should leave Mr McKenna alone now. He's looking tired, if I may say.'

'Thank you, Maggie.' Clifton's voice was frail, but the triumphant look he gave Suzy wasn't. She made an obscene gesture at him behind Mrs Penrose's back and left.

11

In the elegant surrounds of the Connaught Hotel, Alice's progress meeting was going very successfully. She, along with two of her lawyers, Springfields' accountant and a representative from Coutts, were in further discussions with another small group of bankers and lawyers, led by a very wealthy Argentinian whose son had been at Eton with Jem. Don Valmez owned a chateau just outside Versailles, from which he trained world-conquering thoroughbreds for fabulously wealthy owners. Several of them wanted to keep horses in the UK, so he was in the process of finding another stables to enhance his already superlative reputation. He had been speculatively watching Springfields for years, knowing that Clifton would never consider selling, but since the accident Alice had been far more forthcoming about negotiations. However, she was a tough cookie, and although she would be grateful to absolve herself of responsibility for the stables, she didn't want to lose the kudos associated with such a high-class establishment, and she wasn't going to let it go for a bargain price.

The Argentinian listened to her eloquent reasoning. She was an intelligent woman and a greedy one, but he respected that. They had spent an enjoyable two hours over a superb lunch discussing power sharing, future prospects, and potential financial rewards. Now they had all been sufficiently oiled to discuss the sticky technicalities.

'My main concern is Mr McKenna,' the Argentinian

said finally. 'I need to be assured that no problems will arise once he is aware of what is being discussed here.'

'Regrettably, my husband's mental condition is deteriorating daily,' Alice said sadly.

'But while he was still in sound mind he signed the contract disowning responsibility,' the first lawyer interrupted smoothly. 'Mrs McKenna is in control. There is no doubt about that. Why else would she be paying for this excellent lunch?'

There was general laughter. Alice watched Don Valmez. It was a pity he was so loyal to his wife. She could have sewn the deal up by now if he had been accessible in bed. Men were such saps. Even the two legal representatives, unbeknownst to each other, had been given the Alice treatment. How else had she managed to convince them to do as she asked? They were sharks, smelling a killing, one ready to wipe Clifton off the face of the earth if he contested the divorce proceedings she was waiting to slap on him. With the contract he had signed, and the evidence she had of his affair with Kate, plus the various testimonies waiting to be given by her friends concerning his disturbing behaviour, including his inexplicable attraction to Suzy Whitbread, his case was already dead in the water. But bankrupting a crippled man would hardly be healthy for her public image. No, she had been playing for time. Now he was healing physically, the time had just about come.

Much later, when it was dark, she drove back to Springfields in her sporty BMW, feeling as if life could not get any better. Hurtling down the M40, she made one more phone call. When that was done, she shivered with anticipation, thinking of Robin O'Grady. Ever since she had first seen him she had not been able to get that handsome brute out of her mind, and he had not disappointed her. He was rough, seedy, insatiable, and he was greedy, which meant that every time she snapped her fingers he would be there. The money side of it was slightly distasteful, but that only added to the man's grubby appeal.

Suzy spent the day with an old friend in London, thinking it was probably wise for her and Clifton to spend some time apart. She arrived back just after ten, having turned down an invitation to go clubbing. She wasn't in the mood for it. Maybe she was growing up, or growing old. Almost an hour was spent in the bath pondering this point, before she went to bed, still feeling as if her life had changed irrevocably, but not knowing why.

In the dead of night, she heard a sound, or rather, sounds, coming from one of the rooms below. It sounded like soft slaps, and grunts of pain.

All thoughts of sleep gone, curiosity overcame her. Slipping on her short silk robe, she crept out into the corridor. There were plenty of places to duck and hide, and she mapped out each one before advancing towards the top of the stairs, feeling a growing sense of adventure.

The sounds were coming from Clifton's room. Her heart began to beat very fast. She slunk down the stairs and ran to his door, pressing herself hard up against the wall. His door was open, and a risky peep in revealed that his bedroom door was also open. Boldly, Suzy entered the living room and tiptoed over to the sofa, hunkering down behind it. From there she could see the bed.

Clifton was face up on the bed, naked and spread-eagled. His hands had been cuffed to the railings above his head. His face showed conflicting emotions: anger, lust, humiliation. He had been blindfolded. Alice was sitting on his lap, her small silk chemise demurely covering both his and her private parts. She was talking, spitefully and scornfully, and slapping his face every now and then.

'I imagine it's very frustrating for you, seeing all those women looking at you, remembering the man you once were. Do you still wish you were sticking it to them?' Slap. 'What about Kate Palmer?' Slap. 'Not much to look at but she gives good head, doesn't she? Or how about Suzy's large titties?' Slap. 'You like the look of those, don't you?' Another slap, harder this time.

Suzy looked down at her breasts. She didn't think they were that large, but compared to Alice's angry little beestings, she supposed they were.

'I saw you this morning staring at them. Do you like her to rub them all over your face, Clifton? Those fat scratchy nipples tingling against your tongue?'

She was actually quite good, Suzy thought. Way off from the pristine, prim woman everyone saw in public.

'Oh yes, I think we've found your weak spot, haven't we?' Now Alice was gently rubbing him. Clifton whispered something that Suzy couldn't hear, but it didn't sound very pleasant. She knew he would rather hang than admit his lust for anybody, just in case Alice tried to use it against him.

Alice's arm moved rapidly now. Suzy guessed she was masturbating him. Clifton's jaw was clenched tight. Even out in the living room Suzy could sense the effort it took him not to give Alice the satisfaction of seeing him submit.

Suddenly Alice stopped. She climbed off the bed and sat on the edge, stroking Clifton's legs with an ostrich feather. Now Suzy could see his cock, vivid red and massively erect. Alice let the feather drift over his genitals. His chest was heaving rapidly, and his dick bounced against his belly. Against his will he was enjoying every minute. Now Suzy understood what he had said the first time she had shaved him. 'Mine will be the greater pleasure,' he had said. His stunning erection was proof that, ultimately, Alice was not going to beat him.

Suzy's own nipples were erect and her sex was damp, watching him take that exquisite torture, but to stay longer was to risk being discovered. Just as she was about to stand up she heard another person enter the room. In the dim light she saw who it was. Robby, Bonny's brother, intent on ploughing a very personal furrow of his own. He was butt-naked, his penis sticking out in front of him like a club. Alice squealed softly as he picked her up effortlessly and set her down upon his cock. He turned her around and pinned her against the wall of the bedroom, so that Suzy could see his reddened, beer-bloated face. Suzy's snort of laughter almost gave her away. What would Alice think if she knew she was shagging one of the pikeys?

Robby pumped lewdly at Alice against the wall whilst Alice hooted with pleasure like a demented owl. Then, thus joined, they staggered back up the stairs, leaving Clifton bound and helpless on the bed.

Suzy stood over him, wondering how to play it. He was vulnerable, hopelessly aroused, in the perfect position to be punished for his insults the previous evening. It was time to be very, very bad.

She leaned over, and ran her moist, hot tongue all over his balls. His cock slapped audibly against his belly.

'Oh, sweet Mary,' he moaned.

'No, it's Suzy.' She did it again and again, swirling, sucking, until his hips began to churn and he was panting softly. 'Does the Squire want his candy?' She asked, so low it was barely more than a breath, whilst she removed the silk blindfold from him. Upstairs, the sounds of sustained, rigorous coupling could be heard.

He tried to hide his smile. 'What the hell are you doing here?'

She took a deep breath, so that her voice was perfectly calm. 'Considering that you can't come and find me to apologise for your recent behaviour, I thought I would do you a favour and come to you.'

'Does Alice know you're here?'

'Absolutely not. Let's just say it was serendipitous, my discovering you in such a compromising position. If I were you, I'd be rather worried.'

He smiled slightly. 'Go screw yourself.'

Suzy flicked one of his nipples with her tongue. 'No, that isn't quite right. I was expecting more along the lines of "sorry". You know, something simple.'

'So that you would understand it? How about this? "Off" and "piss". Rearrange how you like to make a well-known expression of irritation, normally used at low-lifes who won't get out of your face.' His lips twitched, suggesting that he was enjoying himself immensely.

'How about, "My behaviour was reprehensible and I would understand if you find it impossible to forgive me, but I beg you to try?"'

'How about you take your clever-dick arse back to London and don't come back? Ever.'

'You don't mean that.' She shifted between his legs and ran a pointed tongue around his massive balls.

'Don't I?' He sounded breathless.

Suzy began stroking his nut brown nipples. They instantly hardened between her lips and grew larger. She pinched them lightly, and felt him draw in another sharp breath as she raked her fingertips down his body, lightly so that the marks would not show.

'You better keep quiet, or Alice is going to come back down here,' she warned him.

'I doubt that. Who's she got up there?'

'The gardener.'

Clifton laughed explosively, forcing her to clamp her hand over his mouth. 'Shut up, she'll hear you!'

'Does she know who he is?'

Suzy grinned. 'No. Bonny says she thinks he's a farmer from Ireland.'

Clifton began to laugh again. 'That is so sweet –' His breath caught as Suzy eased her lips over the great red head of his penis. She traced every vein, every fold with the tip of her tongue, kitten-licking him from root to tip and down again, before lavishly sucking him almost to the point of no return.

'No more,' he gasped after the third time.

'You haven't apologised to me yet.' She let a trail of breath trickle down to his cock again.

'I'm sorry,' he breathed. 'How about a pussy kiss, to say you forgive me?'

She laughingly obliged, settling her sex lips against his mouth. She felt his mumble of pleasure, the deep thrusting tongue. He slavishly licked at her, savouring her musk as she let her mouth close over him again. This time she eased him in slowly, right down to the root, feeling him shiver. With her mouth full of cock she rested and let him concentrate on her clitoris. Because she was already highly aroused he hit the spot almost straight away. Her thighs quivered and she came with a deep moan, muffled by his mass of flesh. She held onto him as the tremors continued. After her most intense peak he drew away and licked all around her lips instead, delving, exploring, and she began to suck him again, this time in earnest. The hardness he had lost briefly returned. The bass moan told her he was going to lose it so she cupped his buttocks and lifted, intensifying that jolt of white hot pleasure that forced him deep into her mouth. After a moment she withdrew, her mouth full of his cream. As he watched she deposited it around his navel in pearly pools.

'A nice touch.' He grinned as she replaced the blindfold. She kissed him deeply, sharing the sea-fresh taste of his come, and whispered goodnight.

A few minutes later, Alice came down to his room. She made a sound of disgust, seeing the drops of come cooling around Clifton's navel and his flaccid dick, lying to one side as if exhausted.

'You're an animal, Clifton. You really are.' She unfastened the handcuffs and took the blindfold from his eyes. 'You can clean yourself up. I'm not doing it.'

Early the next morning, Alice put on her Aquascutum tweed skirt and cream cashmere twin set to keep out the misty morning chill. Checking in the mirror, she slicked on light pink lipstick and smoothed away a stray dusting of face powder. She pinned her pale blonde hair back with two tortoiseshell combs and put pearls at her throat. Outside, she looked like the respectable lady of the manor, with her short belted Burberry trenchcoat and Russell & Bromley walking shoes. Inside, where people could not see, her heart was thumping. The thick wad of notes weighed down her pocket as she parked the BMW in a secluded lay-by and walked out onto the dewy heathland beyond.

When she was well out of sight of the road a man stepped out from behind a large, dense bush. His appearance was suspect, to say the least, dressed as he was in a long army coat. He leered at her, showing several gold-capped teeth.

'Mrs McKenna,' he said, dipping his grubby Fedora hat.

'Mr Price.' She thrust the money at him and turned to go. It was a little ritual they went through every single time.

'You're always in too much of a hurry, Alice. That isn't the way to treat the father of your only son now, is it?'

Alice's lips tightened at the familiarity, and the constant reminder of the mistake she had made twenty-six years before.

David Price had caught her eye because he was the antithesis of Clifton. Small, hard, tightly muscled and coarse, with a cheeky grin and twinkling eyes, and already missing two teeth from a pub fight. She could not help wondering what he would be like in bed, and as she was used to getting her own way, set about finding out, even though she and Clifton had just come back from their honeymoon.

He wasn't going to argue when the pretty blonde wife of a rich man suddenly decided she wanted him. After a brief flirtation they were going at it anywhere they could without being caught. After that her obsession with rough men persisted, even after she fell pregnant. She told Price she would bring the baby up as Clifton's, and rather naïvely thought that was the end of it. That was, until he turned up on her doorstep five years previously, bankrupt because of his love of the ponies.

So she reluctantly agreed a sum of cash every month. But that wasn't all.

She glanced down and saw that through his open coat, his trousers were unzipped. He saw the direction of her gaze.

'Oh, come on, Alice. You knew I wouldn't let you go that easy,' he grinned.

She sighed heavily. The Prices had no respect, even though it was Alice who had paid for the large satellite dish stuck on the side of their council house, and the

Ford Cosworth that ripped up and down the road outside the village on a Saturday night. She looked around the heath. No one was about. They wouldn't be at that time in the morning, even in the hunting season. Dew sparkled in the watery sunlight. Their footsteps showed dark in the silvery grass.

Price led the way. He cut a seedy figure in the long coat and pointed unpolished boots, his cheeks unshaven. He was still devilishly handsome, if one ignored the teeth and the ratty long hair under his hat. His trousers were grubby and stained, like the tips of his fingers he ran through her neatly coiffed hair. He pushed her to her knees and guided her head towards his crotch.

As she drew him into her mouth her nose wrinkled at the stale smell of cigarette smoke and cement dust, but the tawdriness of what they were doing still moistened her panties and stiffened her nipples.

'I know you love this, bitch,' he growled. 'Get your tits out.'

She scrabbled at her cardigan and prised her breasts out of their silk cups, offering them to him. They looked creamy, each tipped with an alluring pink nipple. He sucked them one by one, his rough skin chafing the delicate flesh, before standing up again so she could continue to suck him. His girth distorted her pretty mouth but she kept on until he began to thrust hard. He drew out and spurted his seed all over her face and tits, hoarsely telling her to lick him clean. Obediently she did so, swallowing the last drops of smoky semen as if they were life-giving water.

'Now give me your knickers,' he rasped.

Alice's eyes widened. He had not asked that before. Hurriedly, because the less time she spent with him the better, she stepped out of her filmy French knickers and handed them to him. He pressed them to his face for a moment before stuffing them in his pocket. Without further word he walked away.

A few minutes later Alice was back in her car, trembling and weak; her mind was already on the day ahead. She required Mrs Penrose to make an apple cake for the coffee morning, as it was so much better when made on the day. And no one would bat an eyelid when she said she had made it herself out of a recipe from *Country Living*.

David Price drove home first before going to the bookies. Shirley was out visiting her ancient mother and wouldn't be back until that night. He went upstairs, threw off his coat and lay down on their bed, his boots still on. The money seemed to burn a hole in his hand as he counted it out. He didn't need to. Alice always paid what he asked for, but just the feel of it felt good. He was getting stiff again, thinking of Alice's pretty mouth straining around his cock. With the money scattered at his side he freed himself and draped Alice's expensive silk panties around his cock. The friction they made as he rubbed gently made him harden even more. He visualised Alice's soft blonde hair, the pale pink lipstick she had left on his underwear, her expensive scent and fancy clothes, and he felt his orgasm rising with every thrust of his hand.

'What the hell are you doing?'

Peter stood in the doorway, watching him with disgust. Price quickly covered himself and tried to hide the money and the panties, but his son had seen.

'Oh, I get it. You've been to see Alice McKenna.' Peter grabbed his father by the lapels and threw him up against the door. 'She's been paying you, hasn't she? Paying you and sucking your dick!'

Price shook his head, but that enraged his son even

further. He pressed his forearm against his father's neck. 'Tell me the truth! She's paying you hush money so people won't find out you're Jem McKenna's dad! That's it, isn't it! There's us, dirt poor, and you're spending Alice McKenna's blood money on the fucking ponies!'

Price gasped for breath. His son was hard and fast and furious, but he had never laid a hand on him before. Now his eyes were murderous. Whatever answer he gave, he was doomed.

'Yes,' he whispered, and waited for the killer blow.

Peter Price gave him one final hard shove and let him drop to the floor. He gave his crotch a vicious kick.

'See if you can get it up for Alice after that.' He scooped the money and the panties from the bed and walked out.

The Cosworth's tyres screamed as he pulled away from the house. Down the long drive to the stables, horses fled away across the field as the speeding car kicked up plumes of dust. He parked in the middle of the yard and strode into the office, ignoring Jakki. Jem was at his desk, on the phone. Peter snatched it from his hand and slammed it down, then crashed the door shut behind him.

'Tell your cunt of a mother that she can have these back,' he said, throwing the panties into Jem's lap. 'And you can tell her that if she wants her dirty little secret kept quiet, she comes to me.'

'What secret?' Jem looked wary.

Peter leaned on the desk and smiled with vicious satisfaction. 'My dad is your dad, but that don't make us brothers. Not ever. You got that?'

'Loud and clear,' Jem said quietly. His lack of reaction unnerved Price. He backed uncertainly away.

'Fucking freak,' he muttered, his thunder stolen. At least he still had the money to give to his mother. He left before anyone could challenge him.

Jem fielded his staff's concerned enquiries smoothly and told them to get back to work. The panties were hidden in a padded envelope in his desk drawer. He didn't want to touch them. There was no doubt Price was telling the truth. He had suspected as much for years.

He didn't do much work for the rest of the day. There didn't seem to be any point. He left early and went up into the hills. It was the only place he could focus. An hour later he drove home. Alice wasn't around, so he went into the drawing room and looked in the cabinets. He selected a few valuable items, moved the others around so that they would not be missed, and went upstairs to make a few phone calls.

When Suzy arrived back at the house that morning, following her usual bun run to the stables, the house seemed full of people. At first she thought something terrible had happened. In fact, something terrible was happening. Alice McKenna was giving a charity coffee morning.

The drawing room was eventually filled with chirping, self-righteous women, all wearing little blue ribbons and Gabor sandals. Mrs Penrose looked distinctly harassed, running around with delicate china cups and saucers, and pimple-sized cakes. Suzy sat in the gallery at the top of the stairs and peered through the rails like a small child, listening to it all. She didn't want to go down and run the gauntlet just yet. Anyway, it was fascinating viewing.

All was going well until Clifton's door slammed open. She couldn't see him, but boy, could she hear him. Probably the whole village could.

'Alice! What the fuck is that coven of witches doing here?'

There was a delicate pause, and then Alice emerged, looking pained.

'Clifton, really! I told you everyone was coming today!'

A few of the braver souls had gathered behind her. One greeted him with ultra-smooth politeness, delivered in a loud voice usually reserved for the deaf or terminally stupid.

'You're looking very well, Mr McKenna.'

'I would be, if I was allowed to jerk off in peace.' Clifton backed the chair into his suite and slammed the door. Suzy's hand was tight over her mouth, stifling her sobs of laughter. Downstairs, the creak of eyebrows could be heard, lifting into tightened foreheads. Alice's smile had frozen to her face.

'Oh dear, Alice. I'm so sorry,' someone said sympathetically.

'It must be dreadful for you,' said another woman, with delicious enjoyment.

'How you put up with it is beyond me,' said another woman, leading her back into the drawing room. Sympathetic murmurs all round, with Alice's faint voice saying, yes, it was difficult, but one had to understand how frustrated and angry he must feel, etc., etc. The door closed again on her sanctimonious whining.

Suzy was still grinning when she went downstairs, only to be caught by Dr Maloney.

'Can we borrow you, my dear?'

'What for?' she asked as he escorted her back through the house.

'Clifton and I are old friends,' he said. 'We knew each other long before the accident. We know about each other's tastes, dislikes,' he paused slightly, 'needs.' He opened the door to Clifton's living room and guided her in. When the door closed behind them he suddenly grabbed her arms and pulled them behind her back, thrusting her breasts against the buttonholes of her shirt and stretching them dangerously.

'Hey, what –?'

'Be quiet,' he said sternly. With a spare hand he flicked the struggling buttons free, allowing her breasts in their small pink cups to burst through.

Clifton was sitting behind his desk, studying his computer screen as if the episode in the hall had never happened. She noticed that he had been reading blood-stock reports. It was a good sign of his rehabilitation, but something told her that horses were the last thing on his mind right then.

'Here she is,' Dr Maloney said cheerfully. 'Where do you want her?'

Clifton's reply wiped whatever irritated, smug or attitude-drenched expression may have been on Suzy's face.

'Over my knee,' he said severely.

'Damned right, too,' Dr Maloney said, dragging Suzy towards him. Too stunned to struggle, Suzy found she was facing the floor before she could blink. Clifton had dropped the sides of the chair and now she was draped over his lap. He pushed the short skirt up, exposing Suzy's buttocks. Her panties were diaphanous and pale pink, with tiny white flowers; very pretty, but she didn't want them being shown to the world. She struggled uselessly, humiliated beyond belief.

'It's no good screaming,' Dr Maloney said. 'You wouldn't want the good ladies of Great Clutton to realise what was happening, would you?'

'How dare you!' Suzy squeaked, outrage making her sound like Minnie Mouse. 'Let me go!'

A sharp slap halted her struggles. It was the sound

more than the pain that did it. Before she could register the discomfort there came another, and another.

'This is for disrespecting the master of the house, creeping into his bedroom late at night and abusing his helpless body,' Clifton said severely. Another smack. 'And this is for being dirty with Dr Maloney here. He informs me that you seduced him very successfully the other day. This is for every erection you've given him since.'

Dr Maloney was avidly watching. Clifton stopped, and for a minute she thought it was over.

'He's a connoisseur,' Dr Maloney said helpfully. 'He knows that pausing lets the blood flow again, it lets the skin warm up, the nerve endings come alive. Then . . .'

Clifton smacked her again. This time it seemed to hurt more, followed almost instantly by numbing warmth that was intensely erotic. In the large mirror at the other end of the room she could see him, his pale skin flushed, intense concentration on his face as he visually feasted on her glowing buttocks. He motioned to the doctor, who came forward.

'Dr Maloney would like you to suck him off.'

Suzy gave him a horrified glance. He could not be serious. But the doctor was right in front of her, stroking her hair, and she was helpless over Clifton's knees. He spanked her again.

'Do it,' he barked again as the doctor unzipped his trousers. Another slap, and her sex felt as if it were on fire. Suzy was angry that they could use her so easily, yet a heated excitement was flooding through her body, adding to the moisture already between her thighs. Her legs opened slightly and as she felt his finger probe her soaking hole the doctor pushed his pink, hard cock against her lips. She sucked him in, feeling him shudder. Clifton slapped her buttocks again.

'Deeper. Take him all in.'

The doctor uttered a moan as she obeyed, steadying himself with his hands on her shoulders. Clifton was spanking her, alternating with a wanton finger thrusting deep in her hole. Soon she was adding her own small sounds at the pleasure, the sharp sting and the spreading warmth his hands wrought throughout her body. She could feel Clifton's erection, hard against her stomach. He was flushed, breathing hard, enjoying the sight of her reddening buttocks.

'Is she doing a good job?' he asked Maloney.

'Yes,' Maloney spluttered, unwilling to do anything but concentrate on the velvet tunnel his cock was enveloped in. Suzy scooped his balls out of the soft cord trousers and licked them as well. Above her he was rigid, legs apart, his head thrown back. Clifton's fingers pushed deeper inside her, making her want so much more. In frustration she sucked hard on the doctor's cock and he pulled away with a ragged grunt of pain.

Clifton slapped her rump again, harder this time, as Dr Maloney rubbed at his offended cock and whipped her lips with it.

'Be nice,' Clifton said. 'Pretend you're doing me and make it damned good.' He pushed her legs further apart and shoved three fingers inside her oozing pussy as she took the doctor's cock in her mouth again. For a moment she halted, overcome with delight, but another slap reminded her of her task.

'Oh yes,' the doctor murmured. 'That's much better.'

Clifton had worked all of his fingers inside her and was moving them slowly, penetrating her more deeply than she had ever been before. She mumbled around the base of the doctor's penis as she was slowly stuffed from behind, punctuated by a smack whenever she lost concentration on her task. The doctor sighed, enjoying the benefits of her rapture.

'Turn her over,' Clifton said from afar. As if in a dream she was turned and now she lay on her back across Clifton's knees, looking straight up the doctor's stiff cock, balls covered in a fluffy golden down. The men held her secure to stop her from tumbling to the floor, and this time she automatically sucked the doctor into her mouth. She felt wild, abandoned, spread wide before these two salacious men, each taking their own pleasure from her splayed body. Clifton hand-fucked her with such finesse that she could have come from that alone, but the combination of that invading hand, his fingers decisively strumming her clitoris, the hands on her breasts and the doctor's rampant cock now thrusting feverishly in and out of her mouth sent her tumbling into ecstasy. With difficulty the doctor pulled away and splashed come all over her breasts, her stomach, her face, whilst Clifton continued to stimulate her by rubbing it into her breasts, tugging on the slippery nipples, his other hand brutalising her pussy. Suzy came in a series of hard peaks, writhing uncontrollably on Clifton's lap, eventually tumbling off to lie on the floor, panting, gasping and squirming, her hand buried between her legs.

When she had quietened and sat up again, the doctor had gone. Clifton was heading towards the bedroom, the motor on his wheelchair the only sound in the room. Suzy glanced at her watch. Alice's coffee morning would be over very soon.

'Well? What are you waiting for?' Clifton said. His deep voice held a hint of impatience. Suzy climbed stiffly to her feet and went into his room. He had manoeuvred onto the bed and was unzipping his trousers.

'We don't have much time.'

'Why should I?' She folded her arms and leant against the door post.

'Quid pro quo,' he reminded her, unselfconsciously stroking his cock.

He had not pleaded with her, or commanded her. They both knew that if he had, she would not have obeyed him. She allowed him to pull her onto the bed.

Alice went at him full throttle that afternoon. Clifton looked surprisingly relaxed, considering the tongue-lashing. He had been reading his *Telegraph* throughout, punctuating each pause for breath with a 'yes, dear'.

'And if you even think about humiliating me in front of all my friends again, I'll have a few choice words to say to my lawyer,' Alice said triumphantly.

'I can think of a few choice words of my own,' Clifton replied, flicking his lighter. He blew smoke at Alice's spiteful face.

'But mine will actually do some damage. All you can do is sit there like some useless, vindictive old goat and hope that some stupid little scrubber will consent to suck you off. How much are you paying her, anyway?'

'Probably a lot less than you're having to pay our gardener to butt-fuck you.'

Alice paled. 'You'll pay for that, Clifton. Really you will.'

'I've been paying for it since the day I married you,' came the bitter reply.

Whilst they were arguing, Suzy had escaped into the garden and walked down to the lake to lob a few bits of spare bread to the ducks. She scrunched up her eyes and looked out over the Vale, across the river. Oxford was a misty outline in the distance. Christ Church Tower looked as indistinct as her future at that precise moment.

She had long since given up pretending that she was looking for work. A quick check of her finances reassured her that she could probably manage for a year before she needed to think about it again, even though she had refused the money Clifton had offered her for being at his side. He had done it clumsily, in a moment of humility that disturbed her. She warned him that if he was going start behaving like a pathetic old man she would gladly leave. That had led to a violent argument, with him accusing her of prostituting herself. He was so enraged that she had begun to laugh. It was her laughter that calmed him down. That day their relationship subtly changed. That was the day they had become friends. It was as good a paycheque as any.

The one thing she wanted to do was square things with Jem. Since his accusation every one of her attempts to talk had been rebuffed. She found him in his room. A large leather bag lay on the bed. All conciliatory words flew out the window.

'Where are you going?'

'I'm taking Bonny to New York on Concorde. Is that OK with you?'

He was playing it hard, which didn't suit him, but she decided to play along.

'I think you're wasting your money, but that's up to you.'

'Not my money. My mother's.' He pushed past her and rummaged in his wardrobe for black chinos. 'You can tell her, if you like. I don't give a fuck.'

'Whatever, but you're still a romantic devil,' Suzy replied easily. 'I hope Bonny appreciates it.'

Jem shrugged. 'She gives good head and fucks like a rabbit. That's all I want.'

'Strike the romantic bit,' Suzy said dryly.

She waited for him to ask her what she was doing, but he didn't. His face was set as he folded clothes and put them in the bag, as if he were packing for a funeral, not a sex-saturated weekend in one of the hottest cities on the planet.

'Well, have a good time,' she said, turning away. That had been a raging success. Not. She went to see Clifton instead.

12

That Saturday afternoon, Alice was in a luxury hotel in the middle of Buckinghamshire, being fed English strawberries by Robin O'Grady. He looked as smug as a 1970s porn star, with his exaggerated sideburns and bad taste in shirts, the hair on his chest luxuriant and glossy. He had planned a surprise for her later, he said. One of her fantasies was going to come true. He liked listening to her fantasies. In them she was rapacious and greedy, and one man was never enough.

She tweaked one pink nipple between her French-manicured fingers and listened to him talking about his home in Southern Ireland, where his family had a farm. He was in England for a working holiday, looking to buy another farm, perhaps. He had a wife and three daughters living with his old mother in Cork. He would be going back soon to give them a hand castrating the bullocks before they went to market.

Alice gave a tinkling laugh. 'I bet you handle a bull quite well.'

Robin smiled indulgently. 'We used to castrate 'em by hand. Poor buggers. They didn't half yell.'

'And the cows? What did they do when they were taken to the bull that wasn't castrated?'

Robin smiled down at her greedy, feline face. 'They opened up real wide and let that fat old cock in as far as it would go.'

'Was it very big?' Her voice was breathless now. She didn't want to hear about his family any more, or about any other aspects of farming other than the bestial needs of big, brutish animals, bigger than the brute she was currently in bed with.

'As thick as my arm,' Robby replied, holding up and flexing his bulging bicep. 'Some of the young ones, they couldn't take it at first. They would squeal a bit.'

Alice was feeling all moist again at hearing about the farmyard antics. The power of a fierce snorting beast that was hungry to mate – that massive cock, those pendulous balls. Her legs had widened of their own volition, her hand lewdly between them, stroking her slippery sex.

'I'd like that,' she said huskily. 'I'd like to be mated with a great horny strapping farm lad at the same time as the bull is covering the cow. No, lots of them, one after the other, again and again . . .' Her voice faded to a murmur as the fantasy took over. She had been captured and strapped into a harness, her legs splayed wide. She could not see, but she could hear snorting, bellowing, and the heavy clop of hooves. Then the farm hands arrived, already erect and desperate to service her. The biggest one came up behind her. She could feel his rough work clothes and smell his gamy odour, and feel the first nudging of something huge and wet, with a fat, bulbous tip. It was penetrating her, not gently, but with a massive thrust that almost split her in two. Then another and another, deep inside her, all the way in, and a earth-shaking pulse that rippled right through her body as he flooded her with seed . . . and a great cheer went up from 'the lads'.

By now Alice was on her front, her rear in the air as Robby pumped hard from behind. She bucked and pushed back at him as he held her hips and grinned in the mirror beside them. In his wildest dreams he had never imagined the lady of the manor could be so filthy.

After dinner he showed her the clothes he wanted her

to wear. They were cheap and nasty, black PVC and scratchy red lace, but she complied because it felt so dirty to look like a common whore for once. She could hardly walk in the teetering red heels, but that didn't matter because she would be on her back most of the time. She didn't totally trust him, but that was half the fun. Now they were in his grubby white van, bound for destination unknown. She was in the back, on an old mattress he had acquired from somewhere. Her hands had been tied so that she wasn't tempted to remove the blindfold and see where it was they were going.

After half an hour he stopped the van and she heard the doors open. He helped her out and walked her into a place that smelt of beer and cigarettes. Her juices began to flow. This was the sort of place that excited her, usually full of husky men hot and sweaty from a days hard labour. The sort of place she would never dream of entering in real life. She was guided up a flight of steep, narrow stairs. The walls vibrated with the thump of a hip-hop beat from somewhere else in the building, and there was the smell of greasy fried food.

She was pushed down onto a bed and told to wait. She couldn't do anything else. The bedcover smelt slightly musty, mingling with her light perfume. In her prone position her nipples were now resting on the top of the half-cups of her black brassière. She could feel them, erect and tingling, brushing lightly against the red silky material of her blouse. She felt deliciously tarty and wanton, and she stretched luxuriously, opening her legs wide and arching her back.

'Come and get me,' she murmured, to no one in particular.

'Ooh, that's pretty,' a voice said. It made her jump. Her second thought was that it had not been Robin who had spoken. A stranger was in the room. Her nipples pinged against the bra and showed through the red silk blouse. She heard breathing, unsteady, coming at her from all sides. She was surrounded by strangers. She wet her suddenly dry lips with her tongue and held her breath.

Voices, all of them male. She counted at least five of them, including Robin.

'She's hot.'

'Really fucking hot. Who'd have thought –'

That voice was cut off, replaced with, 'Looks like she's gagging for it'.

The voices were Irish, a gentle lilt she found strangely reassuring. Then she felt the bed dip, and a cool, wet tongue thrust deep into her pussy.

She cried out and bucked, but the tongue was relentless, licking her out as if really tasting her. She felt her head being turned and something smooth and rubbery pushed against her lips. Automatically she opened them and found her mouth filled with a very long, fat cock. She couldn't take it all, but she began to suck him properly, eliciting a deep moan.

'The lady's sucking me!' As if he were surprised. He pushed harder, and this time – her mouth slick with pre-come – she managed to take all of him in. The mouth at her pussy was a distraction though, as this man really knew how to work it.

'Robby, is that you?' she asked, before being dominated by that insistent, greedy cock again. There was some laughter.

'No, duchess, I'm right here, waiting my turn,' he said behind her. She purred and widened her legs, communicating to the man below that he was very good at his job. He continued his salacious exploration as the man she was sucking suddenly thickened and grunted, spurting thick cream over her lips. She licked it up and sucked him dry, humming contentedly to herself.

The man at her pussy had changed. She felt another cock push against her lips and she tasted feminine musk. She drew him in but this time she could not concentrate. Her clitoris was as swollen as a grape as the third man lashed it gently, alternating with a deep, muscular thrust up into her pussy. Her hips started to churn, and when she felt her nipples being tweaked through the scarlet silk, she began to moan.

'Oh lady, look at you,' one man said in awe. There was a choked sob and warm liquid spattered over her pussy. The tongue was still there, building her orgasm, the cock still forging in and out of her mouth. Her legs were so wide that they ached, but she didn't care. Her hips rotated crazily. All around her there was heavy breathing, choking cigarette smoke, the smell of hard liquor. She gave in to her first orgasm, flopping around like a fish starved of oxygen stifled by the mass of flesh in her mouth.

At some point they turned her over and took the bindings off her hands. She knelt up and pushed her bottom out to her unseen companions, her sex heavy and gaping with need. It was soon filled, by a cock that felt like Robby's. The jack-hammer energy felt like Robby too, and the vicious digging of his fingers into her hips. It seemed to go on for ever until he pulsed and let go with a guttural grunt. Another cock replaced him straight away, squelching into her pussy and making the sperm already there ooze down her stockinged legs.

'Give me something to suck,' she whispered.

'What was that, duchess?'

'Give me something to suck,' she growled, licking her lips and opening them for the salty member now easing its way between them. 'You boys do have some energy,' she said as she was reamed from both ends. She was enjoying the experience too much to come just yet. In fact, she was getting greedy for even more cock. Her tight hole puckered as someone spat on it and slid their finger in. After initial resistance she was open to him, pushing back against his finger, moaning around the other man's penis. The vibration from her moans made him shiver and bolt suddenly, shooting smoky sperm down her throat. She gulped and swallowed and sucked so lavishly that he kept hard, pumping slowly into her willing mouth.

A cool tongue fluttered against her anal opening, making her whimper and weaken.

'Shove it in,' she hissed greedily, before engulfing another erect penis waiting her attention. There was a little shifting around, in which the man doing her from behind withdrew, leaving her feeling bereft. She was guided sideways, and felt a body on its back.

'Sit on me, there's a nice lady,' a voice rasped. His breath smelt of curry and cigarettes, but his dick was super-hard and filled her up so much her eyes watered. He groped for her blouse and bared her breasts, and began pawing them, pushing them together, tweaking the nipples. His cock throbbed hard, and every time it did he grunted, an animalistic sound that reminded her of the bull he had told her about the night before. Then she felt warm sticky stuff being sprayed all over her backside. Someone was coming, spending their sperm all over her crack. It acted as the finest lubricant, and when it was massaged in she felt as open as the Dartford Tunnel.

'Yeah. Fuck, yeah,' the man underneath her moaned as the second cock eased into her back passage. She was too stunned to moan, her breath coming in tight little gasps. He was so big that she felt split in two, a danger-ous, exciting feeling that worried her simply because after this, normal sex would never be the same again. She would have to have two men, all the time. She began to move, slowly, voluptuously, strange 'ooooh' sounds dripping like molasses from her lips. She was no longer a woman, but a sex machine, her pussy, her arse, her mouth all stuffed with hard, pulsing flesh. The men around her were mostly silent, except for the ones buried deep inside her, and they were moaning as well, stunned at the awesome tightness of her pussy, the wantonness and greed of their conquest. But for Alice, it still wasn't enough. She wanted someone at her clit as well. She frantically licked her fingers and pushed them down there, but it was no good, her balance was shot. Someone else did the job for her, cool, wet fingers sliding between the heaving mass of bodies to stroke her needy clitoris. Now she could buck and squirm and grasp every bit of pleasure she could. A tongue on her nipples, the soaking fingers on her clit, the cocks in her mouth, pussy and arse, she felt like exploding with joy. Her cries as she came were loud and unashamed, the reverberating of her inner muscles too much for the deeply imbedded men. They came seconds after she did, each jolting, cursing, banging hard into her abused and greedy body.

Half an hour later, she dressed with some difficulty, still blindfolded, and Robby led her back to the van. On the old mattress she stroked herself to another orgasm as he drove her back to the hotel. As commanded, she did not remove the blindfold until he had stopped the van. Then she staggered up to the bedroom to clean herself up as he drove away.

After breakfast on Monday morning Suzy went to the stables, hoping to see Jem. He wasn't back yet, Jakki informed her impatiently, so she sought out Alan the Head Lad and offered her services. For four hours she shovelled manure and picked out hooves and brushed chestnut coats, knowing that Alice was at large with more of her hideous friends at the house, before thinking she had better get back to see Clifton. In the village a sleek black Jaguar passed her, all windows darkened. Very nice, and probably not a local, she mused, unashamedly ogling it. It turned in the direction of Springfields and was gone, with a roar of twin exhausts.

She walked the mile back to Springfields, pausing to eat lunch on the way on the hill, surrounded by blue and brown butterflies. Alice came towards her in her blue BMW just as she joined the road again. She stopped and lowered the window, looking slightly flushed, but all sugary sweetness and English roses.

'Suzy, darling, see if you can cheer Clifton up, will you? He's being terribly churlish. I'm nipping into Oxford for a facial and a manicure. I want it done properly for tonight.'

That was a dig, implying that Suzy wasn't up to doing the job properly herself, even though she hadn't even offered.

'If you want something else to do I'm sure Mrs Penrose could use a hand. Clifton has smoked all his best cigars and wants some more, so I had better go.'

Like she really cares, Suzy thought, but she just smiled. 'That's fine, Alice. I'll look after Clifton for you.'

'You do that, darling.' She gave a little wave and roared away in the style that women do when they want to say, 'I have a bigger, better and faster car than you will ever have, poor thing.'

Suzy went back to Springfields the back way, entering from the rear of the house, over the fields. She could see Clifton through the conservatory window, but he didn't see her. She went upstairs and showered away the lingering aroma of horse, before slipping on a short linen dress, spraying a light mist of perfume and going downstairs to see whether he was recovering from their insatiable weekend.

He was sitting on the sofa, and didn't look as if he needed any help at all. In fact, he looked better than she had ever seen him, his glossy black hair brushed straight back, and for the first time he was wearing a shirt and tie. His long legs were casually crossed. He had been reading the *Telegraph*, but now his attention was focused solely on her. She paused in the doorway, letting the light from behind shine through the flimsy linen dress to show her shapely figure underneath.

He opened his mouth to speak but she hushed him with a finger to her lips. Slowly she sauntered towards him, letting her hips undulate gently, slowly pulling the laces that held her dress together. She arrived at his side, and shifted his top leg so it was level with the other. He was totally transfixed as she gathered up her dress, affording him the merest glimpse of her small white thong, before straddling him and nestling comfortably on his lap. She rubbed her hand over her cleft and let him smell her scent off her fingers before opening his mouth and slipping them inside, kissing him at the same time with a wicked, probing tongue. His groan was deep-felt, echoed by a rising of his loins towards her. He grasped her buttocks as the kiss deepened, Suzy drinking in the exciting masculine scent of good cloth, Cuban cigars and an unfamiliar mossy aftershave.

'You smell so good,' she whispered, running her tongue along his jaw line and tugging gently at his ear, breathing him in. He did not reply, but brought her back to kiss him again, deeper than ever, as she felt between their legs for his cock and palmed it, feeling it pulse against her hand.

When the kiss ended he smiled at her and spoke in a distinctly South African accent.

'That's the best welcome home I've ever had.'

13

Suzy leapt to her feet as if scalded, her face flame red. She could not believe she had just attempted to fuck a complete stranger, who was now laughing at her.

'Why didn't you say anything?' she gasped.

'Why should I? It was very pleasant.'

She tried to cover her embarrassment with a pathetic attempt at formality.

'So you must be Clayton McKenna?'

'That's right. I'm the brother who can walk. Just don't ask me to prove it right now.' He smirked, shifting position slightly. 'Who are you, honey?'

'Suzy Whitbread. I'm his relaxation therapist,' Suzy said stiffly, then immediately wondered why such an asinine thing had come into her head.

Clayton McKenna roared with laughter. 'Jesus, woman! I'm surprised he's not dead by now!'

Suzy bridled under his mockery. 'I don't care for you very much. Why don't you go fuck yourself?'

'And deny you the privilege?' He raised one eyebrow, as black as a raven's wing, just like his brother's. Damn, he was attractive. And damn, didn't he know it.

'Don't be fooled by Suzy. If she can handle me she can handle you just as well,' Clifton said, sliding on silent wheels into the room. He was still sporting an unhealthy white pallor, compared to his brother's golden tan. Suzy wondered how she could have made such a crashing mistake.

'Is that right? Wouldn't be the first time we've shared

a woman, eh, Cliff?' Clayton flipped his lighter and held it to the end of a half-smoked cigar. 'So, what is it? Alice has agreed to you bringing your ladies back to the house at last? It's taken her long enough. Of course, if she had chosen me, I would have been shot of her long before now.'

Clifton shot him an irritated look. Suzy went to stand behind him, glaring over his shoulder at Clayton. Her hostility only seemed to amuse him, though.

'I don't think she likes me.'

Clifton squeezed her hand. 'Suzy looks after my interests very well.'

'I bet she does,' Clayton said suggestively, drawing on the cigar.

'What are you doing here?' she asked abruptly.

'This is our parents' house. I am entitled to be here.'

'Yes, but why now? You didn't rush here when he first had the accident.'

'Suzy . . .' But Clifton seemed too weary to carry on. Clayton drew lazily on his cigar again, but he still had the air of a jaguar about to pounce.

'Alice called me. I came from Cape Town as soon as I could. It seems I'm needed here to sort out some family issues.'

'Pardon me for making an observation, but I think you're a bit bloody late,' Suzy said tartly.

'She's savage, this one. Lionesses would run from her,' Clayton said to his brother, half-jokingly.

Suzy suddenly felt very protective of Clifton. She placed her hands on his shoulders. He was very tense, his muscles hard knots. She couldn't think of anything else to say that wasn't rude or defensive. The silence became thick and uncomfortable.

Clayton stood up and picked up his jacket. 'We'll continue this conversation later. Right now I'm bushed.

Ten hours' sleep to catch up on.' He slung his jacket over his shoulder and sauntered gracefully out of the room.

Clifton sagged back against Suzy's breasts. 'That's all I need,' he groaned. 'Just when I thought it couldn't get any worse.'

'What do you want to do?'

'Right now? I want to get drunk on single malt and get fucked until I die. Next question?'

'That isn't an option. Try again.'

He stared moodily out of the window. 'Take me out in the Jag. I don't think I can stand being in this house a moment longer.'

Alice returned late that afternoon, with the requested cigars. She seemed to have undergone a personality transplant along with her manicure, as white light seemed to glow from her newly tinted hair. At the dinner table all her attention was on Clayton. It seemed that baiting Clifton had lost its appeal under the glowing magnetism of his brother. Even Jem seemed pleased to see his uncle. Talk was easy, wine was copious. Under the circumstances, it wasn't a bad evening.

Clayton monopolised the conversation, and turned out to be a gifted raconteur. He was knowledgeable about wine, about horses, about life on the savannah, in fact, about almost anything. He did like to shoot animals, but only as a game warden, one of his many careers. His description of grappling with a dozy hundred-pound lioness to nurse its wounded paw seemed unbelievable, especially as right then he looked too suave to grapple with anything more challenging than a glass of superlative Shiraz.

'Of course, once the lioness knew what it was dealing with, it had the sense to just lie down and let me get on with it, just like every other good pussy I've met in the past.' Clayton winked at Suzy over his wine glass.

'Really, Clayton, you're just like Peter Pan, coming here with all your stories. When are you going to grow up?' Alice asked indulgently.

Clayton shrugged carelessly, slinging his boots up on the table. 'Why should I?'

'Maybe because every time you go you leave your shadow behind,' Suzy said, toasting him with her wine.

Clayton's smile was wiped away in an instant. They both knew that she had seen right through him.

Clifton laughed out loud. 'Trust Suzy to tell it like it is! That's why we get on so well.' He kissed Suzy's hand. Alice glared at him. Clayton's voice had deserted him. It was as if he had been faced with a truth that he had been trying to avoid all his life.

'So tell me about this girlfriend of yours.' Clifton addressed Jem to fill the sudden silence. 'Are you still seeing her or has your mother scared her away?'

'She wasn't my girlfriend, Dad. We were fucking. There's a difference.'

There was a small pause, in which Suzy was aware that her mouth was open, but she couldn't shut it; Clayton's soup spoon had stopped half-way to his lips and Alice was frozen in a state of horrified catatonia. Baker and Mrs Penrose seemed to find the ceiling very interesting.

Clifton continued to smear butter on his bread roll. 'Really? How infinitely sensible. Don't you think so, Alice? I think we could learn a lot from the younger generation.'

Alice spoke, in a high, hurried voice, desperate to change the subject. 'How was New York? It can be very hot at this time of year.'

'Hot as hell, Ma. I sweated like a pig.'

Suzy fled from the room with a muttered excuse. In the gym she let out the guffaw she had been hanging onto. It was weird, laughing by herself, but she held her stomach and sobbed, wiping the tears from her eyes.

Only when she was absolutely sure she could control herself again in polite company did she venture back to the dining room. On the way she ran into Clayton.

'I was sent to find you.' It was a lie, and a lousy one at that. 'You OK?'

'I'm fine,' she said. Suddenly, with him so tall and so close, she didn't feel like laughing any more. It was surreal, hearing a guttural, clipped voice coming from a man so familiar in looks and mannerisms.

'Why don't you like me?'

She looked at Clayton McKenna's achingly beautiful face and thought, but I do, damn it.

'I don't know you,' she started carefully. He started to speak. She raised her hand to his mouth. 'And you talk too much. And you're everything that Clifton used to be and wants to be again. And I don't trust your motives for being here.'

'Anything else?'

'I'll think of something,' she muttered, thinking, and I want you, even though I don't know you from Adam.

'Jem tells me you're responsible for getting Clifton to walk again.'

'He isn't walking yet, but he will,' she corrected him. 'We'd best get back to the table. They'll wonder where we are.'

She found herself pressed against the solid oak wall panel, with no hidden escape route to spin her into another time. His kiss was warm and sweet, not demanding, but assertive enough to quicken her breath.

He caught her arms over her head so she was totally trapped.

'I don't know you!' she protested.

'Yes you do. You've lived with my other half for a month. You know what makes me tick and what turns me on. And you love it.' He swooped down on her but she was quicker. A swift knee between the legs and a rapid twist of her body and she was free, smashing her hand across his face.

'You think you can get a cheap grope out of me because of my loyalty to Clifton? Screw you! You're going to have to work a lot harder than that.'

She walked off in the direction of the dining room. Don't stomp, she warned herself. Walk with graceful indignation. Only look back when you're at the door. He won't be watching you.

He was.

Back at the table, tension had set in. The hissed voices stopped as soon as Suzy walked in.

'I had something stuck in my throat,' she said lamely, taking her seat at the table again. Clayton appeared and picked up the wine bottle, replenishing everyone's glasses as they sat silently.

'I really can't imagine why I've stayed away so long,' he said loudly. 'And now you can tell me about Australia, Jem, and what was so bloody awful about it that you felt compelled to return to the bosom of your beloved family.'

Clifton was about to say something, probably along the lines of 'shut up', when he caught Suzy's eye and closed his mouth again. Jem, relieved at having something to say, talked at length. Most of it was bullshit. Suzy knew for a fact that once he hit the beach he mostly stayed there, and didn't bother venturing into the cities.

Clayton probably knew that too, as he had travelled extensively around the Antipodes, but mercifully he kept his mouth shut and listened.

Eventually he excused himself, blaming jet lag. Alice immediately got up and went with him. Suzy pushed Clifton's chair into his living room and poured whisky for both of them.

'What do you think of him?' Clifton asked as she worked oil into his knotted shoulders. He winced as she dug her thumbs in.

'Who?'

'It's whom, and you know. Clayton.'

'He's like you, but he thinks a lot more of himself.' She ran her hands around his neck in a soothing, circular motion. 'To be quite honest, I don't like him.'

Clifton grunted rudely. 'You're doomed then.'

'Why?'

'Because when a woman says that, you know what she really means is that she fancies the pants off him.'

'I'm sure that's not good grammar.' Rub, rub, smooth, over and over, seeking out those little hard knots. 'Anyway, if I do, it's only because he's just like you.' She kissed the top of his head. He looked back up at her.

'At first Kate said she hated me. I knew then I was in with a chance.'

'You still could be.'

'Don't go there,' he said warningly.

Suzy smiled. She already had Kate's address in Norfolk, but the timing seemed all wrong. Until now. She completed the massage and kissed him again on the back of his neck.

'Is there anything else I can do for the Master before he goes to bed?'

Clifton rolled drowsily over onto his back. 'Undress me,' he said.

'You lazy bugger. You're quite capable of doing it yourself.'

He took her hand and kissed each finger, before guiding her hand down and placing it on his crotch. She could feel him shifting under her fingers as she pulled his zip down. She unknotted his tie and slipped it from his neck, before unfastening his shirt and peeling the fine cotton off his back, feeling his lips against her breast as he leaned forward to help her. Then she removed his socks, his trousers, all whilst he lay there, letting her do it, only moving when he had to. His boxers came off last, and his gasp as she took him gently in her mouth was music to her ears. He stroked her hair as she sucked him, twisted it as she teased him, and pulled hard on it as he came, deep into her warm, tight mouth. Afterwards he thanked her and kissed her, and she slipped quietly from the room, the taste of his sperm creamy in her mouth.

As she closed the door Clayton McKenna pounced and pushed her up against the wall. Paralysed with shock, she had to accept his kiss, so deep that her tongue could not fight back, whilst she cringed because of what she had been doing just seconds before.

After a while he backed away from her, a small smile playing across his lips.

'I trust my brother is now truly relaxed. Would you like to find out if I taste the same?'

She slapped him hard and fled up the stairs, her face burning.

Bonny greeted Jem joyfully when they met on the Mount, just after midnight, but there was trouble on the way. Earlier, someone had lobbed a Molotov cocktail at one of the caravans, from a speeding car. The police didn't seem that bothered. They did point out, though, that for their own protection, it might be wise for the travellers to move on.

The younger contingent disagreed. They would not be run out of town because of a few village idiots. The rumblings grew. In the heat of the night they felt justified in their indignation. The Price boys, and the Fishers, and every other oaf that had crossed them needed to be taught they had better things to do than mess with the O'Gradys and the Donellys.

Bonny hated the fighting talk, but no one would listen to her. She had crossed over to the other side. The slapping her father had given her for defying his orders and going with Jem to New York had left her bruised and defiant. Both she and Jem felt like fugitives. They talked far into the night.

That night Suzy couldn't sleep. Clayton's sudden appearance had troubled her in more ways than one. Clifton had changed since the accident. He was thinner, more drawn in the face, and now his healthy alpha male alter ego was right beside him he had seemed to shrink in his chair, as if he wanted to become invisible. He must have seen how Suzy's gaze kept moving between them. As for Alice, Suzy's presence had ceased to bother her, now she had an old flame to flirt with. Seeing her act like a flighty debutante was revolting.

It was still only six o'clock the following morning when Suzy finally decided to give up on sleep and go to the pool. No one else was up, which was fine as she was in no mood for mind games or being an agony aunt.

But when she went through the changing room to the pool, wrapping a robe around herself that she found there, she heard soft splashing sounds. Someone else had had an attack of insomnia. At first she was half-tempted to give up and go back to bed, but curiosity overcame her.

Whoever it was in the water wasn't ploughing up and down or even doing straight-laced, chin out of the water breaststroke, like Alice usually did. Peering around a conveniently placed palm, Suzy watched him. He had a long, naked body and glossy black hair, and she realised that he was actually *playing*, diving and rolling in the deep water at her end as gracefully as an otter. Transfixed, she continued to spy on him, until he hauled himself out of the water and stood with his back to her, pushing the water back out of his hair. She visually feasted on his dripping, hard body for what seemed like a lifetime. Suddenly he spun around and stared right at her.

She ducked behind the tree, feeling idiotic. The fleeting glimpse of his naked sex burned on her mind like an after-image from the sun.

'You're quite safe, Suzy. I won't eat you,' he said.

'Are you decent?'

'Yes.'

She emerged from behind the palm. He was still naked, grinning at her and pointing to his watch. 'It's a Rolex. Is that decent enough for you?'

'A little nouveau riche for my taste,' she replied archly, throwing him a towel. Still he did not cover up, choosing instead to dry his hair with it. Finally he walked over to where she was standing and stood so close to her that she had to step back to look comfortably at him. He took the lapels of her robe and fingered them thoughtfully. Then he pulled them violently apart, making her jump. She kept very still, trying not to betray how hard she was breathing, as he raked her whole body with his eyes. After the longest time he slipped the robe from her shoulders.

'This is actually mine,' he said, putting the robe on and tying the belt. 'Care to join me in the shower?'

'Why don't you go and have a hand shandy by yourself? You should be good at that, being a prize wanker.' To her credit, her voice didn't betray the thudding of her heart. She turned and walked smartly away, thinking she was getting really tired of doing just that. They had known each other barely twenty-four hours, and already he had gotten under her skin. And, joy of joys, he knew it.

To her relief, he had business up in London for the next couple of days. The house seemed full of people, all Alice's friends, chittering and gossiping like caffeine-fed monkeys. Clifton kept to his rooms and didn't come out. His mood had darkened to the point that even her company wasn't enough to pull him out of his shroud of enervating gloom.

On the Wednesday before the long-planned cocktail party, Suzy spent most of the day at Sammy the ageing rock star's Wiltshire manor house, giving him and his wife their manicure, pedicure and facial treatments. In between, she was plied with good coffee, lunch on the lawn and afternoon tea. It was all very English and sociable, if one didn't look at the black-clad rock groupies who were serving her. Sammy sat in the middle of it all, pinned to the chair by a huge chocolate Labrador, while his ferocious wife barked orders in an East London accent that could strip paint at fifty paces. All in all, it was a precarious, strange environment, but infinitely preferable to the one she had left at breakfast.

She left with a firm offer to accompany them on a tour of the States. Mrs Sammy, as his wife was affectionately known, was organising everything with the precision of an army general. Her bewildered husband was just expected to find his way on to the stage and sing, and there were some privately voiced doubts about whether he would be able to manage that. Even so, Suzy was seriously thinking about accepting the job. She said she would let them know by the following Monday. That was two days after the party.

Feeling high and nervy with indecision, probably due to the copious amount of weed she had passively inhaled that day, she braced herself for the evening ahead.

Dinner was a master class in underlying sexual tension. Alice deliberately put Suzy next to Clifton, who presided as usual at the head of the table. Alice sat at the other end and put Clayton next to her, with Jem in the middle, acting as unwitting referee. Clayton fawning over Alice at dinner was sickening. Even so, she couldn't keep her eyes off him, and Clifton knew it. He watched her broodingly and hardly ate a thing. The meal ground slowly on, fuelled by Alice's constant, inane chatter. Meanwhile, Suzy was increasingly aware of the smouldering looks Clayton kept shooting in her direction when he thought nobody was paying any attention.

It was Jem who finally had enough. He threw down his napkin and stood up.

'I've had enough of this. Why don't you all go and screw each other and get it out in the open?'

With frightening ease Alice switched from ageing sex kitten to appalled mother in less than a second.

'Jeremy! What on earth has got into you? Clifton, make him apologise!'

'Why?' Clifton said. 'He has a point. You want to fuck him,' pointing at Clayton. 'He wants to fuck her,' pointing at Suzy, 'and I can't fuck anybody because my wife has screwed me royally already with her smartass lawyer from Bond Street!'

'This is bullshit!' Jem said, and left the room.

In the silence that followed, Alice delivered her killer blow.

'Clayton rode Sentinel today,' she said sweetly to Clifton. 'He didn't have any problem at all getting on his back. Everyone said he probably thought he was you!'

Clifton's hand shook enough to make his cup rattle on the saucer. Suzy shot him a sympathetic glance.

'It's a pity you're selling him,' Clayton said. 'He's a damned fine animal once you know how to handle him.'

'Which you did, admirably,' Alice gushed.

'And who said anything about selling him?' Clifton's face was white. So were his knuckles, bunched around the linen folds of his napkin. The atmosphere around the table could be sliced and eaten. Alice laughed delightedly when she saw Clifton's face.

'Oh for heaven's sake, darling, why on earth would it matter to you? You're never going to get up on a horse again!'

Suzy put her hand over Clifton's and squeezed it. He was taking deep breaths, trying to control his temper. Clayton watched him curiously.

'Jesus, Clif, I thought you knew . . .'

Clifton threw his coffee cup with some force at the wall. Clayton stared at him as if he had suddenly turned into a stranger. Baker gave Clifton his crutches and stood back to let him up from the chair. Alice was smiling spitefully at him.

'You don't sell my fucking horse,' he snarled back at her as he limped with great dignity out of the room.

Later, Suzy tried to concentrate on her book, but her ears kept tuning in to sounds coming from the next bedroom. Creaking bedsprings, soft sighs, light giggles, but they were all in her imagination. Had they fallen asleep already? It didn't seem possible. Only fifteen minutes had passed since she had first heard them pass her door.

A soft knock made her heart lurch.

'Who is it?'

The door opened slightly. Clayton stood there, but he did not enter.

'Clifton and I were wondering whether you'd like to join us for a nightcap.'

She looked uncertainly at him. 'Where's Alice?'

'Asleep.'

'Already?'

'I gave her something to help her on her way.'

Suzy didn't know whether to believe him at first, but in the end she did. She could believe anything of a man as calculating as Clayton McKenna.

'Are you coming?' he asked.

'Let me get dressed first,' she said, waiting for him to leave.

'Come as you are. We won't mind.'

'I'm sure. Tell Clifton I'll be down in five minutes.' She waved him away.

'If you're not I'm coming to get you.' He closed the door again.

She hesitated, feeling slightly put out. When had it changed from an invitation to a command? Or did he always fail to distinguish the two? And what was she thinking, even considering going down there in the first place?

Because Clifton had sanctioned it, that was why. No other reason, she tried to convince herself as she assessed her reflection in the mirror. Her cream gossamer silk camisole top and French knickers seemed too flimsy for wandering around the house, and she didn't really know what they were expecting. Only they knew the answer to that one. And she guessed that once she had walked through the door, if she didn't like the answer, it would be very difficult to back away.

She decided against lip gloss and perfume, preferring to go au naturel. She didn't want them thinking she had made an effort, just because they expected her to. She pulled on her short silk robe and padded down the stairs in bare feet. The huge house felt dark and cold, and she shivered. A soft light glowed from underneath the door and deep male voices talked quietly, against a backdrop of lilting Chopin.

Clifton was making inroads into a bottle of Rémy Martin. He looked happier than he had been for days. Clayton sat on the other side of the coffee table. He had unfastened his tie and it was dangling loosely around his neck. His shirt was half undone under a black waistcoat, also unbuttoned. Clifton was in a similar state of disarray. It looked as if they had been hitting the bottle for some time. Clayton handed her the heavy Waterford balloon tumbler that had been waiting for her, the cognac already poured. She looked at Clifton.

'Don't worry, Suzy. It isn't spiked,' he said.

She sat next to him, very aware of Clayton's heated gaze.

'We thought we would relive some old times.' Clayton relit his cigar and sent a stream of fragrant smoke towards Suzy. 'Would you like one?'

So they had been talking. She wasn't ready to play into his hands just yet.

'No thank you,' she said coolly.

'That's a shame. I believe that good cigars, like fine wine and expensive women, should be shared between brothers.'

Clifton smiled wryly into his glass.

'But never at the same time, surely? Especially the

women.' Suzy said, feigning wide-eyed naïvete. Her sense of adventure was bubbling up again, together with that now familiar moistness between her legs.

Clayton reached for the cognac bottle. 'On the contrary, my dear. All those virgin debutantes needed to be broken in thoroughly, didn't they?' He laughed obscenely. Suzy shook her head disapprovingly.

'It's typical. A girl walks in the room and the conversation immediately switches to sex.'

'Actually, a girl with hardly any clothes on walks in the room, and yes, the conversation will naturally turn to sex,' Clayton corrected her.

'You can have us both if you like,' Clifton whispered in her ear. This time when her eyes widened it was for real.

'If he's telling you I've got a small dick, forget it. We're identical in every way,' Clayton said, reaching for the Rémy again.

'I don't doubt it for one moment,' Suzy said, injecting a bored tone into her voice. 'Do you ever think about anything else?' She caught Clayton staring at her, and knew that it had riled him. She suddenly felt very self-conscious, her heart beating loud in her chest.

'Take my advice,' Clayton said quietly. 'You either leave now, or stay and face the consequences. You're looking at two very horny men, one of whom hasn't had a decent woman for a very long time.'

'That would be you, I take it?' Though she couldn't quite believe it. He was even more attractive when half-inebriated and looking at her as if he wanted to eat her for breakfast.

He held his cognac up to the light to admire its golden glow. 'I've been in the bush, my love.'

Clifton snorted into his glass. Suzy looked at both of them. Two 46-year-old men, still boys under the skin.

Still, they would have been an intimidating partnership on the upper-class social circuit, back when they were still escorting debutantes to hunt balls. How many cherries had they popped between them, she wondered. She decided to find out.

Clayton rested his head back on the sofa and counted on his hand. 'Cecilia Bonham was the first. Mary Hughes, and the bitch with the glasses,' he held up three fingers, then four. 'And that Russian doll, Tatanya Pilkington-whatserface . . .'

'You had her? She told me I was the first,' Clifton said indignantly.

'When was that?'

'After the ball, in the woods at the back of Huntingdon Manor.'

'You were too late, mate. I had her in the car on the way there.'

'Fucking slapper,' Clifton muttered into his balloon tumbler.

'Is that all?' Suzy asked pityingly.

But Clayton was still reciting names. He had run out of fingers and toes. And at least half of them he had duplicated with Clifton, some at the same time.

'Those were the days, hey, Clif?' he said wistfully. 'Maybe Suzy here could take us down memory lane.'

'That is just so lame,' she said disgustedly. 'What do you expect me to do? Just open my legs and let you get on with it?' She clamped her knees together and folded her arms. Clayton looked at his brother.

'We've got a feisty one here, Clif. You've always had the lion's share of finesse. You persuade her.'

'You got that right,' Suzy muttered. 'I'm not one of your shallow eighteen-year-old bimbos, you know.'

'I know you're not shallow.' Clifton leaned close to her, running his hand up her leg. 'I know how deep you are, my love. Have another drink. Let the boys take care of you tonight.'

Those penetrating amber eyes were hard to resist. If she had been an eighteen-year-old virgin in the early 70s, it would have been almost impossible to keep her virtue, even under the strictest of chaperones. His hand had reached her inner thighs, feather light. Gently he eased between them and stroked her. 'Do it for the Squire. He wants you to.' He attempted to pour more cognac out of the empty bottle into her glass. 'Go get Baker to fetch another bottle, old boy. Suzy needs some convincing.'

Clayton obediently struggled to his feet and left the room. As soon as he had gone Clifton grabbed her. She was almost overwhelmed by his hard, alcohol-laden kiss. It intoxicated her more than any wine would do. He took her hand and guided it to his lap. He was very hard.

'Look at you,' he said, gently opening her legs and showing her the dark patch of moisture on the pale cream silk. 'You can't tell me you haven't thought of this before.'

'But I thought –'

'That I would be jealous? Only if you were alone with him. You can do anything you like when I'm here, but don't fuck him. Ever. Right?'

Clayton walked back in, brandishing a bottle of Sancerre. 'You should sack your supplier: this year was bloody awful.' He looked at the label again before despatching the seal and cork with a flourish. 'Still, might as well try it.'

Baker had followed him in, wearing a pained expression. He put a full decanter down on the coffee table, with fresh glasses, and Clifton dismissed him for the night. Clayton poured some wine for Suzy. 'Tell me what you think.'

She took a sip and grimaced. 'It's very dry.'

'Like the savannah. That's its strength. Maybe it wasn't such a bad year after all.' He tasted it and swore. 'Or maybe you have no palate. It's fucking horrible.'

She opened her mouth to retort, but it occurred to her then that the possibilities were endless. She could passively sit there and let them take control of her, or she could up the ante and make things go her way.

'I just think it needs sweetening up,' she said, taking the glass from him.

'How would you do that?'

Suzy stood up. Clayton settled back on the sofa as Suzy picked up the bottle of Sancerre and poured some into her hand. Smiling at the two men, she poured the wine from her hand down between her breasts. Clayton's jaw dropped. Her nipples crinkled and stretched out as if pulled by invisible fingers, thrusting against the tight wet silk. Clifton licked his lips and beckoned her to him. With a small smile at Clayton she turned her back on him and sat on Clifton's lap, straddling him. She sighed with pleasure as he peeled the soaking material away from her breasts and his hot tongue lashed against her cold, wine-soaked nipples. There was a hurried movement. Clayton had come to sit next to his brother.

'Excuse me, I'm the wine expert in this family,' he said. Carefully he poured more wine from Suzy's glass onto the breast closest to him, and bent to suck the liquid off her nipple. When he looked up, his breathing had turned ragged. 'You're right,' he said hoarsely. 'The acidity has been neutralised very effectively.' He dipped his head again. Clifton's mouth closed over her other breast. She felt dizzy with arousal, watching their reflections in the darkened windows, each lavishing attention on her singing, sensitive nipples, whilst Chopin continued to play softly in the background, and the smoke from rich cigars hung in the air.

'You're a lucky man, bro,' Clayton said. She could feel his hands, stealthily gathering up the back of her chemise, tugging the panties into a thin rope of silk between her buttocks, before running his hands over the smooth skin of her back. She toyed with their clothes, pinching and arousing their nipples through fine silk. Half-dressed men turned her on immensely, so when Clayton moved to take his shirt off all together she stopped him.

'I like you like that,' she said, gathering the two ends of his tie and pulling him to her for a fluttering kiss. His hand dropped to his trousers, but again she stopped him.

'It's beginning to hurt,' he complained. She found the stiff lump at his groin, large and tightly restrained, and she squeezed it gently, eliciting a hard pulse.

'Good,' she said, and gasped as she felt Clifton's fingers pushing deep inside her pussy.

'Why don't you taste her?' Clifton suggested, proffering the hand that was sticky with Suzy's juices to his brother.

Then Clayton did something extraordinary. He took Clifton's hand and licked her essence off his fingers. The tender, yet licentious way he did it warned Suzy that the control had shifted. It was now the two of them against her. The men watched her with their feral yellow eyes, two big cats challenging their prey to take flight.

Suzy's heart lurched. Too late she realised she was overstepping her boundaries in a very dangerous and exciting way. A girl one could reason with if it ceased to become pleasurable, but two men with club-like erections and intuitive knowledge of each others needs? She was out of her depth.

But just as suddenly she knew she wanted to be taken

over, controlled and commanded. She wanted to watch how they reacted to each other, surrounding her, rendering her defenceless. It was like bunjee-jumping into the unknown, not knowing if the cord would snap or hold, but realising as she took that step that she didn't care, and savouring the exhilarating freedom that knowledge brought her.

Clayton kissed Clifton's fingers once more and let them go before reaching for the delicate panties and ripping them as easily as one would rip tissue paper. Within seconds they were somewhere over the back of the sofa.

'Sit on me properly,' Clifton said, lifting her up and undoing his trousers at the same time. She caught her breath as she slid all the way down onto his cock, rearing out of his black trousers. Clayton pulled her arms behind her back and held her there, helpless, then bent his head and fluttered his tongue against the nipple closest to him. Tiny eddies of sweet sensation arrowed down her body, making her inner muscles contract against Clifton as she undulated slowly against him.

'Do that again,' Clifton said to him, and Clayton obediently did so. Clifton groaned deeply with need as Suzy leaned back on his knees and let her hair hang to the ground between his feet. From that position she saw Clayton kneeling in front of them, running his hands over her body as if it were discovered treasure. His groin pressed close to her face. When he felt her nuzzling against him he undid his trousers and let his penis, clad in silk trunks, rub against her lips. He smelled gloriously male, musky and clean. Still comfortable, despite being upside down, she nipped gently at that smooth, firm ridge. He responded just as she wanted him to, by pulling the trunks down just low enough to expose himself to her mouth. In the trapped dark, she closed her eyes and sucked him in, feeling him harden to the point of bursting. And all the while he ravished her breasts, using his lips and rapacious tongue, subjecting each nipple to stealthy attack and sending those sweet, secret messages down to her shimmering pussy. Distantly she realised that he was using her pleasure to heighten Clifton's, as much as he was enjoying losing himself in the delights of her body. He made her hold her breasts together to form a shallow cup in to which he poured more wine. He proceeded to drink, following with long, hungry licks peaking at the tips of her nipples. She was lost, blinded with bliss, so that when she felt the hot breath and the tiny flutter of a tongue against her clitoris she jerked upwards, crying out at the unexpected pleasure. Clifton pulsed inside her as her muscles contracted again. The grip he had on her wrists tightened as her need grew. She was going to come, brought to ecstasy by that skilled tongue and the mass of flesh invading her from both ends.

'Don't stop,' Clifton gasped as Clayton paused before upping the pressure. Suzy locked eyes with Clifton just as the climax hit her. Clifton's iron grip held her safely as she jolted against him, forcing him deeper inside her. He was so close to coming, but it wasn't enough to tilt him over the edge. Instead he had to endure her voluptuous spasms around his dick and watch her body express the wild joy of her orgasm. On and on it went, no escape from either of them as they mercilessly stimulated her beyond endurance. When she finally pushed Clayton away from her he gently eased her upright again. Clifton held her in his arms as her breathing quietened and she became still, but he was still inside her, a constant, thrusting reminder of her recent ecstasy.

Clayton went to the other sofa and collapsed on it on his back. Clifton patted Suzy's backside.

'Clayton wants you to thank him properly.'

'But I might want to continue fucking you,' she said, sinuously moving up and down his shaft.

'You will, but first I want to watch you pleasuring my brother. Squire's orders.'

Clayton had one knee propped up against the back of the sofa. Suzy removed herself from Clifton and took a sip of her wine. It tasted better this time. She took too more healthy swallows and felt it kicking in. It was a surreal experience, going from one man to his mirror image, five feet away.

She poured some wine on his taut, bare stomach. She licked up the drips as they rolled away, leaving him gasping. She removed his trousers and admired his cock packed away again inside tight white trunks. It almost glowed pink through the thin silk, and smelled musky and divine.

'What are you waiting for, woman?' He said huskily. She had the impression that it wasn't going to take very long.

'No stamina,' she sighed, slowly peeling the trunks away and removing them. Now she could actually see it, he had a very attractive penis, just like his brother's. It really meant business. The head was fat and rubbery, a deeper wine red than the rest of the shaft, which was traced with plump veins. What a pity it was out of bounds, she thought, her pussy contracting at the thought of him thrusting hard inside her. His balls were very full. They hardly shifted and felt very heavy as she lifted each one with her tongue. If he came in her mouth he would drown her. No, she wanted that come somewhere else. She wanted to see it. He was moaning almost constantly, a deep rumble echoing throughout her body. She clamped her hand over his mouth.

'I told you before, don't talk so much,' she said sternly.

Leaving her hand where it was she moved down to continue sucking him. By now he was in such a heightened state of arousal she could have done anything to him. His rapture kept him from doing anything but lifting his hips every time she engulfed him to the root. She tasted the sweet pre-seminal fluid. He was close. Once, twice, she brought him to the very edge, until he dashed her hand away from his mouth and swore at her for being a bitch. On the other sofa Clifton was laughing.

'Let me inside you,' Clayton pleaded with her.

'You're not allowed,' she said ruthlessly. Her hand slipped between his buttocks, one finger pressing against his rosy hole. His backside contracted.

'What the fuck are you doing?'

'This is one of your brother's favourite little treats,' Suzy said. He made a strangled sound as her fingertip penetrated his arse, just as her hot lips closed over the head of his cock once more. He squirmed, trapped with pleasure, not knowing how to move to escape her invading finger or her tormenting tongue. Her other hand was on his shaft, rubbing him gently, and then harder as he started to tense. Again he tried to hold on to his orgasm but it was too much. A deep groan warned her to pull back. As she licked slavishly at his balls, the come shot forth, over his stomach, over his chest. He swore hoarsely, unable to resist as she continued the assault on his balls and arse. Then finally, 'fuck,' he spat. 'Fuck and fuck you.'

'There's gratitude for you,' Suzy said, scooping up his seed in her hand. She turned back to Clifton and stood before him, rubbing the cooling liquid over her breasts, teasing out her nipples again. They looked very attractive, glistening in the soft light.

'It's good for the skin,' she said. Clifton pulled her down and gave one of her breasts a lavish lick, sucking the rosy tip until it was clean. Again she was stunned at this act of intimacy between him and Clayton. Clifton smiled slowly at her, his eyes heavy with desire. She knew what he wanted. She knelt between his aggressively spread legs and straightened his cock along his stomach. He still tasted of her as she tongue-bathed him, slowly and sensuously, her rump stuck high in the air. He ran his fingers through her hair, detangling her curly tresses, almost purring with delight as each lick swirled around the top of his dick and back down, around his balls.

A slap on her backside rang through the room. Clayton was on his knees behind her, probing her pouting sex lips with the tip of his cock. Clifton's face grew angry.

'You're not fucking her,' he snarled, pushing Suzy down to the ground. Clayton laughed at him.

'I could take her right in front of you and you couldn't do a damned thing about it.'

'You wouldn't dare.'

Clayton's eyes changed to cobra-like slits. 'You know how dangerous it is to challenge me. Choose your next words carefully, brother. You may have to eat them.'

Suzy watched the power struggle going on between the two men. She slipped out from between them and lay on the soft, luxuriant rug, on her back.

'Be nice to each other, boys, and I might let you both eat me. If not, I'm going to bed, and neither of you can have me.'

Clifton ended the silent duel first. He rolled off the sofa and wriggled between her legs and buried his face in her muff. Clayton joined him, and together they explored, fingered, murmured to each other. She could feel one tongue, then both, licking, flickering, fluttering and probing. Clayton moved around and pressed his come-sticky body right along hers, pushing himself against her lips. As she sucked him in he swelled and throbbed, and all the sensations put together were so overwhelming that she could not help her strangled sounds of pleasure. It was an exquisite form of torture, having these two men feasting on her like lions at a kill, whilst she was too stuffed with cock to help herself.

'Well, isn't this cosy?'

Alice was standing next to them, outraged but still half-asleep. She stumbled backwards as Clayton got up and advanced on her. Her clumsy slap was easily deflected and she was on her knees over the sofa. Clifton pushed Suzy back down.

'He'll keep her happy. And it'll take his mind off you.' He dipped his head and Suzy felt his tongue slide over her folds again. She decided *que sera sera* and lay back down, watching Clayton pull Alice's hands behind her back, forcing her face down on the soft leather couch. He proceeded to spank her bottom, muttering something about fucking the gardener and being such a dirty whore for doing it, and as Suzy watched them she became wetter and wetter, so that Clifton was drenched in her juices and they stained the light wooden floor. Alice's sounds had become abandoned as she submitted to the punishment, and Clayton was so hard he looked like a pagan fertility god, encumbered with that massive tool. When he finally pushed it into Alice Suzy cried out first in sympathy. She wanted it too, but Clifton wasn't going to let her think about that any more. He bit the inside of her thigh so hard she cried out again, this time in dismay.

'That will teach you to lust after my brother while you're supposed to be fucking me,' he snarled, pulling her around to face him.

'I'm sorry,' she whispered, kissing his lips. In the background, Alice was screaming like a cat on heat.

Clayton was fucking her hard, still beating her, the effort showing in the sweat glistening across his back. Suzy turned away and kissed Clifton again. He was appeased by the heat behind the kiss. He drew her down and lay with her on the floor, letting her feel the bruising length of his cock against her belly.

'Get on me,' he whispered, so she did, easing herself down inch by inch. She was so wet that it was easy, but he was so hard that his presence could not be ignored. He lifted her buttocks up and down, controlling the speed with which she fucked him. When he was too overcome to carry on she continued, sinuously dancing for him, a stark antithesis to the rutting going on a few feet away. Clifton's breathing turned shallow again. She knew he wanted release this time. She cupped her breasts in her hands and toyed with them, keeping eye contact with him. For a moment it seemed that it was only the two of them in the room, until Clayton grabbed her hair and turned her head to face him. Alice was a molten, shagged-out heap on the couch, helpless to do anything but watch. Clifton swore and pulsed hard as Suzy took Clayton in her mouth. She would never have believed it of herself to do what she had only seen in hard-core porn flicks, but once she got the rhythm going, it was easy. Her lower body moved as one with Clifton, bringing him to a grunting climax as Clayton withdrew and sprayed come all over her tits, commanding her to rub it in. As she did she felt wild and free, impaling herself on Clifton's erection for a final explosion of pleasure felt from her nipples to her clit and the heavy, swollen walls of her sex. She collapsed on top of Clifton and Clayton landed beside them. The two men high fived lazily and let their arms entwine, Clifton stroking Suzy's back with his free hand.

When she left them a few minutes later they were all

nearly asleep. Alice snored loudly on the sofa, her legs sprawled like a two-bit hooker as the sleeping tablets had at last kicked in. Clifton and Clayton were practically in each other's arms. That would be something for Mrs Penrose to gossip about, Suzy thought, as she dragged her abused body back up to bed.

14

Suzy rolled sleepily out of bed at around six, just after the alarm had woken her. It had been an age since she last emerged so early, but it probably wasn't wise to see Alice that morning. She wasn't sure she wanted to see Clayton either. Besides, there was something she needed to do.

Blindly she went to the shower, and ten minutes later she felt human again. She dressed in silk khaki combats and a small cream vest top with silky spaghetti straps, with a khaki jacket over the top just in case the temperature was cooler by the sea. She padded downstairs, carrying her brown leather sandals with her, and put them on only after closing the back door behind her.

She was just putting the key into the ignition of the Golf when Clayton suddenly appeared by the passenger door, making her jump so high she nearly hit the roof. He climbed in beside her and waited for her to start the engine.

'Well, what are you waiting for?'

She glared at him. 'You, to get out of my car.'

'I don't think so. That journey can be kind of boring without any company.'

'To which journey are you referring?'

'The one you're taking to Norfolk. Are we going to get started or not? Traffic will already be building up on the M25.'

'I'd rather do this on my own, if you don't mind.'

'But Clifton is my brother, and therefore I have a right to know what exactly you're up to.'

'I'm not up to anything!' She sounded too indignant, and, therefore, guilty.

He assessed his surroundings. There were scrumpled up balls of paper, cassette tape cases, old cassettes, a dead Diet Coke can and the ends of numerous cigarettes. Suzy felt supremely conscious of all of it, as she was of his long legs and freshly applied aftershave wreathing around the warm confines of the car.

'Do you drive it or mulch down in it?' he asked casually.

'Do you want to walk?'

'No.'

'Shut the fuck up, then.'

'On second thoughts, we'll take my car,' he said climbing out again. 'Coming?'

He was irritating her. She wanted to listen to Johnno and Erica on Heart FM and sing as badly as she pleased. She wanted to drive without feeling self-conscious. It wasn't fair.

'Look, you can drive this heap of shit and I'll follow you in my clean, air-conditioned, super-charged Jaguar, if you like. Whatever, but you're stuck with me.'

He slammed the door and strode to his own car, climbed in, and waited.

Suzy drummed her fingers on the steering wheel. In the end, pure economics won the day. If he wanted to pay for the petrol, that was up to him. Anyway, she was sure her exhaust pipe was about to fall off.

But it didn't alter the fact that she was now stuck in a small space for three hours with a man she didn't like and whose aroma was sending jangling, confused messages to all her newly awakened nerve endings.

On the other hand, Clayton seemed perfectly at ease.

He played rhythm and blues on the CD player, sometimes broke into melodic song for no reason, and not once did he try and engage her in conversation.

'Do you mind if I smoke? No, I guess not,' he said, lighting up a cigar before she had a chance to protest. After a fraught hour she turned the radio off.

'I need coffee,' she said, motioning to a fast-approaching Little Chef. He made the entrance with inches to spare and they went inside.

Suzy wasn't going to eat, but after smelling the bacon she couldn't resist it. They ordered omelettes with bacon and strong coffee. After the waitress left he took Suzy's hand. She immediately removed it.

'What's the matter? I am on your side, you know,' he said.

'I don't know,' she answered.

'What? You don't know what the matter is, or you don't know if I'm on your side?'

'I don't know why you wanted to come with me.' She toyed with her coffee cup and did not look at him.

'You came with me,' he reminded her.

The food came, and they began to eat silently.

'Actually, it's because I wanted to spend some time with you without my brother looking at me like I'm a cup of arsenic,' he said finally. 'Last night we worked as a team, but woe betide me if I attempt to get you on your own.'

'Just for your information, last night was for Clifton and myself,' Suzy said coolly. 'You were an optional extra.'

The superior look was wiped from his face. 'Thank you for that, Suzy. I do like to know where I stand.'

'Good.' She concentrated on her food.

'So why are we going to Norfolk? Is it some quest for the Holy Grail, or what?'

'Come on!' Suzy scoffed at him. 'You know damned well why I'm going.'

'I don't! I honestly don't.' He spread out his hands. The look on his face was totally open. For the first time, she began to believe him. She took a speculative sip of her coffee, and began to grin.

'Then I think it's a damned good idea you've decided to come along,' she said cheerfully. He looked disconcerted at her sudden change in mood. She ignored him and cleared her plate.

'What's going on?' For the first time, he was the one to look suspicious.

'Finish your food. We need to hit the road,' she said, draining her coffee.

'But that doesn't answer my question,' he said, following after her.

She stopped and stroked his cheek, very lovingly. 'You shall find the answer you seek. Just be patient, and trust in the lady with the forget-me-not eyes.'

Two hours later they were cruising along the great beachfront at Great Yarmouth. It was relatively quiet, with a few joggers and strollers dotted along the wide promenade, but promised to be busy later on. They drove past the amusement arcades and gift shops, some of them still shuttered. A gang of youths stared at the car as it growled past.

'Shit, this is worse than Jo'burg,' Clayton muttered.

Now they were passing in front of a long row of Victorian terraced houses. All of them advertised Bed & Breakfast, most of them had vacancies. Some were lush with hanging baskets filled with geraniums. Others looked as if the sea had eaten away most of the paint, leaving a shabby, faded exterior that matched the limp grey curtains inside. Suzy checked the address she had been given. It was up one of the side roads, Albert

Street, number 29. She found it almost immediately and they parked on the opposite side, within sight of the front door. There was a neat sign bearing the name of the house, 'Seagull Cottage'. It looked pleasant and well-cared for, although a good deal of money had yet to be spent on repainting the outside. As with the majority of the other houses, the East wind had taken its toll.

'Now what?' Clayton asked, looking up at the house.

'I go in. You wait here.' Suzy's attention was on the door. It had opened and a large man came out. He was very large, lumbering and thick-necked. He lit up a cigarette as soon as the door had closed, and walked down the street away from Suzy and Clayton. Suzy undid her seatbelt.

'Where are you going?' Clayton asked her.

'Give me five minutes, then ring the bell. Will you do that?'

Clayton shrugged. 'Sure.'

Suzy walked over to the house and rang the bell. The door opened and a woman opened it.

There was no mistake. This was definitely Kate, albeit a pale, insipid version of the woman Suzy had seen in the photograph. Suzy introduced herself and said that her mother had told her about the guest house. She would like a room for a night, if possible.

Inside, the house smelt of baking and building plaster. Out the back, someone was using a plane saw. Kate apologised for the noise and the dust. They were supposed to be opening for business in a week, and it just wasn't going to happen. She was sorry if Suzy had a wasted trip, but in the meantime, would she like to look upstairs. If she could tolerate the building work, she was welcome to stay for a night, she said as Suzy followed her up three flights of narrow, squeaky stairs.

The room was flooded with light from a large bay window, which looked out over the sea. The decoration was Laura Ashley and fragranced with rose pot pourri. Suzy complimented her on it and they talked about Great Yarmouth and the surrounding area. Kate seemed very knowledgeable. As Clifton had said, she was the perfect hostess, warm and approachable. Suzy felt like a complete heel.

The front door opened. Kate hurried down the stairs ahead of Suzy. In the middle of the last flight, she almost cannoned into her. Kate had frozen mid-stride and was staring at the man who had walked in through the front door. He was staring back but only because he couldn't understand why she had reacted so dramatically to his appearance.

There was a small, thick silence, during which Kate walked gracefully down the last few stairs and approached Clayton McKenna. And, with as much force as she could muster, she slapped him across the face.

Clayton took an involuntary step backwards at the blow, stunned by its power and the anger that was behind it.

'How dare you walk in here as if nothing has changed!' she flared at him, advancing upon him like a small, furious cat. 'How dare you!' She punched his chest with both fists, driving him against the wall. 'All this time I've waited for you! Where were you? You lousy bastard!' Her voice cracked into sobs as she continued to pummel him. Suzy sat on the stair, rather enjoying the sight of Clayton helplessly fending off this furious woman. As she exhausted herself he put his arms awkwardly around her and looked over her head at Suzy, who shrugged innocently.

'I told you it was a damned good idea,' she said. At her voice, Kate suddenly remembered her presence.

'What the hell is going on?'

'This is Clifton's identical twin brother, Clayton. I'm sorry for the deception, but –'

The door opened again. Kate thrust away from Clayton and dashed the tears from her eyes. Alfie Palmer walked in and frowned, first at Suzy, then at his wife.

'What's going –' In the reflection of the hall mirror he spotted Clayton. Again, it was as if his presence had lit a blue touchpaper, but this time Clayton was ready for him. What the big man lacked in speed, Clayton made up for in sheer power. As Alfie went for him with a bellow of rage, Clayton floored him with a single punch. Alfie went down like a felled log and lay still.

'Sorry,' Clayton said to Kate. 'Why don't we go in the kitchen? Then Suzy can explain, to both of us,' he added with a pointed glare at Suzy.

Kate blinked at her prone husband, clearly in shock. Suzy led her into the kitchen, where she started making tea. It was automatic. Kettle, tap, water. Mugs, teabags, spoon. And cookies. There they were, freshly made, moist and delicious, heaped on to a Denby plate. Alfie was still out for the count in the hallway. All was normal.

'Explain,' Kate said succinctly. She had recovered her composure and her anger had come back. She kept staring at Clayton as if she would like to hit him again.

'The reason he didn't find you is because he believed you didn't want to see him anymore. And until recently he hasn't been in a position to do anything about it.'

'So there aren't any phones in his house? Has he lost his ability to make enquiries? Alice told me he was no longer interested.'

Suzy went through Alice's trickery, the contract, the state of Clifton's mind. Kate heard it all, but Suzy could tell she was still not impressed.

'So why isn't he here? Why him?' She motioned at Clayton as if he were an inferior substitute.

'His coming was unfortunate. I was lumbered with him unexpectedly this morning,' Suzy confided, as if he was not there.

'So what are you telling me now? That Clifton wants me to go and see him?'

Suzy paused. 'He loves you. You're his world, but he's a very stubborn man and won't swallow his pride enough to back down. He thinks you don't want him any more because of the accident.'

'That's ludicrous,' Kate said impatiently. 'He should know me better than that.'

'So it's up to you to tell him.'

'No, it's up to him to come to me.' Kate's sweet full lips were set firm. 'You can go back, today, and tell him that. I won't expect anything less.'

'Oh well, that's another beautiful ending fucked up,' Clayton muttered. 'What do you want me to do about him?' He nodded at Alfie, who was groaning and struggling to sit up. Kate's eyes narrowed at her husband.

'He doesn't know who you are, does he?'

Clayton rubbed at his jaw. 'Unfortunately not.' He understood what Kate was getting at. He went out into the hall and dragged Alfie to his feet, and pinned the dopey man to the wall.

'Listen to me, fuckhead. Don't even think about touching her or I'll come and slice off your nuts with my hunting knife and force you to eat them. Got it?'

Alfie's stupid, piggy eyes showed real fear. He nodded slowly.

'I'm the fucking Terminator, Alfie. Whatever you do to me, I will always get up and come after you. Got that?'

Another nod. He looked over at Kate, helplessly, as if

she were the one to save him. She stood watching, impassively. Clayton gave him one final hard shove and let him sag back down to the floor.

Suzy opened the front door and went out into sweet fresh freedom. Clayton followed, looking as relieved as she did. Kate stood at the door.

'Thank you,' she said.

'You'll be OK?'

Kate glanced back at Alfie. 'I can handle him,' she said grimly.

'Thank you for that,' Clayton said as they climbed back into the car. 'Would it be redundant to suggest you knew that was going to happen?'

'Actually, it turned out even better than I thought it would,' Suzy said smugly. He gave her a terse look. At Seagull Cottage, Kate had closed the door on them.

'That is one scary lady,' Clayton muttered, dabbing at a scratch on his neck.

'Scarier than Alice?'

Clayton shuddered. 'When I think how close I came to marrying that woman. Mind you, I would have divorced her within five years.'

'I think Clifton would have, but he didn't want to leave Jem.'

Clayton fell silent. Suzy could tell he was thinking about his brother. Maybe they were not as alike as he thought. Maybe he was learning more about Clifton than he knew. It was hard to tell. Even so, the superiority of the first few days had mellowed somewhat into a grudging respect. Not that he would ever admit it, of course. Hell would probably freeze over first.

The mist that had been encroaching from the sea had accumulated into fog, which turned to grey rain the further inland they drove. It was now a miserable, wet afternoon, with a long, boring journey back home to Oxfordshire ahead of them.

Just outside Cambridge Clayton turned off the road, into a long, leafy driveway. The building at the end was grand, dollhouse Georgian, with many uniformly sized windows.

'Time for some afternoon tea, I think,' Clayton said lightly.

'I hope they don't have a dress code,' Suzy said, glancing down at her silk combats and spaghetti strapped top. The temperature had dropped, but the khaki jacket she had hardly seemed suitable for such grand surroundings. Fortunately, Clayton looked far more in keeping with the lush reception area in his dark trousers and cream linen shirt.

The man behind the reception desk eventually furnished Clayton with a key, at which point Suzy started to protest.

'I thought you said tea!'

'Save it until we're alone,' Clayton whispered harshly, taking her upper arm and guiding her up the wide staircase behind the porter, who did not seem surprised at their lack of luggage.

'Isn't this a bit presumptuous?' Suzy demanded as the door quietly closed, leaving them in a sumptuous suite, dominated by a bed at least seven feet wide.

Clayton was perusing the menu. 'We can order food up here if you don't feel comfortable in the restaurant. They have an excellent selection. Care to look?'

Suzy's stomach said, 'yes, please'. Ungraciously she snatched the menu out of his hands.

'They also have a superb wine list,' Clayton said, leafing through a leather-bound volume. 'Excellent! We'll have the Etienne Sauzet 1998. White is acceptable to you, I take it?'

Suzy tore her attention away from the seductive menu just as his hand reached the phone.

'Wait! What the hell are you doing? I didn't say anything about this! You didn't even ask me!'

'The wine list is right here. If you want . . .'

'That isn't what I meant and you know it.'

Clayton looked exasperated. 'The hotel has a four hundred foot driveway. Why didn't you object on the way in?'

'I don't know! I guess you were just . . .'

'Driving up to have a look at the place?' He stepped back and regarded her intently for a moment. 'Tell me, what is it that my brother finds so attractive about you, apart from your great tits and arse?'

When she lashed out at his face it was almost as if he were expecting the blow. He caught her hand by the wrist and for a moment they were locked together.

'I know now,' he said softly, pulling her towards him. Reluctantly, hesitantly, she accepted his kiss. It was sweet and slow, non-invasive. It made her want much, much more. But first, other physical needs had to be met.

'I'm really hungry,' she whispered.

'So am I.' And he wasn't thinking about filet mignon and delicate raspberry soufflés, unless they were purely euphemisms, she thought, as he kissed her again, more insistently this time, his tongue sliding between her lips.

OK, time to stop playing the disapproving vestal virgin. She never had before so it was too late to start now, especially after their drunken binge the night before. Besides, she had known since the first day that they were destined for something more intimate. She moulded her body into his, returning his kiss with a fervour that made him whimper against her eager lips. Together they tumbled on to the bed, their hands eager to fumble through their clothing to find warm, naked flesh. The mattress was firm, the sheets cool and crisp, but that was nothing under the luscious shock of having a man who could move freely, who could take control. He pinned her arms above her head and ground his pelvis against hers, letting her feel his rock solid arousal. She felt weakened by its presence, frightened almost, at the raw need she had invoked in him. But he was kissing her too deeply for any communication other than body language. This was the kiss of a man whose feelings could be shown only occasionally, when his guard was down. She had stripped it from him, and what was left awed and turned her on more than at any time in her life, with any man. When he drew away to look down at her his lips were soft and bruised looking, his eyes feverish.

'Damn!' he said explosively, and kissed her again, this time for even longer, whilst she gathered up his shirt and stroked his long back, and wrapped her silk-clad legs around his and rocked him into her loving grasp.

Much, much later, she woke up with a start. The light in the room was dim, but outside it was still broad daylight. How long had she been here? Not that it mattered. Oddly, she felt so much more grown up than she had when they had first begun to make love. Or, to put it more accurately, he had begun to make love to her.

But where was he now? She sat up suddenly, her ears tuning in to small sounds in the bathroom. The door opened and he came out, still naked. He crawled on to the bed and kissed her.

'Still hungry?'

She stretched luxuriously, letting the sheet drop to her waist. 'Actually, I feel rather full.'

He nuzzled at her nipple and gave it a crafty lick that sent shivers down her spine. 'That's a shame.'

'And why's that, Mr McKenna?'

'I was thinking of treating you to dinner by the river, complete with champagne. Then I was going to bring you back here and make love to you until you begged me to stop. Of course, that wouldn't be until early tomorrow morning, such is my skill and stamina.'

She stared at him, open-mouthed at his self-belief, before the sparkle in his eyes and the twitching around his mouth suggested that he may have been joking.

'How can I resist an offer like that?' she murmured. 'Although you're forgetting that I have more stamina than you.'

'Is that so?' He shifted so that his body effectively pinned her to the bed. 'I would suggest that my added experience and maturity might beg to differ on that score.'

'And I would suggest that my relative youth might disagree with you.'

He rolled her over and over again, until she was trapped in the sheets and completely at his mercy.

'The best wines are those with a few years behind them,' he countered.

Suzy reached up to nip his chin with her small white teeth. 'I started very, very young,' she whispered. His answering shudder was felt down the whole length of her body. After that there was no more talk. She had no desire to fight him, or to be clever, or to out-fox him. That womanly feeling she had woken up with was still there, making her a languorous goddess that he was happy to worship with his tongue, lips and cock. Never before had a man spent so much time giving her pleasure, she thought happily, as he pressed small kisses up the inside of her thighs. He blew gently on her sex before continuing on his way, leaving tiny imprints of passion on her belly, her breasts and neck. He held her hands to her sides so she would not wriggle, but she had no desire to. Her breath caught as he flicked at one breast, gently, curling his tongue around the nipple. He watched it swell with greedy eyes, before suckling it tenderly again, sending tiny arrows of electricity shooting down her body. Then the other breast, the same arrows of pleasure, until they were one coursing channel, surging down into her clitoris and swelling it, making it sing. Then he was at her throat, tasting, sucking, breathing on the cool saliva left behind. Suzy felt so overwhelmed with sensation that she could not have moved anyway. After a long, deep kiss that left her breathless he crawled around and buried his face in her sex.

It was all so unhurried, so measured. He knew what he was doing and had no desire to prove himself. He tilted her body towards his so that they were effectively side by side, and with his head resting on her thigh he pushed his tongue lazily into her pussy, all the way. She shivered and moaned, and the meaty cock, so close now to her lips, swelled in appreciation. It too was half-erect, waiting, again not worried about proving how hard it could get. She knew that already. He had left her feeling as tender as a virgin the first time they had made love, earlier that day. With the same dreamy lack of speed she sucked him into her mouth. He moaned against her pussy and thickened instantly, filling her mouth so suddenly that her lips hurt. His moan reverberated through her body and she answered him, letting him feel the same sweet eddies of pleasure. For a while they stayed like that, lazily eating each other, until she felt him becoming even more tense. Sweet liquid coated her tongue. He struggled to a sitting position and kissed her mouth, sharing her musky juices. This time, the kiss was hard and needy.

'Present yourself to me,' he said hoarsely.

Instinctively she knew what he wanted. She rolled over onto her hands and knees and thrust her backside out at him, looking over her shoulder at him.

'Like this, Master?'

The words came out automatically, and as soon as she said them, she regretted it. He would know that it was the game she played with Clifton. Nothing like reminding a man of one's affair with his brother at the wrong moment.

But she was wrong. They were identical, and inevitably, found the same things exciting. His eyes were narrow with lust as he kneeled up behind her, forcing her buttocks apart and licking all along the deep crevice. She cried out and thrust harder, like a horny cat, her sex lips puffed up and gaping. She wanted him so badly, but he was drinking her in, his finger probing her tiny puckered hole. When it went in she tossed her long black hair, glaring back at him for the indignity he had thrust upon her. But he was guiding his cock between her sex lips, holding back slightly, torturing both her and himself, before sliding all the way in with a deep, satisfied, 'oh yesss'. He paused, his eyes closed for a moment, and when he opened them again she knew she was in trouble. He drew out, almost to the point of departure, and slammed back again, almost knocking her into the wall. She slapped her palms against it to steady herself as he began to fuck her hard and rhythmically. Even when indulging in this basest of acts he was still elegant, his fingers digging deep into her hipbones, every measured thrust a masterpiece of pleasure for them both. As the assault went on he grabbed at her hair, twisting it around his hand and pulling her head ruthlessly back. After being lulled into a false sense of serenity this sustained attack was brutally exciting. He stopped fucking long enough to kiss her, a hard, biting kiss before pushing her back on to all fours. He was strangely silent, apart from the physical effort it took to keep going at such a pace. Suzy wanted him to come, to release her and let her rest. When he did it was tight and hard.

'Foxy ... little ... bitch,' he spat, every word an ejaculation timed with each hard pulse. He collapsed on to her back and they fell on to the bed, he still buried deep inside her.

A few minutes later he had fallen asleep, still inside her. It was a strange sensation, feeling him deflate and slowly fall out of her bruised and swollen pussy, leaving behind a cooling stream of juice that very soon began to trickle down her thigh. She reached over him for the sheet and pulled it over them both, wrapping them up in a cocoon far removed from the outside world.

It was another twenty-four hours before she looked at the clock again. In that time she had forgotten everything but the most basic human needs. Food, alcohol and sex, lots and lots of it.

And talking. Clayton liked to talk. It was as if he had not seen another human being for a decade. But it was what he didn't say that told her more about him. Underneath his insouciant attitude, resentment burned like a hot brick in his chest whenever he saw his wiser, older brother in their father's house, comfortable, respected, seemingly content. That jealousy had been deep-rooted from an early age, yet he still clung to Clifton emotionally, coming back to home base when he needed a dose of security.

When he did eventually crash out he was a heavy sleeper, so she took the opportunity to check her text messages undisturbed. The first one was from Jem, and it was like a kick in the stomach.

'WHERE R U? DAD GOING BALLISTIC.'

She had felt no guilt at sleeping with Clayton. She had not thought of Clifton at all in the time that they were entangled in cool Egyptian cotton sheets. Now she felt sick. After their bawdy evening Clifton's fevered imagination would have been working overtime. She looked over at Clayton. He was breathing softly, wrapped in a deep, sated sleep, looking slightly smug. As well he might. He had walked in, conquered both Alice and Suzy in a matter of days, and had every right to assume that he had finally got one over on his superior twin brother, after waiting all his life to do so. He would be insufferable when he arrived back at the house, and then he would disappear without warning, leaving a trail of destruction behind him.

Suzy knew she had to talk to Clifton before he did. She dressed quickly and quietly, considered leaving a note, then decided against it. He was a resourceful man. He would find his own way home.

15

It was after midnight by the time she hit the M40. Half an hour to go. Her foot squeezed down on the accelerator. She tried Jem's mobile, but was still shocked when he answered.

'He's gone to pieces. Is Uncle Clayton with you?'

'No.'

'Thank Christ for that. I wonder where he is?'

It was a rhetorical question, so she didn't answer it. 'Tell Clifton I'm on my way.'

Alice pounced on her as soon as she walked through the door.

'Where's Clayton?'

'He's up in London. He said I could borrow his car. I visited friends in Suffolk.' It was the story they had worked on the day before, to field awkward questions.

'What's he doing up in London?'

'He said he had business up there. I dropped him off at Oxford station.' She held her breath. The lies came too easily, as if she did it for a living. Alice regarded her suspiciously for a few moments. In the background she heard the piano. It sounded as if a cat was tiptoeing across the keys. Alice cast her eyes to the ceiling and sighed heavily.

'Clifton didn't know where you were. Next time let him know, for goodness sake, so we can avoid all these ghastly dramatics.' She led the way into Clifton's room. 'She's here, darling. You can relax now,' she said sarcastically.

To say that he looked terrible was an understatement. Around lunchtime the previous day he had hit the bottle, and now he was slumped over the piano, his head resting on his arm on the keys. He was plinking the white ivories he could reach, playfully, toying with them. The high, jarring sound was sinister, as if shrieking at Suzy not to get too close.

She walked around the piano to face him. His eyes were blank, staring through her.

'Feeling OK?' she asked wryly.

Inexplicably, he started to laugh. Only it wasn't a laugh, but a creepy, psychotic giggle. She wanted to slap his face, but if she did, he would have fallen on the floor. He reached with the hand that had been playing with the keys to the top of the piano and groped around for a finger-marked whisky tumbler. She moved it out of his reach. Something slipped to the floor. She picked it up. It was another photograph of Kate, smiling, her head thrown back, posing somewhat self-consciously on a grass bank somewhere near the house. It wasn't in a frame, but part of a collection that was sliding slowly off his lap. She gathered them up.

'I'll put these in your bedside drawer.' She did so, and when she came back he was reaching weakly for his whisky glass again. In doing so, he lost balance and slithered to the floor. He lay as if stupefied, unable to move. Suzy attempted to pick him up under the arms to drag him to the sofa, but he was over six foot tall and it just wasn't going to happen. She went to the drawing room where Jem was waiting anxiously.

'He's totally plastered. I can't move him.'

Together they manhandled him into the bedroom. Jem exclaimed at the fading marks on his back.

'Ask your mother,' Suzy said shortly, stripping Clifton's clothes away. Eventually they rolled him between the sheets. Clifton opened his eyes and seemed to see Suzy for the first time. She expected the abuse to start immediately, but it was worse than that. He started to weep.

'No, no, absolutely not,' she said firmly. He grasped her like a drowning man and she held him, grimacing at Jem over his shoulder. He shrugged helplessly.

'Go,' she mouthed at him. Gratefully, he complied.

Once they were alone Suzy extricated herself from Clifton's tentacle grip and forced him to look at her. She wiped away the moisture from his face.

'You are going to be so embarrassed by this tomorrow morning.'

'Where's my brother?'

'He isn't with me.' Again, the truth. Just.

'He didn't go with you?'

'Do you know where I went?'

Clifton shrugged, too drunk to notice that he had been diverted from this awkward question. 'To the coast?'

'That's right, and before I tell you why I want you to promise me that you won't start crying again. I don't need it.'

Clifton attempted to smile. 'Shit, I am wasted, aren't I?'

'Yes. Go to sleep.'

'Give me your tits and I will.'

She obediently unbuttoned her blouse. There was a certain erotic contentment in having him fall asleep on her, sucking at her breast like a large lion cub.

Fortunately, there was no further interrogation from Alice at breakfast. She was preoccupied with retail therapy, so stressful had the previous day been for her. Clifton's questions were a little more barbed, but Suzy stuck to her story, hating herself for deceiving him. Jem had guessed the truth, but he kept his own council. After all, he owed Suzy a lot for her discretion about his relationship with Bonny. And, quite frankly, his own love life was complicated enough without him getting involved in his father's.

That morning Suzy had a long swim as Clifton watched. He was calm, a different human being from the one she had left the night before. She wondered how long it was going to last after what she had to tell him. Approximately five minutes, tops, probably. She dried herself and, still in her bikini, she sat at his feet to begin his foot massage.

'I went to see Kate.'

Make that five seconds.

'She loves you to bits, but she ain't happy,' Suzy continued hurriedly, before the explosion. He looked like a volcano ready to erupt. 'Reading between the lines, she wants you to go in there, broadsword and white horse at the ready, and haul her ass out. Then take her somewhere very quiet and spend the rest of your natural life ravishing her.'

'So why hasn't she come to see me?' he asked tightly.

'Because Alice had told her that you didn't want to see her ever again.'

'And she believed that after the way our relationship had worked? Has the woman no sense?'

'She loves you.'

'She's still stupid.' He glared into the contents of his coffee cup before engulfing them in one swallow.

'So . . . does this mean you won't go and see her?'

'Why should I? If she had any strength of character she would come here!'

'That's funny. She said something very similar about you.' She picked up his other foot and began the process again. Gradually he started to relax.

'So are you going to see her?' Suzy asked.

'Who?'

'You know, the woman who has dominated your life for the past year. Kate.'

'I've told you, she's got to come to me.'

'You're a fool.'

'She's a fool.'

'Fine, you're both fools!' Suzy dropped his other foot on the floor with a thud. 'You're pissing your life away over a principle. Swallow your pride and get over there!'

'I don't think so.' Clifton picked up his newspaper. Suzy snatched it back from him.

'Only because you're scared. Why? The grief she'll give you for not going earlier is nothing to the grief I'm giving you now!'

'Fucking women! In my next life I'm going to come back queer. Get the hell away from me!'

'Oh, don't be so grouchy. You know I'm right.' She picked up his foot again and continued filing his toenails. He picked up the newspaper and continued to read.

A car drew up outside the house. She heard distant voices and the slamming of a door. Then footsteps, coming closer. Clayton had arrived home, not in the best of humours. As he entered the pool house she did not have to turn around to know that he wanted to haul her outside by the scruff of the neck and demand to know what she was playing at.

'You look stressed, Clay,' Clifton said cheerfully. 'Bad day in the big city?'

Clayton looked at them, apparently unsure how much Clifton knew. Suzy set his other foot between her breasts before squeezing exfoliating cream into the palm of her hand. She began the same soothing movement, up, down, between the toes. Clifton closed his eyes and relaxed back on the sun lounger.

'Go and tell Mrs Penrose to make some more coffee,' he said lazily, waving a manicured hand in Clayton's direction. 'You're ruining my karma, standing there like a bad-tempered monkey.'

Clayton looked as if he would like to punch him. He turned on his heel and stalked away, with one final evil glare at Suzy.

'What was the matter with him?' Clifton drawled.

'Jealous, probably,' Suzy said lightly.

Clifton grinned, still with his eyes closed. 'What a pity.'

Suzy deftly avoided Clayton all day, but sooner or later he would capture her. He finally did, just before the nightly pre-prandial drinks in the drawing room. With a firm hand around her upper arm he guided her into the library and shut the door.

'Why did you walk out on me?'

'Clifton needs me. You don't. He was upset last night so I came home. I knew you wouldn't understand if I gave you my reasons.'

'How do you know I don't need you?'

'You hardly know me! We had great sex but that doesn't mean –'

'What? That you love me? That you feel anything for me?'

His mentioning of love threw her into a panic. She tried to push past him, but he wasn't going to let her.

'How do you know I don't need you?' he asked again. 'You don't know how I feel, because you've not bothered to find out!'

'I don't need to! You obviously want me because Clifton has me instead. To you I'm a possession to be fought over. You probably haven't even thought about how I feel! All you're interested in is yourself!'

He stepped back from her. 'Hold on a minute. I was

under the impression that the pleasure was mutual. I wanted us to get to know each other before other people got in the way. I really felt we were getting on ...'

'Listen to yourself! It's all about you, what you want, how you feel. What about me? I listened to you last night and it was wonderful, but did you ask about me? No! Not once!'

'You didn't give me a chance!'

'You had your chance. How long does the average first date last? Four hours? You had forty-eight and you still blew it!'

She found herself up against the wall. Her protest was stalled by a kiss so masterful she had to take it like a horrified maiden, her hands batting uselessly against his broad shoulders.

'You once accused me of talking too much. Now I don't talk enough! What do you want from me?'

Distant voices, getting closer.

'Don't hurt Clifton. That's all I ask.'

'Do you love him?' he asked quietly.

'Yes, but not in the same way as I love you.' The words were out before she could stop them. She winced. 'Oh shit, I didn't –'

'Mean it? Don't lie to me, Suzy. We feel the same about each other, but let's just get lust out of the way before we start talking, OK? Before I self-detonate.' He kissed her again, but this time she matched him in urgency, her arms twining around his neck. Their breath came hot and thick and fast, as each kiss merged into the next, deeper and more demanding. Alice was just outside the door. In moments she would discover them, ravishing each other as if there were no time at all left on earth.

The door opened. Alice saw Suzy on one side of the room, Clayton on the other.

'Clayton, drinks are being served in the conservatory. Clifton is waiting for you, Suzy.' She said the last bit with a malicious smile. If Suzy wanted damaged goods, it was up to her.

Much later, when the house was quiet and Alice had been helped to sleep with another pill, they met in the White Garden, where the smell of mock orange blossom and honeysuckle perfumed the warm night air. Suzy's feelings were ambivalent. She had had to watch him flirting with Alice over dinner, oozing so much charm that the woman was panting by the time coffee was served. Suzy wondered why he bothered, especially now. And there was still that sneaky seed of mistrust, because he had not fully explained his motives for coming back.

'What's wrong?' he asked. 'You hardly spoke a word at the table.'

'I'm surprised you noticed,' she said archly. 'Are you sleeping with her as well?'

'Alice? No. She'd like me to. I'm just keeping her sweet.'

'Why?'

Clayton pulled her into his arms. 'Do you trust me?'

'No,' she replied, almost laughing.

'You can, but she can't. That's all I'm prepared to say. Do you want me?'

She did not answer him, although her answer was an unequivocal yes. The moon was nearly full, and they could see clearly as they circled one another like wary animals. Clayton reached for her hand, and this time she allowed him to take it. He kissed the palm and very deliberately placed it on his cock. He was already very hard. She squeezed, feeling the reverberations shudder throughout his body. With her hand still in place she put his hand on her breast, over the thin silk blouse. He moved it around, letting her nipple play through his fingers. A distant owl and their breathing were the only sounds in the stillness of the night. They were spinning out the moment when they could feel skin on skin to a tortuous degree, daring each other to be the first to crack. Suzy pinched his nipple with her other hand, again squeezing his dick. The hard throb made his legs give way. He sank to his knees and pulled her towards him, gathering up her skirt and pressing his face between her legs. She felt his warm breath drift against her inner thighs, and the questing hot tongue flicker across the damp patch in her silk knickers. He eased them to one side and probed further, in between her engorged pussy lips, as she bit back a cry and steadied herself on his shoulders. But the exquisite pleasure was too much and soon she was on the ground, on a cashmere blanket he had brought out for them, her skirt flaring around her waist, her pale skin silvery in the moonlight. Her hips lifted as his tongue played with every secret place, the cool breeze his accomplice to drive her wild with lust. She spread herself like a banquet before him, her fingers toying with her nipples, made stiff in the coming coolness of the night. She used the dew in the grass to stimulate them further, and gasped delightedly as his hot mouth covered them and sent electric ripples of sensation down her body, whilst at the same time he entered her with a need so fierce it swept them both away. She heard the faint snap of elastic as her knickers were lost somewhere in the flowerbed, forgotten instantly as he pushed in all the way, letting out a harsh sigh of joy. With the hard ground instead of a mattress beneath her, there was no escape. His kiss was scalding on her neck as he pulled back and thrust into her again, her hands on his buttocks driving him deeper, her husky whispers telling him to fuck her harder. He obeyed joyfully, driven by her soft voice, her sharp nails, her silky, tight body rising up hard and fast to meet his.

With supreme self-control he went back down to finish the job he had started, sweeping his tongue first around her pussy lips, now much engorged and open, before moving on up, towards her clitoris, playing it with the virtuosity of one dedicated to his craft. Suzy bit her hand to stop the moans rising in volume, but she could not stop her body, lifting, undulating, stretching itself wide open to take more and more pleasure. Her orgasm was deep, gut-wrenching, stars exploding behind her tightly closed eyelids. When it was over she still hadn't had enough, whispering greedily for him to fuck her, to make it good.

'You're a hard woman to please,' he growled, thrusting deep inside her again.

'You're not up to the job?'

'Live and learn.' And he proceeded to screw her so hard she knew that the chafe marks would show on her back and shoulders the following day. His bruising attack was relentless, until she had to tell him to stop for hurting her.

'I'm not used to it,' she said. They both knew what she meant. Clayton lay back on his elbows and let her tongue-bath her essence from his cock. Naked except for his shirt, he looked both vulnerable and devastatingly lewd, with his great erection lying along his taut belly. His head fell back as she lapped slavishly at his balls.

'Do that again,' he murmured, so she did, watching his hips lift with every lick up his scrotum, right to the tip of the head, descending as she traced the fat central ridge back down. Again and again, until he said he was going to come if she did it any more.

'We don't want to waste it,' she said, climbing on his

lap. By now the dew was seeping through the cashmere rug but neither of them intended to leave yet. She uttered a tiny sound of pleasure as she sank onto him, making it take a long, long time, as if his cock were endless.

'You fill me right up,' she murmured, gently nipping his earlobe. There was an answering appreciative pulse. This time their fucking was slower, less frantic, their eyes locked as gradually ecstasy took hold. At the last moment he flipped her over and lunged into her with three desperate thrusts, forcing her to look at him, his lips drawn back from his teeth in a primeval grimace.

At breakfast next morning, his appearance in tight jodh-purs and leather riding boots made her feel hot and weak.

'Do you ride, Suzy?' he asked, cracking a crop against his palm.

She coughed to steady her voice. 'Not horses,' she said.

Clifton laughed explosively from the end of the table. Alice scowled at him and beamed widely at Clayton.

'I'll come out with you, darling. Suzy's always been afraid of horses, haven't you?'

It was the first she had heard of it, but Suzy decided to play along. 'Terrified, but Jem's helping me overcome my fear by making me clear out the stables. I'll be there until midday.' She looked at Clayton as she said it. He nodded very discreetly. Message received and under-stood. After that Suzy couldn't look at him any longer. Suddenly they were lovers, but paradoxically it felt as if she was being unfaithful to Clifton, and Clayton was being unfaithful to Alice. She felt as though a big neon sign had appeared over her head, screaming 'I'm fucking Clayton McKenna'. When she felt a hand squeeze her knee she immediately looked at him, but it was Clifton.

That look must have given her away, she thought, but Clifton was talking easily to Jem, otherwise paying no attention to her. She immediately sensed the tightrope she had started walking upon, and vowed to be more careful.

The horses' hooves rang loudly on the tarmac as Alice and Clayton approached the village. On the other side the road led to a bridleway at the bottom of the hill, which opened out into fields where the horses could stretch their necks and really fly. As they approached the village green they saw the mothers dropping their children off at school, parked haphazardly along the kerb. It was an eternal problem, one that Alice had also been fairly vociferous about in recent months. And although she had a valid point, she had not offered any solutions, and her manner had made her unpopular with some of the younger mothers in the village.

Several women admired Clayton as he rode by on Sentinel. He rewarded them with a tip of his hat and a knowing smile. Alice's attention was on a man hovering outside the Spar. He was unshaven, filthy ragged jeans and a checked shirt open to reveal his hairy torso. Despite herself, Alice felt a prickle of lust. Then another man joined him, tall and gangly, with a wiry pony tail. Seamus Donelly, leader of the gypsy clan. Her nose wrinkled in disgust

'Hey Dad, give us the fags,' the younger man said. As he caught them he turned and saw her, and his face lit up. He scratched his hairy belly and tugged his forelock at her.

'Morning, Mrs McKenna! Great day for a ride!'

Alice had gone a sick cream colour under her riding hat. Robby was approaching them, still grinning. The mothers seemed to have gathered, like crows smelling carrion. Clayton had stopped a few yards ahead, watching their encounter with unhelpful curiosity.

'What do you want doing today?' Robby asked loudly. 'A bit of bush trimming, perhaps?'

One of the women snorted with laughter. Alice gave him a supercilious smile and carried on walking. Robby walked along side her.

'There's a lot I could do for you, Mrs McKenna. Offer me a fair price and I'm all yours.'

They had moved away from the gathered women. When Alice was sure they were out of earshot she turned on him.

'Don't bother turning up today, Mr O'Grady. Your employment has been terminated!'

'You're firing me? Why?' He looked regretful and hurt.

'For gross insubordination, that's why! If you harass me again I shall call the police!'

O'Grady looked up and down the street. No one was near. 'I don't think that's a very good idea, Alice. After all, I have something all your posh friends might be very interested in. A little home movie. I'll let you know when I want to discuss it.' He melted away from her as Clayton came back. Alice looked as if she were about to be sick.

'Is everything all right?'

'Fine!' Alice snapped. Then she simpered at him, all sugary sweetness again. 'Let's go through the fields. I know a lovely little spot we can rest a while.'

When they arrived back at the stables, Suzy was with Jem in the office. Clayton dismounted, removed the tack and began to brush Sentinel down. Alice thrust her reins at a passing stable girl and told her to deal with it. Then she went home, complaining of a headache. Suzy could not keep her eyes off Clayton as he dealt with Sentinel, treating the huge horse with macho affection, his tight buttocks and long legs irresistible to watch as he leaned and stretched, giving Sentinel a rub down. Her legs felt weak as he caught her eye and smiled, before taking Sentinel into his stable and closing the door on him. When he finally led her into a dark, quiet corner, filled with warm hay and horse oats, the first thing she did was seek out his cock.

'I'm sorry,' she said, 'I can't help it.' It took seconds to massage him into full hardness, and then she took her time ogling the tightly restrained outline, running her fingers over that long, plump ridge, pressing her lips against it and breathing in musk and saddle oil and hot horse. He leaned against the stable wall, breathing heavily, his hand in her silky black hair.

'Don't apologise,' he gasped. 'Just make it worth my while.'

She eased the zip down slowly, enjoying the sight of him bursting through the opening as if angry at her for making him wait so long. She turned, gathering up the skirt she had worn on purpose, revealing her lack of panties. She braced herself against the stable wall and let him enter her from behind.

'You're so fucking sexy,' he muttered, pushing all the way into her hot, tight pussy. Outside, the stable hands were leading horses through the yard. In the stable next door, someone was mucking out. If they stopped to listen, or even if they looked carefully through the wide cracks in the wooden planks, they would have seen Suzy's lily white haunches, and Clayton McKenna's muscular jodhpur-clad legs, slightly bent as he plundered her flesh with mounting desperation.

Seconds later, their breathy, heated coupling came to a head. She purred with pleasure, feeling him spend the last pulses of pleasure into her trembling body, hearing his bitten-back grunts of joy. He pulled away and sagged back against the wall, his eyes closed. She made him cry out by giving his cock one last cheeky suck, before melting away, out of the stable, her long skirt hiding the rivulets of come dribbling down her legs.

That evening Robby stopped off on the way back to the encampment and slumped on the roadside to enjoy the six-pack he had bought from the off-licence. He wanted to drink it before anyone else tried to get it, especially his little half-brother, pain in the arse that he was. He closed his eyes and lugged down the beer, imagining Alice's face when he told her how much he wanted for the video tape. And she would still fuck him. He knew she would. She was dirty and desperate, just like him. He could feel his penis thicken, just thinking of her bending over for him, her tight, hard buttocks clenched in protest until he slapped them hard to make her comply. He knew he would have to go to the other side of the hedge to wank if he thought about it any more, but he couldn't be bothered right then.

He didn't notice the man watching him from the other side of the road at first. When he did, he felt his bowels weaken. The man looked just like the Squire, only he was walking, as straight and strong as any man who hadn't yet fallen off his horse. It was the man Alice had been with when he had seen her that morning. He approached with menacing grace, his hand reaching inside his jacket pocket.

'I want a word with you,' he said.

16

The first cars began drawing up soon after seven. Alice greeted her guests with copious 'darling's, and air kisses. She wore a coral palazzo pants and halter neck ensemble, which showed off her St Tropez tan to perfection. Her fingers and toenails had been painted a pearly white to match the pearls at her throat and ears, below hair coiffed to within a millimetre of its life. She was hanging on to the arm of a stunning man with Mediterranean skin, a flute of Veuve Clicquot complementing her slender, pearl-enrobed wrist. The talk was of business, tropical holidays, public schools and horses, always horses.

'A smashing little filly. I've just bought her for two fifty.'

'I paid a million and a half for mine, but her bloodstock is top notch.'

Were they talking about horses or women? Suzy pondered this point as Clayton cruised up next to her, stunning in a white shirt and bow tie. His dinner jacket was already slung carelessly over his shoulder.

'Hey, you.' She wanted to kiss him, but dared not.

'Can we go somewhere quiet?' He leaned down to whisper in her ear. 'The sun shines right through that dress. It's given me one hell of a hard-on.'

'Hush!' She hit him playfully and noticed several arched eyebrows. 'Later,' she whispered. 'Meet me in the bowery at ten o'clock.'

'It's a date,' he murmured. Alice approached and introduced him to a couple from New Zealand, blatantly ignoring Suzy. The talk turned to wine. After a few moments she made her excuses and left. She wanted to check up on Clifton.

Men turned to stare as she went past. The simplicity of her outfit made the rest look like gaudy parrots. She had chosen ice blue to match her eyes, with slim diamante straps that crossed over at the back. The insubstantial dress came just above the knee, and she wore blue diamante strappy sandals to match. She had bought one of Lena's wire and jet creations, lacy and delicate, to wear around her throat, and had put new blue streaks in her hair. She felt funky and good, and knew she looked it.

When she went in to see Clifton he was on the bed, fast asleep, still dressed in his black silk Dunhill robe. She prodded him.

'Hey, sleeping beauty, wake up. You've got a party to go to.'

He did not move. She saw the whisky tumbler on the bedside table, and the bottle, almost empty. She was sure that it had been full that afternoon. Frowning, she picked up the glass. At the bottom, almost so fine they could not be seen, were a few transparent grains. She shook the glass and sniffed suspiciously. No discernible odour, but she was sure that he had been drugged. He looked too unconscious for it to be alcohol alone. Anyway, when she had spoken to him that afternoon, he had been quite happy to join the party. If he had not wanted to go he would have just said so, not drunk himself into a stupor.

There was nothing she could do, so she went back outside. For a while she cruised around, listening rather than talking, trying to pick up any murmurings about Clifton's absence. At last, her eavesdropping paid off. Alice was talking to an earnest Clare Rayner type, systematically destroying Clifton's reputation with horribly convincing stories of drunken rages and mental cruelty. When she saw Suzy she stopped, tight-lipped, and changed the subject. But Suzy had heard enough. So that was her game, to win support before she announced that the stables would be sold, presumably to the highest bidder. She remembered the tall, well-dressed man Alice had been attached to earlier, and decided to seek him out. He was charming when she introduced herself as a 'friend of the family', but it was obvious he wasn't giving anything away. Frustrated, she went back to find Dr Maloney.

'Who is that man?' she asked him.

Maloney craned his neck to see. 'Him? Bad news. I didn't realise this party was for the competition as well.'

'What do you mean?'

'He's a trainer. I worked on his boy after a fall a couple of years ago at Cheltenham. Clifton can't stand him. At the time he was considering opening stables in the UK. It never happened.'

'Until now. Maybe,' Suzy suggested.

'Where's Clifton?'

'Out for the count. She slipped a Mickey Finn in his Scotch.'

Maloney's eyes widened. 'You're joking!' He saw she wasn't laughing. 'Leave it with me. I'll see what else I can pick up.' He smoothed his way into the crowd.

Jem sidled up to her.

'There's enough mutton dressed as lamb down there to start a Cornish pasty factory,' he muttered darkly. 'Still, you'll slay 'em.'

'Thanks. Does that mean you forgive me?'

'I've been a bit of a shit, haven't I?'

'A bit!'

'You know what Dad said to me the other day? "She

brought me back from the dead." He adores you, and so do I.'

He gave her a quick hug. Suzy felt her eyes prickle. She didn't cry easily but the thought of Clifton McKenna crediting her with skills of Lazarus-like proportions was too much. Jem laughed at her.

'Don't get all soppy about it. He also said you were a bigger cunt than my mother.' He kissed her affectionately on the cheek and then he, too, slipped away through the crowd.

No one saw him go upstairs. In his room he dragged the bag he had packed out of the wardrobe and checked the contents again. It was all there, passports, plane tickets and ten thousand dollars in cash.

He swiftly went down the corridor, into Alice's room, pulling on soft latex gloves as he went. There was a safe, hidden behind a picture of a woman holding a small dog. He dealt with it efficiently, as he had practised many times before very recently. Within seconds he was inside. He swept the Mappin & Webb diamond necklace, various rings and other jewellery into a velvet bag and shut the safe again, replacing everything exactly as it was. Outside, Alice stood out like a beacon in her coral silk. Suzy was there too, effortlessly flirting with an old gentleman with a monocle. Jem blew her a silent kiss and went to the door.

He listened in the corridor for a moment before walking back to his room. Once inside, he opened the velvet bag and wrapped the jewellery properly. He already had a buyer lined up in London, waiting for him. Then he and Bonny would be on the redeye to New York. After that, who knew?

The security staff were the only people who saw him

leave the house. One even opened the front door for him. His car was prominently placed, facing the gate. He threw the bag in the boot and, with one last look back at the crowd, he climbed in, gunned the engine, and drove away.

He stopped at a letter box and posted the letter he had written to Clifton. It was brief, thanking him for supporting him and apologising in advance for the fall-out that would undoubtedly arise when Alice discovered what he had done. The one thing he didn't say was where he was going.

He parked in the lay-by and walked up to the Mount to wait. Below him he could see Springfields House, and hear the strains of Elgar drifting up in the cooling night air. Beyond, the lights of Oxford cast an orange glow over the lower sky, like distant fire.

And between, on the long stretch of Roman road that led to Great Clutton, he could see a purposeful line of headlights, coming towards the village.

Suzy saw Clayton again an hour later, when it was nearly dark. They seemed to be in orbit around each other, moving ever closer, as the high-octane small talk fizzed all around them. When he eventually appeared at her side again, it was almost ten. Silently, they communicated their need and began to move very subtly towards the edge of the crowd.

As soon as they reached the bowery he pulled her to him and kissed her so deeply it was as if he were trying to fuck her from the inside out. Never before had she been kissed so thoroughly, so greedily, as his hands stealthily crept under her flimsy dress and stroked her bare buttocks. The Aubade thong she was wearing was nothing more than a jewel on a piece of silk rope, with a tiny triangle of black silk at the front. As he stroked her he exclaimed in delight.

'What the fuck is this?' He had found her smooth and silky pussy, Brazilian waxed that morning.

'Surprise, surprise,' she whispered, lifting one leg to hook around his waist so that he could continue exploring her.

'And you're saying we're not going to fuck right now? Think again.' He reached above their heads and tore at the white roses hanging down, showering them both with soft petals. There were roses in her hair and down the front of her dress. Their heady scent acted like a drug as he kissed her again, his hands back where they had been before, their breathing wet and hot and heavy. Suzy pressed herself against his bruising arousal and moved slowly from side to side, feeling him throb hard against her stomach.

'I'm surprised you haven't been scaring the ladies with that,' she murmured.

'I'll shoot in my trousers if you don't stop,' he whispered, tugging at her neck with his teeth.

'Good,' she replied, slipping a hand between his legs. His cock felt so good in her palm that she suddenly wanted him, then and there. In the darkness she felt her way, her tongue brushing against the sweet stickiness at the gaping tip of his cock. She licked him clean and sucked him all in, hearing his sawing breath above her as her mouth hugged him hard and tight. His protests became staccato curses as he tensed and let go, flooding her mouth with hot, creamy spunk. She drew back a little so he would not choke her, and swallowed and sucked until he was dry. As he leaned back against the trellis, breathing heavily, she zipped him up.

'Now you won't embarrass the ladies.' But he was

kissing her again, thrusting his tongue down her throat, tasting his essence.

'You'll be punished for that later,' he said.

The sky lit up with green and white stars, followed a second later by a deafening bang. He looked at his watch.

'Right on time. Come on. We'll miss the show,' he said, taking her hand.

'I don't care about a few fireworks. We can see them from here.'

'That isn't what I meant,' he said with a wolfish grin.

Night had drawn in. The lads of Great Clutton had congregated around the bar at the Red Lion with their girls, who were all made up to the nines, in skinny tops and pelmet skirts. They snapped gum and looked tough and didn't do much talking.

After a while a convoy of souped-up hatchbacks ripped into the village and parked behind the pub. Some of them were from Blackbird Leys, one of the toughest estates in Oxford. The word had been spread that the gypsies were going to get a thrashing that night.

Robby was in an ebullient mood, flashing his new-found wealth around. Everyone was getting tanked up, their numbers boosted by the travellers drawn in for the horse fair in Carterton, just outside Oxford. In the increasingly rowdy crowd he felt his Nokia vibrating in his pocket. Surely Alice didn't want him now, in the middle of her posh party, he thought.

It was his father, telling him to get the hell home, and bring reinforcements. If the village boys wanted a fight, they were damned well going to get it.

The first scuffles broke out just after closing time. Bolstered by bored teenagers with nothing else to do, the evening descended into chaos. With no one in the part-time police station to restore order, the destruction spread out to the smaller roads like an octopus regenerating its tentacles. The Spar was raided and eggs and flour taken to throw at the immaculately kept houses and their expensive cars, carefully washed that day. More alcohol was taken. Wine, spirits, lager, it didn't matter. Anything that they could throw down their throats and keep that fierce fire burning as the greed for wholesale damage grew. The good residents of Great Clutton looked on in horror behind their leaded glass windows, battened down the hatches, and jammed Oxford police station switchboard with calls to assist them.

Blissfully unaware of the wholesale rioting taking place not a mile away, people congregated out on the patio to watch Alice's fireworks. Reflected in the still waters of the lake, the display was quite stunning, Alice thought proudly. She looked around for Mr Valmez and could not see him. There were still quite a few people in the marquee where the screen had been set up. She couldn't believe they would find horses more interesting than the fireworks.

Huge star bursts lit up the sky, silver and gold. Alice dreaded to think how much ten minutes was going to cost her, but it was worth it if the Argentinian was impressed enough to buy Springfields. Another green burst, followed by machine-gun fire silver explosions. She saw Mr Valmez in the marquee, watching the screen. The atmosphere was strangely quiet, as though the occupants had been mesmerised.

Then she saw what they could see. The champagne flute slipped through her fingers and smashed on the ground.

Up on the sixty-inch screen, instead of Double O

Seven's victory at Doncaster, Alice was busy giving an unknown man a blowjob, whilst another pumped vigorously at her from behind. From the voracious expression on her face, there was no way she could argue that they had forced her into it.

The picture changed and she was on her back, gulping down wads of sperm and growling in a very unladylike fashion, 'shove it in me!' Two of the women gasped and ran from the marquee. They brushed past Alice without looking at her. But other people were now gathering round, drawn by Alice's aghast expression. The fireworks reached a crescendo, accompanied by Beethoven's *Ode To Joy*, and on the screen Alice screeched like an alley cat as her four gypsy companions whipped her with their cocks and bathed her in their sperm.

Alice fainted.

When she came to seconds later, aided by a hard male hand slapping her face, she saw shocked and appalled people. The fireworks had finished, but the string quartet, ludicrously, had started again, presumably because they were at a loss to know what else to do. There was a vaguely Titanic atmosphere about the whole place.

And then there was a commanding male voice, casting a spell over all who heard it.

'The roomy Lydia's private parts surpass
The lusty dray horse's elephantine arse;
Capacious as some old and well-worn shoe
That's trudged the muddy streets since first 'twas new;
Loose as the bracelet gemmed with green and scarlet
That mocks the arm of some consumptive harlot;
'Tis said, while bathing once we trod love's path,
I know not, but I seemed to fuck the bath.'

Looking around, Alice saw Clifton, leaning on his crutches, the glitter of revenge in his eyes.

I'm sure Martial wouldn't mind me paraphrasing him in this instance,' he added, with a sardonic smile.

'Well said, old boy,' crowed an aristocratic voice from the back. Suzy heard murmuring in the crowd. It seemed that no-one had expected to see him, especially walking and articulate.

'I believe the Romans had poetry for every occasion,' he said, with mock gravity.

'How dare you!' Alice spat, slapping him as hard as she could. Clifton stumbled backwards and fell against a terrified waitress bearing a full tray of champagne flutes. He hit the ground in a shower of champagne and broken glass.

Uproar. Dr Maloney restrained Alice, still screaming and struggling, whilst several people ran to help Clifton. The photographer from the *Oxford Herald* took pictures, unchecked, whilst his journalist colleague nearly came in his pants.

Suzy and Clayton arrived, only slightly dishevelled, to witness the almost unbelievable sight of Alice fighting with Dr Maloney whilst a hard-core porn movie played on the screen behind them. Clifton lay sprawled like a black mantis on the ground, covered with blood and Veuve Clicquot. Suzy rushed to help him, but as she drew near she saw that he was laughing his head off.

As Jem sat on the hill top he knew that Bonny would not come.

'At least I saw the fireworks,' he said to himself. Police sirens in the distance made him jumpy. He looked at his watch. It was time to go, with or without Bonny. He stretched his legs, shook them, and turned to leave. As he did, he heard soft footsteps. Bonny launched herself into his arms. Jem kissed her and hugged her and carried her down the hill to the waiting car.

They cruised past the burning gypsy camp, and drove unchecked through the village, where people were running amok and fighting on the green. Three cars had been turned over and set alight. It was like a heavy night in Liverpool, Jem thought in disbelief. He saw someone point to the car and start running, so he put his foot down, and drove out of the mayhem, into darkness, towards the comforting ribbon of lights that marked the M40 towards London.

17

The following morning it was obvious that it would take a damage limitation exercise of Labour government proportions to claw back Alice's reputation. Mr Valmez made his excuses and left, their business arrangement in tatters, and Alice spent all of Sunday under sedation, the discovery of her missing jewels being the final straw.

The gypsies had gone. They had disappeared in the night, along with a few lawn mowers, some garden furniture and an old Landrover that wasn't worth reporting stolen. The rumour was that Robby had caught the ferry back to Southern Ireland to lie low for a while. On Tuesday, Clifton received Jem's letter. He didn't tell Alice about it. Instead he burned it, and had a laugh at the audacity of his son.

By Wednesday afternoon Alice had wheeled in the heavy artillery: her two sharp Bond Street lawyers. Clifton's legal representatives were there too, in one final showdown in the regal drawing room. There she announced she was divorcing him.

'Thank Christ for that,' he muttered.

'And I'm citing Kate Palmer as the cause, a fact that you cannot deny, because the evidence is right here in front of us, as we shall now see,' she said triumphantly.

'Is that right?' Clifton's voice was dangerously quiet.

Alice drew a large brown envelope out of her Mulberry bag and spread the photographs across the table, like the winning hand in a high stakes game of blackjack. On top of them she placed the letter Kate had written. And on top of that she placed the framed photograph of Kate, facing it cruelly towards Clifton.

'Excuse the pun, but I don't think you've got a leg to stand on,' she said with mock regret.

Clifton did not speak. It was as if he had frozen in his chair. Then Clayton coughed and stood up.

'I think you'll find that it was me.'

Alice's eyes bulged. 'No! It was him! How could you have . . .'

'I came back whilst you were skiing, just before last Christmas.'

'But you could only have been here a week!'

Clayton gave her one of his trademark smirks. 'You of all people, Alice, should know how fast I can work.'

There was a cough, smothering laughter, from Clifton. Alice stared from brother to brother. It was almost impossible to tell the difference between them. The letter she had produced had no names, just initials. It could have been either one of them. There was no way of telling. Clayton was speaking again, but she hardly heard him.

'I think you'll find that this "evidence" is inadmissible in a court of law, and it would be a waste of everyone's time, not to mention publicly humiliating, if this ever went to court. After all, who's going to believe anything you say now?'

Alice's jaw sagged. 'But –'

'So if I were you,' he continued inexorably, 'I would pack as many Louis Vuitton bags as you have in your closet, and catch the first plane to Cannes. From there you can wait for your decree nisi. If Clifton is feeling generous, he might let you keep the apartment. Or he might not. Either way, you are finished here, so do us all a big favour, take your bespoke-suited lawyers and get the hell out of town.'

Alice whirled to face him. 'You evil, revolting man! How could you do this to me! How?' Without waiting for his answer she stormed out of the room.

'It was so, so, sweet,' Clayton said later to Suzy. 'And now she's gone.'

'I almost feel sorry for her,' Suzy said. 'So many things going shit-shaped at once.'

'It's called rough justice, sweetheart. Anyway, I think we're moving away from the most important subject.' He moved closer, allowing her to wrap her legs around his waist. She was sitting on the marble worktop in the changing area, where he had caught her after her work-out. They were still sneaking around like forbidden lovers, trying to protect Clifton from any more shocks that week.

'And what is that?' She asked playfully.

'How am I going to cope without you for six months?' His face was serious again. 'I know you have to go, but –'

She stalled him with a kiss. 'I don't have to go, but I want to go. And if you promise to behave yourself, maybe I'll give you my itinerary. We could meet up in New York.' She kissed him passionately. 'Or San Fransisco.' Another kiss. 'Or even, if you're really lucky, Missouri.'

'Missouri?' He laughed. 'That's a date.' Then his expression changed. Over his shoulder, she saw what he had seen in the mirror.

'You treacherous bastard,' Clifton said coldly. He was standing in the doorway, watching them. Clayton moved away and Suzy quickly adjusted her clothing.

'Clif ... please ...' Clayton seemed at a loss for words, for the first time ever.

'Please? You should have asked that before you screwed her!' Clifton smashed one of his crutches against the mirror, splintering it with a deafening crash. With only one support left, he could no longer stand. He sagged against the wall and slid to the floor, his head in his hands. Clayton looked stricken.

'Go,' Suzy commanded him. He did not move. 'Get out of here!'

The harshness of her voice snapped him into action. He stormed out of the room, slamming the door. Suzy knelt next to Clifton. She wasn't going to make any trite apologies. Her betrayal had gone far deeper than that.

'He could never keep his hands off my women,' he whispered. 'Everything I had, he wanted so he took it. Every fucking girl, every fucking time.'

'But I'm not your woman,' Suzy said softly. 'Kate is. And he hasn't had her, has he?'

'Not yet,' Clifton said grimly. 'Anyway, she isn't mine. She doesn't want me, and now neither do you.' He looked up at her. 'Not that I blame you. I –'

She kissed his lips. 'I love you.' She kissed him again. 'But your heart belongs to someone else, and I will always be second best. I've found someone who loves me as much as I love them, and I know you would want that for me. Wouldn't you?'

Clifton pulled her into his arms and held her. They stayed that way until Baker found them.

18

Clayton McKenna was a man in turmoil. Suzy's declaration had seared to his brain, and he had not stayed to hear the rest. He had gone straight upstairs, packed his things and left, driving away from the village at mach speed until a police car had stopped him for speeding. After enduring the paperwork, the humiliating experience of being breathalysed and discovering he was only just under the limit, and the tedious lecture about road safety, he was on the M40, bound automatically for Heathrow. He would get the first flight to anywhere, book into an expensive hotel with two hookers and three bottles of Chivas Regal, and when all had been exhausted maybe he would have erased the memory of the young woman with curly black hair and eyes like forget-me-nots.

Suzy joined Meathead's entourage and flew to New York, thankful that she had something to take her mind off Clayton's disappearance. Before she went she gave Clifton Kate's telephone number.

'You're free now. You can do what you want,' she said.

'What you want, you mean,' he grumbled at her.

They talked most days, usually when it was evening in England.

'Have you called Kate yet?' she would ask.

'Have you called Clayton?'

The answer to both these questions was always no.

'He has to call me. He's the one that walked out.'

'I'm sensing a feeling of déjà vu,' Clifton said wryly.

'Oh be quiet. In a few weeks I'll be back home to sort you out myself.'

'Yes, please. The Squire misses his maid. Could you tell me a bedtime story?'

Then she would shut the door to her trailer and they would indulge in a little sensual fantasising to help him get to sleep. She loved doing it, but her own sex life was feeling a little arid since Clayton's departure. Ageing roadies wearing Meathead T-shirts just weren't her thing.

Kate was taking her usual evening walk on the beach. It was her time to regain her sanity, after the builders had gone and Alfie had retreated to the pub. She had given Alfie the warning when they first came. The building work had to be completed before she agreed to open for business. And he still had not done it. The kitchen was in the same state it had been in when Suzy Whitbread had come and thrown her life into the wringer.

The tide was fully out, and she could pick up her pace on the firm, golden sand. The few brave souls who had spent the day on the beach had long gone, and an unseasonal North wind snapped at her hair, whipping it around her small, heart-shaped face. The thin blouse she wore was woefully inadequate, but she couldn't face going back to the house just yet.

Ahead, up on the promenade, she saw a huge black stretch limousine. It was an incongruous sight in Great Yarmouth. A man was standing beside it, his legs planted firmly apart, both hands resting on a cane. He seemed to be waiting for someone. As she drew closer, her heart began to beat rather fast.

She walked up to him and gave him the once over, from the tips of his black pointed boots to his black leather trousers and the black cashmere polo neck sweater. The cane was tipped with an ebony falcon. Inwardly she smiled. The Squire had got his groove back.

'You took your time,' she said.

He threw his cigarette down and ground it to dust beneath his boot.

'At least I bothered to come,' he replied.

'So why are you here? To talk?'

'There's time for that later. I've come to take you home.'

'Just like that.' Kate pulled stray hair from her lips and let it fly back to join the others.

'Just like that.' He reached back and knocked on the car window. A chauffeur climbed out and opened the door. Kate looked into the velvety dark interior and laughed incredulously.

'I can't just leave!'

'Why not?'

'Well ... there's the house and the business, not to mention my clothes and –'

'I'll buy you more.'

Kate shook her head sadly. 'You can't buy me, Clifton. You should know that.'

Clifton handed the cane to the chauffeur and very deliberately pulled her towards him. 'If you had a price, I wouldn't be able to afford you.' He thoughtfully fingered the lapels of her thin blouse, then decisively ripped it apart, spraying buttons at their feet. She gave a horrified gasp, clutching herself, looking around quickly to see if anyone had noticed. The prurient looks from passers-by made her flush with shame.

'Oh dear,' Clifton said. 'You can't go home like that, can you?'

She allowed him to lead her into the womb-like car. It was gloriously warm away from the vicious wind. They sat side by side, neither one speaking. The chauffeur got behind the wheel and waited.

'There are a lot of things I can't do yet,' Clifton said, somewhat tentatively.

'Tell me what you can do.'

'I can walk, just. I'll be driving soon. And I can get it up, faster than your average spotty adolescent.' He looked at her. 'Is that enough for now?'

'I must get back. Alfie will be waiting for his supper,' Kate said mechanically, staring straight ahead.

'No, he won't. I posted a letter through his door, telling him you weren't coming back.' He leaned over and kissed her open mouth to stall any protest. The feel of him, pressing against her, his familiar woody fragrance, the increasing passion behind the kiss, all served to weaken Kate's defences, if she ever had any. As the kiss grew more heated, his thumb grazing her nipple, her body responded of its own volition. She slipped her cool hand inside his shirt and found his hard, warm body, as addictive as opium. She dug her fingers in, hard, and he grunted in pain and pleasure.

'Is this you whisking me away on your black steed, intent on ravishing me for the rest of my natural life?' she asked playfully.

He grabbed her buttocks and pulled her on to him. 'Damned right.' He kissed her again, so deeply she could hardly breathe. She wrenched away and glared at him, before grabbing him and kissing him, hard and biting, as her hand came up and knocked on the glass. The car automatically purred to life.

'You have to tell him where to go,' Clifton said, through bruised and abused lips. 'Your place or mine?'

'No.' Kate smiled. 'Ours.'

* * *

When Suzy arrived back in England she spent three days at the flat sleeping before driving down to Springfields in the silver Mercedes SLK that was waiting for her at Heathrow. Clifton had bought it for her, saying that as she wouldn't be able to afford the insurance premium up in London she might as well come to stay at Springfields until she decided what to do next.

She couldn't help feeling a certain amount of smugness as she drove down the familiar driveway. The house was lit up like a palace, and the car park to the side was packed with vehicles. A doorman opened the car door and proffered his hand. He gave the valet the keys and guided her into the house.

The Hunt Ball to mark the start of the season was already in full swing. As Suzy took a flute of champagne from a passing waiter she smiled to herself. The last time she had been to a Hunt Ball she had been outside, in the mud, placard-waving and shouting insults against the elite. Now she wore Prada sandals and a long black Versace dress that made her feel like a 40s film star.

A goddess was walking towards her, in bias-cut cream satin that hugged her curves like a lover's hands. She was smiling and holding out her hands. It was Kate. They hugged like sisters.

'We're so glad you made it! Clifton is dying to see you.'

The well-heeled crowd parted in a wave of silk and black cashmere to let them through. Suzy saw Clifton before he saw her. He was resplendent in a black dinner suit, red bowtie and cummerbund. And he was standing up, without the support of the cane. When he saw her he dropped the conversation he was having like a hot brick and took her into his arms, holding her for a long time.

'I'm going to cry,' she sniffed as they broke apart.

'No, you're not,' Kate said firmly. 'And neither are you,' she said, wagging her finger sternly at Clifton. He caught it and pulled her towards him for a kiss. Only it wasn't just a kiss, but a full-scale ravishment of Rhett Butler proportions. In the ensuing laughter, Suzy caught the difference in atmosphere. They were amongst friends, people who actually cared about them. It made her feel all warm and fuzzy inside, until she remembered Clayton, and the ache she felt every day at his absence.

She felt a tap on her shoulder. She turned around, and nearly dropped her champagne. She squeaked with delight as Jem picked her up and whirled her around.

'Where's Bonny?' she asked breathlessly.

'Oh, she met a Harley's Angel and married him in Las Vegas,' he said carelessly. He dragged an outstandingly pretty redhead to the fore. 'This is Rhiannon. Her father owns half of Idaho.'

'That should cheer Alice up,' Suzy said, grinning at the girl, who seemed totally bemused.

The next three hours passed in a haze of Mozart and Veuve Clicquot. There was so much to talk about, so much to tell. It was magical, but Suzy still felt somehow empty inside. She went out onto the veranda to get some air, and it was there that Baker found her, and told her that Mr McKenna requested her presence in the conservatory.

It was dark when she went in, lit only by a hundred tiny candles. From the garden it had looked enchanting. The smell of stephanotis and fat, waxy lilies was as rich as honey, enrobing her with its perfume as she went in and saw Clifton. He had dispensed with his jacket and tie and was sitting on a red Jacquard chaise longue, smoking a cigar, waiting for her. Two flutes of champagne, together with the bottle in an ice bucket, sat on the table before him.

'Come here,' he said, in a voice unlike the one he had used before that evening. She recognised the lust behind it, the need for something other than just friendly conversation. Warily she sat next to him.

'I've missed you,' he said. He placed his hand on her breast and squeezed it gently. She moved away.

'No! You belong to Kate now,' she whispered fiercely.

'And who do you belong to?' His voice was odd, gravely with desire.

'No one,' she said shortly.

'Not even Clayton?'

'It's obvious he doesn't want me, isn't it?' She reached out to touch his face. 'You're so gorgeous, but I would be using you. Go back up to Kate. You've waited so long for her. Don't blow it now.'

'Do you love him?'

'I haven't allowed myself to. What's the point?'

He ran his fingers tenderly over her lips. 'One kiss, that's all I ask. For old times' sake.'

She hesitated. Of course she wanted to kiss him, but in doing so they would both be cheating Kate. But it was just one kiss.

'All right, just one. But that's the only one. No more unless Kate's in the room whipping me into submission, making me do it.' She gave him a chaste, soft kiss on the lips. He shook his head sadly.

'No tongues?'

What the hell, thought Suzy. She grabbed his head and planted her lips firmly on his. He tasted sweet and smoky as their tongues met, slid together, fought each other. It was a stormy marriage of a kiss, Clifton growling softly in his throat as she tried to devour him. Suzy felt a mounting passion, tempered by the fact that he wasn't hers, she couldn't have him. He would be in someone else's bed tonight. She broke away, near to tears. Clifton savoured the last vestiges of her taste on his lips. Then he smiled vividly.

'I should leave more often, if I'm going to get a welcome home like that every time.'

Suzy blinked, slowly registering the truth. He had tricked her once, and now he had done it again. Her eyes met Clayton's, and although her first instinct was to throw herself into his arms, she followed her second, and slapped him hard on the face.

'You bastard! Why did you walk out on me?'

'You loved Clifton. You said so yourself. He and Kate had to come to Cape Town to convince me otherwise.' He rubbed his sore cheek. 'I'm still not convinced, though.'

'You should have called me!'

'Why didn't you call me?'

'I thought you didn't want me! Why would I call you?'

He stood up and pulled her into his embrace. 'Maybe if you thought I was worth pursuing?'

'I couldn't have stood it if you had rejected me,' she muttered, not looking at him.

'I think,' he said, pushing her away just enough so that he could look at her properly, 'that we have both royally fucked up six months of our lives. Let's not waste any more time.'

Suzy felt a swooping, fearful joy, unlike anything she had felt before. Her feet felt as if they were six inches off the ground.

Actually, they were six inches off the ground, because he had picked her up. Their bodies slid intimately together as she curled her arms around his neck. For a long time, neither of them moved. His kiss was so sweet and so deep she felt drunk with longing. He led her back to the chaise longue and lay with her, kicking off their shoes, manoeuvring until she was lying full length on top of him. Between them, she felt a lump as hard as rock, and a driving, throbbing force that made her wet with anticipation.

'I know this is supposed to be a romantic reunion,' she said, 'but when are we going to fuck?'

'I love a woman who cuts to the chase.' He shifted so that she was on her front, trapped against the back of the chaise longue. He knelt on the floor and flipped up her dress, stroking her long thighs and admiring her delicate black lace panties. They were cut to enhance her pert backside, and when he saw the pale globes just peeking out from under the lace he hissed lasciviously.

'Oh yes, little maid, just perfect for spanking.' He grabbed them and buried his nose between them, inhaling her womanly fragrance. His hot, moist breath only added to the steamy heat of her sex. He made her turn over and peeled the panties away.

'Fur,' he said, stroking her soft black pussy hair. 'I don't know which I like best, the mink or the silk.' He spread her legs, hooking one over the back of the chaise longue, and opened up her pussy with his thumbs, looking intently right up inside its dark velvet depths. Then he ran his tongue over her labial lips. 'Tastes good, like warm muffins,' he murmured, making her laugh and catch her breath as he did it again, round and round, up, deep inside her, and all around the outside until her hips moved voluptuously against him.

'What's this?' he gasped suddenly. 'Buried treasure.'

'Oh god,' Suzy moaned as his tongue flickered over her clitoris. She was streaming wet, her juices seeping into the expensive upholstery, but he kept going, relentlessly, his fingers now sliding in and out of her oozing pussy. The aroma of lilies, the skill of his tongue, the very fact that he was here at all, eating her out with the same finesse that his brother had at the piano, all served to intoxicate her with increasing sensation.

'More,' she moaned, as the orgasm hit. 'More, you fuck. Give me more!' And then she was screaming unashamedly, not bothered who could hear her. She felt him retreat, leaving her to quiver in the afterglow, but he was freeing himself, fumbling, desperate. He pulled her to her feet and turned her around, bending her over so that she had to brace herself on the back of the seat to stop from toppling over. He plunged inside her with a rasp of delight, grasping her hips tightly, slamming into her with a pent-up lust that left her breathless. Distantly she knew they could be seen from outside, but she didn't care. She tossed her hair and pushed back at him with every ounce of strength.

'Come on, baby,' she murmured, looking back at him with sultry eyes, 'you can do better than that.'

Clifton walked in at that moment. There was no way they could say they had been looking for a contact lens. He leaned against the doorframe, grinning at them.

'The reunion went well, then.'

Kate appeared behind him. She slipped her hand around his waist and down, down, into his black trousers. Clifton let her fondle him, leaning back to kiss her with lazy intimacy. Suzy realised it was incredibly arousing, watching Clifton submit to another woman's spell. Kate beckoned to Suzy.

'Come in. No one can see you then.'

As if hypnotised, Suzy left Clayton and went over to where Kate had led Clifton. He was now lying on the sofa, his cock rigid and thrusting obscenely out of his smart black trousers. Kate gracefully sank to her knees and continued to kiss him, slipping one arm out of her dress and offering him her breasts to feel and suck.

'Why don't you blow him?' she said to Suzy.

She didn't need to be asked twice. She knelt next to Kate and took Clifton's cock in her mouth. He made an indistinct sound of pleasure and thickened against her lips. Clayton had come into the room and was lifting Suzy's dress up to her waist, stroking her liquid, beckoning pussy and pushing in again, making her moan. This time his fucking was leisurely, the initial heat dissipated, as Suzy undulated against him, reassuring him that he was her main man.

Outside, guests milled around the large gardens, laughing, drinking, dancing. Inside, the hosts of the occasion were slowly losing themselves in erotic bliss. Now both Kate and Suzy were at Clifton's cock, Suzy lapping at his balls, Kate sucking him with surprising skill. Clayton had retreated to the other sofa to watch, waiting his turn. When it came he lay down and let it happen, stroking their hair, one black as thunder, the other the bright white gold of lightning. Clifton perused each peachy female backside, wondering which one to plunder first. Suzy gasped as he thrust into her, but he was soon magnetically attracted to Kate, who looked like a Grecian maiden bathing in a pool of cream satin. Suzy was so busy watching them couple she almost forgot about Clayton, waiting with swollen, aching balls for her to finish him off. Clifton swore copiously and came quickly, up hard and tight against Kate's slim haunches, and Suzy was given a very wicked idea. Clifton slumped on the sofa with a glass of cognac to recover. Suzy whispered to Kate, who obediently lay on the rug in front of the mirror on her back. Suzy parted her legs, her own heart thumping. The woman's pussy looked so sweet and fluffy and inviting, but it was the first time she had tasted another woman since Lena. As she scooted her hands underneath Kate's buttocks she looked back at

Clayton, highly aroused, breathing unsteadily. Her back arched as she displayed plump pussy lips, slightly open and inviting him to sink between them again.

'Oh yes,' he murmured, watching greedily as Suzy bent to her task, kitten-licking Kate's frilly pink pussy lips, lapping up Clifton's come as it oozed creamily between them. Clifton was watching with disbelief, his cock swelling again. Kate's moans took on a new, bass edge as they made and held eye contact. Then Clayton pushed into Suzy and began to fuck her steadily, forcing her tongue deeper into Kate's cunt. Kate's firm, swelling breasts and long, raspberry nipples were being teased cruelly under her cool fingers. Clifton poured cognac over them and licked it off as Clayton's thrusts became faster, more desperate. Kate motioned to Clifton that she wanted to suck him. As she licked slavishly at his balls she stuck one perfectly manicured finger into his backside. The two men braced themselves against each other above the women, each too turned on to grin at each other. Clayton shot first, deep into Suzy, as Kate submitted to Suzy's relentlessly flickering tongue. Kate's orgasmic cries and invading finger in his arse were enough to tilt Clifton over the edge. He let fly deep in her throat, hissing his pleasure, before they all collapsed in a molten heap on the floor.

'Just like old times, bro,' Clayton murmured from somewhere underneath Suzy.

Clifton sat up. 'Yes, but we never intended to marry them.'

Kate was struggling to get back into her dress. She stopped and looked at him.

'Was that a proposal?'

Clifton brushed himself down, zipped his trousers and smoothed his hair. 'Actually, it was. Well?'

'Well what?'

'Will you marry me?'

'We've just had a group fuck and now you're asking me to marry you?'

'Yes!' Clifton, Clayton and Suzy said it together.

Kate looked at Clayton and Suzy. 'Would you excuse us for a while?'

Clayton led Suzy from the room. Clifton looked crushed. Suzy mouthed 'good luck' at him.

'And what about us?' Clayton asked, pulling her into a dark corner of the hallway. 'I'm flying back to Cape Town in three days. Would you come with me?'

'Only if you promise not to leave it another five years before we come back,' she said, kissing him.

'We can come back whenever we want. The jet is fuelled and waiting.'

'The jet,' Suzy repeated, thinking how extraordinarily her life had changed in the course of one year.

'That's right. It's a Gulfstream, leather upholstered, with . . .' he faltered as she unzipped him and drew him into her mouth. He tasted of her, musky and sweet, with a hint of Issy Miyake perfume. 'Please say yes,' he whispered hoarsely.

'Can't,' she mumbled, 'I've got my mouth full.'

A few minutes later, after sharing semen-slick kisses, they paused outside Clifton's door. No one had come out since they left. Suzy tentatively knocked, and when she received no answer, quietly opened the door and looked in.

Clifton was sprawled over the desk on his front, watching his flushed reflection as Kate caned his bare backside with the riding crop. The look on his face was ecstatic, as pain and pleasure mingled in a burning glow of sexual anticipation. Suzy shut the door again, quietly so as not to disturb them. Clayton waited anxiously in the hall.

'Well?'

'She said yes,' Suzy replied, and eased back into his arms.

LOOK OUT FOR THE ALL-NEW BLACK LACE BOOKS – AVAILABLE NOW!

All books priced £6.99 in the UK. Please note publication dates apply to the UK only. For other territories, please contact your retailer.

LA BASQUAISE
Angel Strand
ISBN 0 352 32988 2

The lovely Oruela is determined to fit in to a lifestyle of opulence in 1920s Biarritz. But she has to put her social aspirations on hold when she falls under suspicion for her father's murder. As Oruela becomes embroiled in a series of sensual games, she discovers that blackmail is a powerful weapon that can be used to obtain pleasure as well as money. **An unusual, erotic and beautifully written story set in the heady whirl of French society in the 1920s.**

Coming in May

BLACK LIPSTICK KISSES
Monica Belle
ISBN 0 352 33885 7

Sultry and mischievous Angela McKie loves dressing up in fetish clothing inspired by Victorian decadence. Perfecting an air of occult sexiness, she enjoys teasing men to distraction. She attracts the lustful attentions of two very different guys: Stephen Byrne is a serious young politician with a bright future; Michael Merrick is a cartoonist for a horror comic. Both want her, and set out to get her, but quickly discover they have bitten off more than they can chew when they allow themselves to be seduced by Ms McKie. **A witty, well-crafted, naughty story set in the fashion-conscious London Goth scene.**

THE HAND OF AMUN
Juliet Hastings
ISBN O 352 33144 5

Marked from birth with the symbol of Amun, the young Naunakhte must
enter a life of dark eroticism as a servant at his temple. She becomes the
favourite of the high priestess but, when she's accused of an act of
sacrilege, she is forced to flee to the city of Waset. There she meets
Khonsu, a prince of the Egyptian underworld whose prowess as a lover is
legendary. But fate draws her back to the temple, and she is forced to
choose between two lovers – one mortal and the other a god. **Highly
arousing and imaginative story of life and lust in Ancient Egypt.**

Coming in June

MIXED SIGNALS
Anna Clare
ISBN O 352 33889 X

Adele Western knows what it's like to be an outsider. As a teenager she
was teased mercilessly by the sixth-form girls for the size of her lips.
Now twenty-six, we follow the ups and downs of her life and loves.
There's the cultured restaurateur Paul, whose relationship with his
working-class boyfriend raises eyebrows, not least because he is still
having sex with his ex-wife. There's former chart-topper Suki, whose
career has nosedived and who is venturing on a lesbian affair.
Underlying everyone's story is a tale of ambiguous sexuality, and Adele is
caught up in some very saucy antics. **The sexy *tours de force* of wild,
colourful characters makes this a hugely enjoyable novel of modern
sexual dilemmas.**

WHITE ROSE ENSNARED
Juliet Hastings
ISBN 0 352 33052 X

England. 1456. The young and beautiful Rosamund finds herself at the mercy of Sir Ralph Aycliffe when her husband is killed in battle. Aycliffe will stop at nothing to humiliate Rosámund and seize her property. Only the young squire Geoffrey Lymington will risk everything to save the honour of the woman he has loved for just one night. Against the Wars of the Roses, the battle for Rosamund unfolds. Who will prevail in the struggle for her body? **Vicious knaves and noble gentlemen joust in this tale of courtly but not so chivalrous love.**

Black Lace Booklist

Information is correct at time of printing. To avoid disappointment
check availability before ordering. Go to www.blacklace-books.co.uk.
All books are priced £6.99 unless another price is given.

BLACK LACE BOOKS WITH A CONTEMPORARY SETTING

☐ IN THE FLESH Emma Holly	ISBN 0 352 33498 3	£5.99
☐ SHAMELESS Stella Black	ISBN 0 352 33485 1	£5.99
☐ INTENSE BLUE Lyn Wood	ISBN 0 352 33496 7	£5.99
☐ THE NAKED TRUTH Natasha Rostova	ISBN 0 352 33497 5	£5.99
☐ A SPORTING CHANCE Susie Raymond	ISBN 0 352 33501 7	£5.99
☐ TAKING LIBERTIES Susie Raymond	ISBN 0 352 33357 X	£5.99
☐ A SCANDALOUS AFFAIR Holly Graham	ISBN 0 352 33523 8	£5.99
☐ THE NAKED FLAME Crystalle Valentino	ISBN 0 352 33528 9	£5.99
☐ ON THE EDGE Laura Hamilton	ISBN 0 352 33534 3	£5.99
☐ LURED BY LUST Tania Picarda	ISBN 0 352 33533 5	£5.99
☐ THE HOTTEST PLACE Tabitha Flyte	ISBN 0 352 33536 X	£5.99
☐ THE NINETY DAYS OF GENEVIEVE Lucinda Carrington	ISBN 0 352 33070 8	£5.99
☐ DREAMING SPIRES Juliet Hastings	ISBN 0 352 33584 X	
☐ THE TRANSFORMATION Natasha Rostova	ISBN 0 352 33311 1	
☐ SIN.NET Helena Ravenscroft	ISBN 0 352 33598 X	
☐ TWO WEEKS IN TANGIER Annabel Lee	ISBN 0 352 33599 8	
☐ HIGHLAND FLING Jane Justine	ISBN 0 352 33616 1	
☐ PLAYING HARD Tina Troy	ISBN 0 352 33617 X	
☐ SYMPHONY X Jasmine Stone	ISBN 0 352 33629 3	
☐ SUMMER FEVER Anna Ricci	ISBN 0 352 33625 0	
☐ CONTINUUM Portia Da Costa	ISBN 0 352 33120 8	
☐ OPENING ACTS Suki Cunningham	ISBN 0 352 33630 7	
☐ FULL STEAM AHEAD Tabitha Flyte	ISBN 0 352 33637 4	
☐ A SECRET PLACE Ella Broussard	ISBN 0 352 33307 3	
☐ GAME FOR ANYTHING Lyn Wood	ISBN 0 352 33639 0	
☐ CHEAP TRICK Astrid Fox	ISBN 0 352 33640 4	
☐ ALL THE TRIMMINGS Tesni Morgan	ISBN 0 352 33641 3	

□ ARIA APPASSIONATA Juliet Hastings   ISBN O 352 33056 2
□ THE RELUCTANT PRINCESS Patty Glenn   ISBN O 352 33809 1
□ WILD IN THE COUNTRY Monica Belle   ISBN O 352 33824 5
□ THE TUTOR Portia Da Costa   ISBN O 352 32946 7
□ SEXUAL STRATEGY Felice de Vere   ISBN O 352 33843 1
□ HARD BLUE MIDNIGHT Alaine Hood   ISBNO 352 33851 2
□ ALWAYS THE BRIDEGROOM Tesni Morgan   ISBNO 352 33855 5
□ COMING ROUND THE MOUNTAIN Tabitha Flyte   ISBNO 352 33873 3
□ FEMININE WILES Karina Mooree   ISBNO 352 33235 2

BLACK LACE BOOKS WITH AN HISTORICAL SETTING
□ PRIMAL SKIN Leona Benkt Rhys   ISBN O 352 33500 9 £5.99
□ DEVIL'S FIRE Melissa MacNeal   ISBN O 352 33527 0 £5.99
□ DARKER THAN LOVE Kristina Lloyd   ISBN O 352 33279 4
□ THE CAPTIVATION Natasha Rostova   ISBN O 352 33234 4
□ MINX Megan Blythe   ISBN O 352 33638 2
□ JULIET RISING Cleo Cordell   ISBN O 352 32938 6
□ DEMON'S DARE Melissa MacNeal   ISBN O 352 33683 8
□ DIVINE TORMENT Janine Ashbless   ISBN O 352 33719 2
□ SATAN'S ANGEL Melissa MacNeal   ISBN O 352 33726 5
□ THE INTIMATE EYE Georgia Angelis   ISBN O 352 33004 X
□ OPAL DARKNESS Cleo Cordell   ISBN O 352 33033 3
□ SILKEN CHAINS Jodi Nicol   ISBN O 352 33143 7
□ EVIL'S NIECE Melissa MacNeal   ISBN O 352 33781 8
□ ACE OF HEARTS Lisette Allen   ISBN O 352 33059 7
□ A GENTLEMAN'S WAGER Madelynne Ellis   ISBN O 352 33800 8
□ THE LION LOVER Mercedes Kelly   ISBN O 352 33162 3
□ ARTISTIC LICENCE Vivienne La Fay   ISBN O 352 33210 7
□ THE AMULET Lisette Allen   ISBN O 352 33019 8

BLACK LACE ANTHOLOGIES
□ WICKED WORDS 6 Various   ISBN O 352 33590 0
□ WICKED WORDS 9 Various   ISBN O 352 33860 1
□ THE BEST OF BLACK LACE 2 Various   ISBN O 352 33718 4

BLACK LACE NON-FICTION

❏ THE BLACK LACE BOOK OF WOMEN'S SEXUAL   ISBN 0 352 33793 1   £6.99
FANTASIES Ed. Kerri Sharp

To find out the latest information about Black Lace titles, check out the
website: www.blacklace-books.co.uk or send for a booklist with
complete synopses by writing to:

Black Lace Booklist, Virgin Books Ltd
Thames Wharf Studios
Rainville Road
London W6 9HA

Please include an SAE of decent size. Please note only British stamps
are valid.

Our privacy policy
We will not disclose information you supply us to any other parties.
We will not disclose any information which identifies you personally to
any person without your express consent.

From time to time we may send out information about Black Lace
books and special offers. Please tick here if you do <u>not</u> wish to
receive Black Lace information.   ❏

Please send me the books I have ticked above.

Name ....

Address ....

....

....

....

Post Code ....

Send to: Virgin Books Cash Sales, Thames Wharf Studios, Rainville Road, London W6 9HA.

US customers: for prices and details of how to order books for delivery by mail, call 1-800-343-4499.

Please enclose a cheque or postal order, made payable to Virgin Books Ltd, to the value of the books you have ordered plus postage and packing costs as follows:

UK and BFPO – £1.00 for the first book, 50p for each subsequent book.

Overseas (including Republic of Ireland) – £2.00 for the first book, £1.00 for each subsequent book.

If you would prefer to pay by VISA, ACCESS/MASTERCARD, DINERS CLUB, AMEX or SWITCH, please write your card number and expiry date here:

....

Signature ....

Please allow up to 28 days for delivery.